Kismet

www.noexit.co.uk

Other books by the same author

Kismet

Jakob Arjouni

A Kayankaya Novel

Translated from the
German by Anthea Bell

NO EXIT PRESS

This edition published in 2007 by No Exit Press,
P.O.Box 394, Harpenden, Herts, AL5 1XJ
www.noexit.co.uk

Supported by Arts Council England, through Grants for the Arts.

A CIP catalogue record for this book is available from the British Library.

ISBN 10: 1 84243 235 4 (paperback)
ISBN 13: 978 1 84243 235 8 (paperback)
ISBN 10: 1 84243 046 7 (hardcover)
ISBN 13: 978 1 84243 046 0 (hardcover)

2 4 6 8 10 9 7 5 3 1

Typeset by Avocet Typeset, Chilton, Aylesbury, Bucks
Printed and bound in Great Britain by CPD, Ebbw Vale, Wales

Kismet

Chapter 1

Slibulsky and I were crammed into the china cupboard, emptied for the purpose, of a small Brazilian restaurant on the outskirts of the Frankfurt railway station district, waiting for a couple of racketeers to show up demanding protection money.

The cupboard was about one metre twenty wide and seventy centimetres deep. Neither Slibulsky nor I would be giving the clothing industry cause for concern about the sales of their XL sizes. Furthermore, we were wearing bulletproof vests, and when it came to the crunch we hoped at least to get a pistol and a shotgun into position where we wouldn't shoot ourselves in the foot or blast our own heads off. I could just imagine the racketeers entering the restaurant, hearing pitiful cries in the corner after a while, and opening the cupboard door to find two total idiots squashed inside, arms and legs flailing helplessly. And I pictured Romario's face at this sight. Romario was the owner and manager of the Saúdade, and he had appealed to me for help.

I'd known Romario since his first gastronomic venture running a snack bar in Sachsenhausen. Until now he'd only been an acquaintance. I was glad to know him when I was skint and he stood me dinner. I wasn't so glad when I was in funds and met him in a bar and he came to sit at the same table, and we had to talk about something or other just because we knew each other. So if this evening's operation came into the category of a favour done for a friend, then it was mainly because Romario hadn't offered me any payment and I couldn't really ask for any either.

Just after midnight. We'd stationed ourselves here half an hour ago, and for about the last twenty minutes my legs had been going to sleep. It was unusually warm for early May. Daytime temperatures were up to twenty-seven degrees, and by night they didn't fall below fifteen. Which did not keep Romario from turning his central heating up to maximum – from force of habit and because complaining about the German weather was, in a way, one of his last links with Brazil. He'd lived in Frankfurt for the last twenty years, he went to the Côte d'Azur on holiday, and I didn't know if overcooked sweet-and-sour chicken and tough pork chops with canned peas were typical specialities of Brazil, but you couldn't really wish them on his native land. Anyway, the whole city might be going around in T-shirts, his customers might be dying of heatstroke, but Romario insisted that it was always cold in Germany and the sun always shone in Brazil – whether he was in a generally bad or a generally good mood.

So I wasn't going to make any money out of this, I couldn't feel my legs any more, the temperature inside the cupboard was approaching jungle heat, and from time to time I heard this barely audible hissing.

'Slibulsky?'

'Hm?' Brief, unemotional. The sweet he was sucking clicked against his teeth.

'What did you have for supper?'

'Supper? What do you mean? Can't remember.'

'You don't remember what was on the plate in front of you a few hours ago?'

He cleared his throat, the way other people might give a little whistle or roll their eyes, indicating that they'll try to answer your question in friendly tones, but naturally it doesn't for a moment interest them.

'Let's see… oh yes, I know. Cheese. *Handkäse*. That was it. Gina went shopping this morning and…'

'*Handkäse* with onions.' And you can't get much smellier than *Handkäse* anyway.

'Of course with onions. You don't eat cheese with strawberries, do you?'

I put a good deal of effort into giving him as contemptuous a glance as I could in the dim light of the cupboard.

'Didn't I tell you we'd be spending some time together in this hole?'

'Yup, I believe you did mention it. Although I remembered the cupboard as kind of larger.'

'Oh yes? Like how large? I mean, how big does a cupboard have to be for two people, one of whom has just been stuffing himself with onions, to breathe easily inside it?'

In what little light filtered through the keyhole and some cracks in the sides of the cupboard, I saw Slibulsky make a face. 'I thought we were here to scare off some sort of Mafia characters? With our guns and bulletproof vests, like the good guys we are. But maybe Miss Kayankaya fancies running a hairdressing salon instead of a detective agency?'

What did I say to that? Best ignore it. I told him, 'I've got sweat running down my face and into my mouth, I have a feeling your stink is condensing, and I don't reckon the good guys have to put up with other people farting.'

Slibulsky chuckled.

Cursing quietly, I bent to look through the keyhole. I could see Romario's bandaged arm the other side of it. He was sitting at the bar doing something with a calculator and a notepad, as if cashing up for the evening after closing the restaurant. In fact he was too nervous to add up so much as the price of a couple of beers. They'd paid him their first visit a week ago: two strikingly well-dressed young men not much older than twenty-five, waving pistols and a note saying: *This is a polite request for your monthly donation of 6,000 DM to the Army of Reason, payable on the first of each month. Thanking you in advance.* They didn't say a word, they just smiled – at least until Romario had read the note, handed it back, and believing, not least in view of the sheer size of the sum, that he was dealing with a couple of novices said, 'Sorry, I don't see how I can go along with your request.'

Whereupon they stopped smiling, shoved the barrels of their pistols into his belly, crumpled up the note, stuffed it into Romario's mouth and forced him to chew and swallow it. Then they wrote *Back the day after tomorrow* on the bar in black felt pen, and went away.

In spite of this little demonstration, Romario didn't really take the matter seriously. He'd been running his place here near the railway station too long to panic the first time a couple of young tearaways tried extortion. As everyone knows, the big protection rackets, the ones you have to take seriously, have a whole crowd of small-time con men following in their wake, thinking they might as well give it a try. Like when you're sixteen you say hey, why not just take a look and see if that bike over there is padlocked.

Romario threw up the note he'd swallowed, knocked two nails into the side of the bar and hung his pistol on them. When they came back they'd see how a real man dealt with such outrageous demands. But they didn't come in the evening, as he had expected, and Romario wasn't behind the bar. It was morning, and he was in the kitchen putting meat in a marinade with oil and seasonings when they suddenly turned up. Still smiling, and with another note. *Your monthly donation to the Army of Reason is now due. Many thanks for your commitment to this good cause.*

When Romario, with the pistols pointing at him and his hands in the marinade, said he didn't have six thousand marks, just how much profit a month did they think a little place like this made, he might as well close down right away if he paid up, they twisted his arms behind his back, tied him to the radiator, and nipped his thumb off with a pair of pliers. The cleaning lady found Romario lying unconscious in a pool of blood. His thumb was on the bar, with the words *Back on Thursday* written beside it.

This was Thursday, and the bandage round Romario's arm looked bright white against the wood-panelled wall. They'd sewn his thumb back on at the hospital. The doctor hadn't been able to say whether he was likely to keep it, and how much use it would still be if he did. Romario's explanation that he'd done it chopping onions was received with scepticism, but it had stopped the hospital reporting the incident to the police. Now and then Romario glanced at the china cupboard as if to make sure that we hadn't disappeared through some crack in it. Whenever he did that I knocked my Beretta quietly against the door to reassure him. Cutting off his thumb was a brutal business and I was sorry about it, no question.

I didn't want to stop and work out whether I was particularly sorry because, but for that injury, a flat-rate payment plus expenses might at least not have been beyond the bounds of possibility.

The hissing sound came again.

'Slibulsky, you're an arsehole!'

'And you're a fucking queen.'

I sighed. 'If I was, I expect I'd have hired this cupboard on purpose to be shut up with you and your fragrant aroma.'

'Oh yeah? The things you know about... is that the way a man starts thinking when he's gone without a girlfriend so long?'

'Oh, Slibulsky.'

'And don't say "Oh, Slibulsky" every time I mention it. If you ask me...'

'Quiet!'

A car had drawn up outside. The engine was switched off; doors slammed. Soon afterwards feet climbed the steps, stopped briefly, then there was a knock. Romario rose from the bar stool and went to open the door. I took the safety catch off my pistol. In so far as it was possible in the cupboard, Slibulsky got on his marks as if to run the hundred metres, ready to leap out with his shotgun levelled. Through a second hole in the cupboard, one we had bored on purpose, I saw two young men in cream linen suits coming into the bar in silence. Both had pale, clean-shaven faces and thick fair hair with short back and sides. At first sight they looked as German as the young men on the German Mail advertising posters, so the obvious deduction that they never said a word because they didn't know any words in German seemed to have been wrong.

One of them handed Romario a note. Romario read it and waved them over to the bar. Black automatics gleamed in their hands. We'd hoped they would leave the pistols in their holsters – now Slibulsky and I would have to delay our appearance until Romario was out of the firing line. Romario knew that.

'Would you like a drink?' I heard him ask, his voice trembling slightly. I saw them both shake their heads. One pointed with emphasis to the note in Romario's hand.

'Sure, right away. I'd just like to know whether this monthly donation will really settle everything?'

They nodded.

'And if… well, suppose there's other organisations asking for, er, donations… I mean, does this payment mean you give me some kind of protection?'

They nodded again and raised their pistols, smiling.

'Fine, so where do I reach you if I need you?'

One pointed the barrel of his pistol at his ear and his eyes, which probably meant: we know what goes on in this city, no need to call us, we'll call you.

Where did these characters come from? I knew German, Turkish, Italian, Albanian, Russian and Chinese racketeers who extorted protection money – but speech-less racketeers were something new.

'Okay,' said Romario, 'then let's see about…'

'Then let's see about' was our signal. While Romario flung himself to the floor behind the bar with a single movement, and then crawled towards the kitchen door, Slibulsky and I burst out of the cupboard shouting, 'Hands up and drop your guns!'

However, they did neither, and if I hadn't got hold of bulletproof vests for us, that would have been the last mild spring night we ever saw. They fired at once. I felt the bullets hit my chest, threw myself to one side and fired back. We'd agreed in advance to aim at their heads if it came to a shoot-out; after all, we weren't the only ones who could lay hands on bulletproof vests. I hit one of them under the chin. Blood spurted over his cream suit, he dropped his gun and clutched his neck with both hands as if trying to strangle himself. He swayed briefly, fell backwards and hit the floor. Slibulsky blasted the other man's forehead away with his shotgun. The wooden panelling was peppered with a hail of shot. While the man who had lost his forehead was still falling I got behind the bar and switched off all the lights.

In the dark I called, 'Romario!'

'Here,' came a voice from the kitchen.

'Slibulsky?'

'Oh, shit!'

I went to the window, peered past the curtain at the street and the buildings opposite. No pedestrians, no lights coming on, all quiet. There was stertorous breathing behind me, not very loud.

I snapped my lighter on and bent over the man who was still clutching his neck. Blood was running through his fingers. His large, pale eyes looked at me, bewildered.

'Who sent you?' He didn't react.

'I can call a doctor or not, as the case may be. I want your boss's name!'

But he couldn't hear me any more. His hands dropped from his neck, his head fell to one side, and he made one last choking, gurgling sound. Then there was nothing to be heard but the hiss of my lighter. The flame cast a yellow light on the dead man's face. It was made up, or anyway powdered, that's why it had looked so pale just now. The skin was darker on the ears and the ragged remains of his throat. I closed his eyes. A young, pretty face with long lashes and full lips. I let the lighter go out and stared into the darkness. It wasn't the first corpse I'd seen, or the first time I'd been in a gunfight with fatal consequences either – but this was the first human being I'd killed with my own hands.

I felt his chest. Like us, he was indeed wearing a bullet-proof vest. So the only place to shoot without killing would have been his legs. If he'd realised in time that he couldn't wound his opponent's chest, would he have spared *my* head? And do injured legs stop a man shooting in a life-and-death situation?

A strip of faint yellow light fell into the room. When I turned my head Romario was standing beside me. The light came from a street lamp outside the kitchen window. Romario was hugging himself with his unbandaged arm as if he were freezing. Lips pressed tight, he looked at the body.

I cleared my throat. 'Er…' And added, for something to say, 'It all happened so fast.'

He kept looking down. 'If that Army of Reason thing really exists, whatever's behind it, then this,' he said, jerking his chin in the direction of the body, 'this means I'm finished in Frankfurt.'

'Mm,' I said noncommittally, getting up and lighting a cigarette. We stood in the dim light like that for a while, listening to the noises in the street. Cars drove past, further away a tram rattled along.

I asked, 'Got any large plastic bin liners?'

'In the kitchen.'

I trod out my cigarette. 'Okay. While Slibulsky and I get rid of the bodies you clean this place up, put a notice on the door saying *Gone On Holiday*, and go home. And tomorrow get out on the first train or flight.'

'Get out? Where to?'

'How should I know? Mallorca? Call me and give me a number where I can reach you. In two or three weeks' time I ought to have found out who's running this racket and whether they're after you.'

'Tell me one reason why they wouldn't be after me.'

'Well, they're certainly extorting money from other people too, so they ought to be suspecting all their victims for a time.' Oh yes, a long time; about one or two days, I should think. By then at the latest they'd have tracked Romario down, and they'd beat everything they wanted to know out of him – Slibulsky's name and mine included.

I saw Romario's outline as he turned away, while his unbandaged arm gestured dismissively in my direction. I guessed what he was thinking: a pity he hadn't asked someone else for help, someone who worked for money and got a bonus if he succeeded, and for that reason alone would have fixed things to the satisfaction of all, no dead bodies, no need for Romario to close down his business. The problem with friends doing you a favour, is that if they fail then the fact that they came on the cheap just proves how incapable they were anyway.

Apart from that, if Romario was thinking what I thought he was thinking, he wasn't far wrong. Yes, sure, I'd gone out and got bulletproof vests, I'd persuaded Slibulsky to join us, I'd discussed the showdown in advance with both of them. But really I'd been annoyed all along for feeling that unwritten laws obliged me to help Romario, and for agreeing to meet him at all four days ago instead of making some excuse, say flu. In other words, at this moment, with one body to my left, another to my right and my feet in a pool of blood, I realised that I didn't like Romario. I didn't like him at all. He let other people suffocate in the dry air of his central heating because he couldn't cope with having been born at some time in some place in another part of the world, he was a terrible cook, he thought he was helping me out by inviting me to eat the leftovers now and then – which was true, and that made it all the worse. But it was about ten minutes too late to do anything about this realisation of mine. I was involved now. Even if Romario ran for it, never to be seen again, there were plenty of people in town who'd wonder about his sudden disappearance, and sooner or later it would get around that I'd been seen with him rather often these last few days. Maybe these Mafia characters couldn't talk, but they could hear and they could probably do their sums too, and if they put two and two together they weren't likely to think I'd come here for a game of dice. And Mafia outfits aren't exactly famous for letting you kill their men with impunity.

All things considered, then, our operation had been a total fiasco. In addition, now I had a guilty conscience. Not only did I not like Romario, I really had done him out of his job, his home and his city in one fell swoop. And that when he'd lost his thumb only five days before.

'Er, Romario…'

'What?' a voice barked behind me. Next moment neon tubes flared on, and cold light from the kitchen fell into the dining-room. Sticky patches of red were spreading over the floor and walls around the corpses, which had now stopped bleeding. The red patches were scattered about like exploded paint-bombs. Slibulsky was sitting on a table, cradling his shotgun in his arm like a baby, dangling his legs and staring ahead of him, nauseated.

I turned to the kitchen door. 'How could I have known they'd shoot straight away?'

Romario's head briefly appeared in the doorway. 'It's your job to know these things! Whether you can do your job is another question!'

Oh, for God's sake! A couple of smart remarks, that was all we needed! Apart from the fact that it wouldn't have been entirely inappropriate for him to ask if Slibulsky and I were all right. After all, it was a miracle we'd got out of this intact. Not to mention any feelings we might have about the dead men and how upset we were. I mean, they weren't just a burst water pipe, and not simply because they did much more damage.

I reached behind the bar, picked up a bottle of schnapps and took a large gulp. Then I bent over the corpses and searched their suits. A silver lighter, a small bottle of mouthwash, two phone cards, half a packet of Dunhills, a nail file, five hundred and seventy marks plus a few coins, three condoms, car keys and two pairs of sunglasses. No ID or driving licences, nothing to give me a clue. I pocketed it all and was about to see what make their clothes were when I found a mobile phone on one of the corpses, tucked into his belt. It was as small and almost as flat as half a postcard. You flipped it open, three fine grooves above and below indicated the receiving and speaking areas, and you keyed in the numbers on a glowing blue touch-pad. I found out how to switch to *receive* if the mobile rang and put it in my breast pocket.

Romario brought in a stack of folded grey bin liners and a roll of sticky tape. Slibulsky and I packed the corpses into them. Both of us in silence, both trying not to feel anything much. The central heating was still full on, and our hands, damp with sweat, kept slipping off the plastic sacks and the dead men's limbs.

When we'd finished I went out and looked around for the BMW that went with the car keys. It was black and new and had a Frankfurt registration. I got into it, felt under the seats, opened the glove compartment, looked behind the sun visors, but apart from empty energy-drink bottles, some blackcurrant-flavour sweets, tissues and a big box of powder the car was empty. I noted the registration number, opened the boot and went back into the Saudade.

By now Romario and Slibulsky were scrubbing the floor and walls. Romario glanced up at me, and judging by the look in his eyes he wouldn't have minded if the blood he was scrubbing away had been mine.

I went into the kitchen and looked for something to help us carry the bodies to the car as unobtrusively as possible. I found a huge double-handled aluminium pan. It was over a metre in diameter and about the same depth. You could cook a whole pig in it, or several hundred-weight of vegetables, or anything else that would feed a medium-sized village for a day.

'What are you doing with that?' asked Romario as I dragged this monster into the dining-room.

'It's never a good idea to load sacks two metres long into a car boot at one in the morning. A pan full of pota-toes, on the other hand...'

'Are you crazy? I'll never find another pan like that!'

'You'll get it back.'

'You don't think I can ever make soup in it again after this, do you?'

'You think the customers will be able to taste them?'

His eyes widened, and for a moment it looked as if he was going to throw his floorcloths in my face.

'Yes, I do! *I'll* be able to taste them! Every time I use the pan I'll be thinking…'

'Hey, hang on!' Slibulsky looked up from his bucket and broke his silence for the first time since the gunfight. 'What's all this about your pan?'

Romario turned to him, and his expression softened. I'd been noticing for some time that he was trying to make Slibulsky his ally against me.

'Yes, exactly! What *is* all this? It's my special soup pan for festive occasions!' he exclaimed, obviously in the belief that for a civilised man like Slibulsky that would close the subject.

'Oh yes? And what festive occasion do you want to keep it clean for? Your funeral?' asked Slibulsky.

'Or your arrest?' I suggested, leaving the pan beside the grey plastic sausage shapes. Taking no more notice of Romario, we squeezed up the first of the bodies – they were still warm – and rammed it into the aluminium pan, treading it down.

'Did you notice their faces? They were powdered white,' said Slibulsky.

I nodded. 'As if they'd been rehearsing how to be dead.'

After we had looked to make sure the street was empty, we dragged the pan, which now weighed about eighty kilos, to the BMW. We heaved it up and tipped it over the open boot, but nothing happened. The man was stuck. We held the pan in the air with one hand and one shoulder each, tugging at the plastic with our other hands. The bin liner tore, and something slimy trickled over my hand.

'I'm going to throw up any moment,' gasped Slibulsky.

I heard a crack. Slibulsky had broken something in the corpse, and it finally gave way. It landed in the boot with a dull thud. We looked at each other's red, sweating faces and gasped for air. I wiped my hand on my trousers.

When our breathing had calmed down a little I said, 'Sorry. I really thought we'd only have to put on a tough guy act.'

Slibulsky flicked a damp bit of something off his T-shirt. 'I only hope Tango Man doesn't try pinning it all on us.'

'Pinning it on…?'

'Well, in theory he could go to the police and say gangsters started shooting his place up. He knows you slightly as a guest, he could say, but he had no idea of your Mafia connections.'

'Slibulsky, I'm a private detective!'

He stopped, looked incredulous, then uttered a sound between a laugh and a cough. 'Have your neighbours said a friendly *hi* to you very often recently? You have a Turkish name, Turkish parents, and since starting this job you've infuriated every second cop in town. You don't think a silly little nameplate on your door will stop them for a second if they have a chance of arresting you as an Anatolian terrorist baron, do you?'

'It's not just a plate on the door. I've got a licence too.'

This was weak, admittedly, and Slibulsky didn't even take the trouble to answer it. In fact he was pointing out a possibility that hadn't for a moment crossed my mind before.

On the way back I said, 'He's Brazilian. The tango comes from Argentina.'

'So what? You knew who I meant, right?'

He was correct there too.

Tango Man was sitting on a chair, feet up on the table, and seemed to have put back several glasses of liquor to calm his nerves while we were outside. 'Tango Man' fitted him perfectly: a long, tough-looking face with small, quick-moving eyes, a sharp nose and a cleft in his chin; mid-length hair, black and shining like lacquer, brushed well back and moving when he moved as if it grew from a single root; a body that was big and broad anyway, but looked even bigger and broader in a T-shirt and trousers that might once have fitted him in a school yard in Rio; and his obvious conviction that no one's ever too tall to wear shoes with five-centimetre heels.

Those eyes, not so quick-moving now, stared at us. We could see how he had to strain his lips to bring out any sound at all. Had he perhaps been putting back not glasses but whole bottles of liquor to calm his nerves? What and how much did you have to drink in just under twenty minutes to reach a state where you couldn't articulate? There was an empty glass beside him. I looked behind the bar, where I found an empty bottle. He hadn't eaten anything that evening, what with all the agitation, and normally he stuck to fruit juice.

'Hey, Romario, this is all a bit much for you, right?' I went over and put my hand on his shoulder. He looked up at me and gave me a long glance which, I suspected, was meant to express pain, but was only glazed and blurred. Then he silently raised his bandaged arm, looked at it and nodded at it, as if to say: what the pair of us go through together! He looked up at me again, reproachfully this time, until his face suddenly twitched and tears ran down his cheeks. As he wept a kind of whinny escaped him. I kneaded his shoulder, said something like, 'It'll all work out,' and looked around for Slibulsky to come to my aid. But he only shrugged and set about fitting the second corpse into the pan. The whinny finally became sobs, the sobs turned to gulps, the tears abated, I gave Romario a handkerchief and he blew his nose.

'I… the restaurant's like a girlfriend to me, see… and the way you'd give a girl jewellery and clothes, I bought it wood and tiles and tablecloths. To make it look pretty, see?'

'Yes, sure,' I said, wondering what kinds of presents, judging by the chipboard, fake marble tiles and check polyester tablecloths in this place, he gave his girlfriends.

'I promise you'll soon be able to come back here.' As I said that, the pushing and shoving behind me stopped for a moment, and I sensed Slibulsky's eyes on my back. Of course, it was more realistic to expect that the Saudade would be blown up some time in the next few weeks, and Romario would have to start all over again with kebabs and canned beer somewhere far away.

'Sorry about just now,' said Romario. 'You're right, how could you have known they'd start shooting straight away? But I was in shock…' He looked at me out of eyes that were still moist, and I nodded understandingly. It was just after one, according to my watch. 'So if you really could fix it, Kemal, I'd be eternally grateful!' He tried a smile. 'And you'd have free meals for life!'

Now it was my turn to try a smile. 'Well, great,

Romario. Thanks a lot. But,' I said, this time glancing at my watch as ostentatiously as possible, 'we ought to get a move on. By tomorrow this place must be as clean as if nothing had happened.' I pointed to the bullet-holes in the wooden panelling. 'You'll have to fill those in with something and paint them over. Better make yourself a coffee and then see how far you can get with one arm.'

I didn't want him to stop and think about his chances of getting safely out of this business. I wanted him to work until his other thumb was practically falling off too, and first thing tomorrow I'd put him on a plane with a bottle of schnapps. Once he'd left, it would be difficult for him to convince the police that he'd been a mere spectator. Particularly if I said otherwise, giving my word as a private detective, which I did think weighed just a little more than Slibulsky thought. I was in my mid-thirties and rather too old for snap judgements to the effect that I wasn't either popular or taken seriously in my profession – even if we were only talking about the police.

'Okay,' said Romario. 'I'll do my best.' Then he stood up, and he was on his way to the kitchen when he turned back again, pressed my arm with his sound hand and looked at me in a funny way. 'Thanks very much, Kemal. You're a real pal.'

Fortunately he was decent or drunk enough not to wait for an answer. He turned on his heel and staggered off with a few final sniffs. I watched him go, wondering if he believed what he said, or if he believed I believed what he said, or whether he simply thought that an extremely large amount of soft soap was advisable in an extremely tricky situation. You had to remember that Romario's moods swung back and forth wildly, and it was far from certain how long he would do his best. The sooner he was on that plane the better.

'Hey, real pal,' said a voice behind me. 'How about helping me pot up that other character now?'

Chapter 2

Ten years ago Slibulsky had been a small-time drugs dealer plying his trade between the station district and the smart set in the Westend quarter. He smuggled, cut, and sold whatever he could lay hands on that didn't mean instant death to his customers. Himself, he stuck to beer. On the side he was open to any kind of deal that in the worst-case scenario wouldn't get him more than five years in jail. We met in the course of one such deal. He helped me to break into Frankfurt police headquarters. A little later he was picked up with coke on him and served a year behind bars. I sent him parcels of World Cup football videos and beef sausage, and he thanked me with a box of clothes pegs he'd made himself. To this day that box stands in my kitchen, and I think every week or so how nice it would be to have a garden or a yard with a washing line in it.

Once he was out on parole, Slibulsky went to work as a bouncer for a brothel, then as a DJ in assorted discos on the outskirts of town, and finally as a bodyguard to a local politician. This man had nothing to fear from anyone, but he was campaigning on the slogan of *No Daily Violence On Our Streets – I'll Be the Enforcer*, and dragged Slibulsky around with him to election meetings as some kind of reverse evidence of the state of affairs he deplored. In the part of the city for which he was standing, criminality reached its height in the form of chewing-gum wrappers dropped on the pavement, and the worst violence seen on the streets was done by barking poodles and grumpy senior citizens. The election was won and Slibulsky was fired. He went back to drug-dealing for a while, until three years ago he had an idea and started an ice-cream business. It used those little carts, mostly drawn by a bicycle and usually adorned with pennants in the colours of the Italian flag, that were familiar to us all as part of our childhood Sundays, going around ringing their bells – or at least that's how we remember it today. No idea if I ever ate ice cream from a cart like that as a boy, or even saw one, but now, when one of them came down the street or stopped outside the swimming pool, for a moment I was eight years old again. And because I wasn't the only one to feel like that, and because almost everyone who remembered or thought they remembered the carts was now able to afford the super-size seven-scoops cornet without making too much of a hole in his pocket-money budget, Slibulsky's business was a great success. Children bought his ices too, but he really made a killing from people who'd pay ten marks to bring back the summers of the past. He had nine employees who worked for him seven days a week on commission, while he sat in an office with cable TV, counted the money and watched Formula One racing. A few repairs now and then, the occasional employee who made off with the day's takings, twice reported to the police for food poisoning – the rest of the time raking in a thousand marks, two thousand marks, Schumacher in pole position. By now he had earned enough for him and his girlfriend Gina to start looking for a house of their own with a warehouse and workshop, and then he'd be able to run the business more or less from the bedroom.

The fact that Slibulsky was helping me tonight, risking everything he'd built up in the last three years, and I don't mean just financially, was... well, it was very impressive.

'Not that way!' He waved a hand. 'There's a disco there, a hundred metres further on they do regular breathalyser checks at night.'

We were on our way to the Taunus to bury the bodies somewhere in the forest. The mere thought of coming up against a police road block and being asked for our papers brought me out in a sweat. Even if the Frankfurt police had awarded me their big Friendship Prize, even if the name 'Kayankaya' had been proverbial as the shorthand for an honest man who could always be believed, I'd have had all kinds of difficulties in explaining where the car came from, the contents of its boot, and the two spades from Slibulsky's garage on the back seat.

'Turn right up ahead there,' Slibulsky told me. 'And don't crawl along like that.'

'I'm driving at fifty. That's the speed limit.'

'Nobody sticks to the speed limit in a car that can do two hundred, not at two in the morning.'

I didn't reply to that, but I went on at the same speed. I'd rather end up in jail through stupidity than arrogance.

'And you could shake off any flashing blue light in this car.'

'Oh, for God's sake, Slibulsky!'

'Well, what is it?'

Yes, I was impressed by the way he was helping me, and the fact that he was doing it at all. But for him I'd never have got through the night intact, let alone been able to fix things so that Romario had half a chance of getting off safe and sound – but I wished I was on my own just now.

Over the years Slibulsky had become kind of like family to me. Sometimes a big brother who could give me advice and make me see reason, who backed me up or shielded me, depending on circumstances, and I had no secrets from him. But now and then he was a little brother driving me crazy with his quarrelsome obstinacy, getting in my way, and I wouldn't even want to give him the time of day for fear it might offer him a chance to poke his nose into my business.

'Let's bury these characters, clear up the bar and take Romario to the airport, OK? If we're in luck we may even get a bit of sleep afterwards. We can discuss everything else in the morning, right? Like how to drive a car.'

Slibulsky looked askance at me, and I could sense the retorts passing through his head. But then he just growled something to himself, put another sweet in his mouth and leaned over to the music system. When he pressed the *on* button it began shining and winking in umpteen different colours like a little fairground. He pushed the only CD lying around into it. Some kind of techno gabba delivered in a poofter sing-song tone. Slibulsky let it play. At full volume. I couldn't make him out.

'Switch that crap off, Slibulsky!'

Head nodding forward and back, he shouted through the din, 'Wait a moment! Listen to this! It's not so bad!'

But I wasn't waiting. And since I was under fire from four bass loudspeakers, and what with images of exploding faces in the back of my mind and two bodies in the boot, and the flashing lights of the music system in front of me, I felt for a moment that I was racing straight to hell, I didn't press the *off* button but took my foot off the accelerator and kicked the fairground to pieces.

'…Are you crazy?'

'You're the one who's crazy! "Listen to this!" I think I'm going nuts!'

For a while there was no sound but the quiet purring of the engine.

Finally Slibulsky cleared his throat and said coolly, 'It wasn't my idea to shoot a couple of guys down and bury their bodies. But that's what's happened, we have it all there in our heads, and it won't go away just because we stick to the Highway Code. You don't want to talk about technical questions, like for instance how no cop with his VW banger could ever overtake us in this car, and you don't want a little music, however horrible, to give you something else to think about – but maybe I do. So for all I care you're a super-killer who shoots a man and then settles down for a nice little nap – speaking for myself, after all that death I'd like something a little livelier!'

I didn't react. I stared straight ahead, gritting my teeth, and meticulously stuck to my fifty kph as if I could prove something that way. It was a fact that driving at such a slow speed on an empty, straight, well-surfaced road was a real strain on the nerves. I carefully stepped on the gas. When we were driving at eighty I'd reached the point where I could mutter, 'Sorry.'

Slibulsky shook his head. 'Oh, what the hell!' And after a pause, 'You know what would be a good idea now?'

'No, what?'

'A good screw.'

'What…?'

'To take your mind off things,' said Slibulsky. 'As I always say. What you need is a steady girlfriend. And don't go saying, "Oh, Slibulsky," again. I bet if you had someone waiting for you at home you wouldn't be so… so edgy.'

'Edgy? When we have a shoot-out behind us and two dead bodies in the boot!'

'Like I said, you need something to take your mind off it. And there's going to be more evenings when you need that too.'

'Oh, really?'

'I mean it, seriously.'

'Slibulsky! If you ask me, we've got plenty of other things to think about tonight, we can leave my private life out of it.'

Slibulsky looked at me and scratched his ear. 'You always do.'

'I always do what?'

'Leave your private life out of it.'

I briefly turned my head and caught his challenging look.

I wondered what Gina thought of being described as a good screw to take his mind off things in the evening. If Slibulsky said things like that in front of her. And if she was listening. Gina didn't often listen when Slibulsky was talking. There had to be some reason why two people with such different routines had stuck together for over ten years, and still seemed relatively happy. Gina was an archaeologist, and paid almost no attention to anything that wasn't to do with ancient potsherds. Whether Slibulsky was in jail or making millions with his ice-cream carts, she was always flying off to assorted desert countries, digging in the sand and discussing the results at congresses all over the world. She sat over her microscopes and dust samples at home, and when Slibulsky had visits from thugs whose bosses claimed there were old drug-dealing accounts still outstanding, Gina shut her door. Perhaps she actually didn't mind just being something to take his mind off things. Perhaps she saw Slibulsky in the same light. Perhaps Romeo and Juliet would have come to some such arrangement if they'd survived.

'In case you're really interested, I still have Deborah.'

'Deborah? Don't you mean Helga?'

'She calls herself Deborah, so I call her Deborah too.'

'But she's a tart!'

'So what?'

'I meant something else.'

'You said "a screw".'

'All the same, there's a difference.'

'Between a tart and a good screw to make up for things? Not much of one, if you ask me.'

'Don't start going on about true love.'

'I wasn't going to.'

'Good.'

A little later we reached the spruce wood where we were planning to dispose of the bodies. I looked in the rear-view mirror to make sure there was no car behind us and no one could see us, turned off the road onto an unmade path, and drove on the sidelights. The path came to an end after about a hundred metres and branches slapped against the windscreen. When we got out we were surrounded by the smell of resin and earth. The ground was covered with a thick layer of spruce needles. No sign of forestry workers or people going for walks.

While Slibulsky took the spades off the back seat, he asked, 'What are you going to do with the car?'

I ducked down under some branches, shining a flash-light as I looked for a suitable place to dig. 'Leave it somewhere near the rail station, as bait. The thing's worth so much, even a successful gangster would be glad to have it back. And perhaps someone will get behind the wheel and be idiot enough to lead me to his boss.'

'Well, just in case you change your mind, we'd get a year's earnings for that car.'

'A year of whose earnings, yours or mine?'

'Mine, of course. With yours you could just about buy the music system,' he said, opening the boot. 'In its present condition.'

'Very funny,' I muttered. Then I found a place. A large root stuck up above ground and could be pushed aside.

We spent the next forty minutes digging. Our faces were dripping with sweat, and blisters formed and broke on our hands. When the hole was wide and deep enough we pushed the bodies into it. We shovelled the earth back, trod it down, covered it with spruce needles, and finally I put the root back in place.

While Slibulsky reversed the car out of the wood, I tried covering up the tyre tracks as best I could. Back on the paved road, Slibulsky asked, 'How exactly did you see that, about using the car as bait? Are you going to stand beside it the whole time?'

'I'll get Max to build in a transmitter with a signal that I can follow by radio.'

'And then what?'

'How do you mean?'

'What will you do then? March in, say: "Hey, I shot a couple of your gorillas, but if you let my mate go on running his bar we'll say no more about it?"'

'What are you talking about? Do you tell people: "Hey, buy my ice cream, there's nothing in it but sugar and milk

33

powder and sometimes a couple of salmonella bugs, but give me ten marks for a cornet and I'll turn a blind eye?"'

Slibulsky made a face as if I were slow on the uptake. I lit a cigarette.

'OK,' he said, 'you'll be cleverer than that, but however clever you are this is a team that drives BMWs, wears Italian suits, and asks six thousand a month from the manager of a miserable little place serving warmed-up beans – about as much as all the furnishings are worth, if that. What I mean is, these guys don't do things by halves. Maybe they'll go crazy and overreach themselves, and then their outfit won't last long, but while it does last there's no compromising with them, no negotiating, nothing. Either you get rid of the rest of them or they'll get rid of you.'

'So what do you think I should do?'

'Tell Tango Man to clear off and forget the whole thing. He'll be up and running again soon. We don't have to worry about a character who's worried about his aluminium pan, not in the kind of situation we were in just now. And you'd better close your office for a few weeks and go to the country. Anywhere this bunch can't find you and you'll get a little colour in your cheeks.'

Before I could say anything, Slibulsky made a dismissive gesture. 'That's all right. About how much?'

I hesitated, knowing that I wasn't going to accept what Slibulsky was offering, but I did the sums all the same. 'Well… I'm two months behind with the office rent, I haven't paid the phone bill yet, and I owe someone three thousand marks.'

The someone was Slibulsky.

'Right, I'll give you seven thousand for the rent and the

phone, you can have a holiday with what's left. And just forget the three thousand…' Slibulsky paused, and then grinned broadly. 'The guy you owe it to has enough anyway.'

To please Slibulsky I grinned too. My thoughts were somewhere else entirely. Refusing his money had nothing to do with pride or a sense of honour. I'd have taken twenty thousand without bothering too much, because there was no doubt about it, Slibulsky did have enough, or anyway as much as we both thought was enough. But I'd been fool enough to accept a job from Romario, and I'd mucked it up, and a lot of blood had been spilt and energy wasted for no good reason. If two men die and everything's still the same as before, or worse, then something's wrong. I had to make sense of it all, even if only by making sure that Romario could carry on acting the typical Brazilian at the Saudade in peace, complaining about the German weather and wearing an apron with parrots printed on it.

Or I could have put it to myself more simply: I wished I hadn't shot anyone.

'Thanks, Slibulsky, but as I see it Romario may be an idiot – well, he *is* an idiot – but it all turned out this way on his account, and I think someone ought to get something out of it. And I have to know who those two were. I can't just shoot a man like that. I won't forget it.'

Slibulsky looked straight ahead, driving the car gently along. I couldn't see his expression in the faint orange light of the dashboard. We drove on to the next village in silence.

'Look,' he said at last, 'It's not a complete disaster because just once you really mucked up.' They didn't exactly leave us much room to manoeuvre. But do it if you must. Three things: keep my name to yourself, pay your rent with my money, and when we've taken Tango Man to the airport let's go back to my place. We'll have a bite to eat and you can sleep on the sofa.'

'Stinking cheese?'

Slibulsky nodded. 'And there's a crate of beer in the fridge.'

When the skyscrapers of Frankfurt appeared ahead of us I slipped lower down in the passenger seat and enjoyed the sight of the lights of the management offices on the top floors shining next to the moon. Whatever I'm feeling like, every time I drive into Frankfurt my heart lifts for a moment at the look of the skyline. In the normal way it's probably just the image of such a concentrated, powerful place with those densely crowded tower buildings you can see miles away, giving a man who has his own little room somewhere among them a momentary illusion of being concentrated and powerful too. But this time those concrete pillars gave off another aura. As we drove past the Trade Fair Tower and I looked up at the façade that seemed to go on up and up into the sky, I felt a little calmer for the first time since the shoot-out. Was it my stupid subconscious whispering: a small-time character like you can't really do anything too terrible? Or was it just the sight of such a mighty building making me feel that the world has seen and survived worse things than two dead thugs who were extorting protection money? Anyway, it was something to do with the fact that the building belonged to my home town, and I had a friend in that home town with a place where I could spend the night and eat, and if some Mafia outfit from somewhere else got a bloody nose from us, it was their own fault!

So far, so locally patriotic. A few cops I knew would have been surprised. They might even have spoken to me politely for a change.

But it wasn't just the management floors lighting Frankfurt up tonight. As we drove past the station and I turned my head to ask Slibulsky if he knew whether there were any flights to the south at this time of night, I saw a red glow in the sky. Roughly in the direction of the Saudade. People sometimes like to say, after the event, that they knew something at a certain moment, although they really just mean they were afraid of it. All the same, I did know. And I felt I had only to reach out my arm and point a finger for Slibulsky to know too. Anyway, he opened his mouth and left it open for the rest of the drive, his gaze becoming more and more fixed. The closer we came to the Saudade the stronger the smell of burning was. When we finally turned into the road where the Brazilian flag had hung on one street corner for the last seven years, flakes of soot flew to meet us, and the blue lights of police cars were circling the place. The street was sealed off, curious onlookers were standing to right and left, and the Saudade was blazing fiercely.

We stopped the car at the road block and watched the fire-fighters running back and forth among ladders, hoses and pumps. Several jets of water were directed on the flames. The building, an old one with wooden floors and window frames, had four storeys, and the fire had reached the third. Meanwhile the blocks of flats to left and right had been cleared, and a bunch of sleepy children wrapped in blankets, unkempt men in dressing-gowns, and women with handbags and carrier bags were spilling out into the street. A tart was arguing with her client about payment for their unfinished business, and a drunk was offering the fire-fighters hurrying past him cans of beer out of a carrier as if he were in charge of a refreshment stop for marathon runners.

When the flames reached the fourth floor Slibulsky turned his head. 'Now what?' he asked.

I think I meant to shrug my shoulders, but I only succeeded in hunching them even further. Five hours ago we had set out, we'd had a quick drink in a bar, squeezed into Romario's cupboard, and all things considered we'd been in a pretty relaxed mood. A stupid job, yes, but not one you couldn't get done with the help of a spot of bad temper and a few moderately funny jokes. I mean, what were two racketeers come for their protection money who never opened their mouths…? Come on, Slibulsky, we can do this standing on our heads, we just have to puff air in their faces and they'll leave Romario in peace…

'…Do you think he got out?'

Slibulsky raised his eyebrows. 'Drunk as he was?'

I lit myself a cigarette. My hands were trembling. 'I don't think I feel well.'

'I told you, they don't do things by halves.'

'How could they find out what had happened so quickly?'

'Maybe there was a third man in the car.'

My mouth dropped open, and I goggled at Slibulsky as if he'd just conjured up a whole flock of pigeons or something. Of course! Why hadn't we thought of that before? And how come I myself hadn't worked it out?

'What do you think, have we been acting like idiots?'

'Look, we had a couple of dead bodies on our hands! And if there was a third man it wouldn't have made any difference.'

'But we could have taken Romario with us.'

'We ought to have got that tall bastard to pay them the six grand.'

That had been Slibulsky's view all along. Protection money to the Mafia was just taxation, he thought, only you got a better return for your money. He knew what it was all about. In his time as a bouncer for that brothel he'd also been responsible for getting the whores to pay up the few hundred marks they owed for round-the-clock guard and their mouldy rooms. He didn't like to talk about that, and the methods he sometimes had to use.

'But he didn't,' Slibulsky went on, 'and then this happened. He knew what tangling with characters like that could mean. Well, nothing we can do here now, and I guess we'd better go home.'

'But whoever started the fire is still around. He's not going to miss the show...'

'So? You think he's standing around somewhere with a big cigarette lighter? Come on, we've had enough for one day.'

Slibulsky started the engine of the car and turned it. I didn't protest. We really had had enough.

After we'd gone round two corners the glow of the fire disappeared behind buildings and neon ads. As we crossed the bridge to Sachsenhausen the sky in the east turned blue. I thought of Romario's one-room flat in the Nordend district. Photographic wallpaper showing a palm-fringed Brazilian beach, plus a bed with a sagging mattress and dirty grey sheets. Slibulsky was on the wrong track if he thought Romario could have paid six thousand marks just like that. He had put all his money into the Saudade, his one true love. But apart from farmers and folk from small towns who wanted to round off a weekend visit to the red-light district of Frankfurt with an exotic supper, scroungers like me and a handful of Brazilian transvestites, hardly anyone had wanted to be witness to his love. From Monday to Thursday the place was empty. If Romario had a special soup pan for festive occasions the size of a rain-water butt, and had objected to its use as a receptacle for corpses, he'd only been putting on a desperate act. There were never any festive occasions at the Saudade, let alone enough customers to put back as much soup as the pan held. And anyway the characters who got lost and found their way to the Saudade were not the kind to waste their capacity for liquid intake on soup. I wondered who would break down the door to Romario's flat, and hoped he'd changed the sheets recently.

After we had pushed a number of ice-cream carts in need of repairs out of Slibulsky's garage and into the yard, and got the BMW under cover, we went up to his flat. Slibulsky took the crate of beer out of the fridge, and we sat down by the living-room window with it. Neither of us felt like food any more, let alone the cheese – a yellow stinker which, if you had enough imagination, looked like a clump of calloused skin collected from mortuaries, kept moist and stored in gumboots for years. Outside it was getting light. We drank beer and watched the first rays of the sun falling on the rooftops. We were too exhausted to talk and too churned up inside to sleep. Only when the sun was shining in our faces and school-kids were shout-ing out in the street did Slibulsky rise to his feet, put a blanket on the sofa for me, and wish me a sceptical, 'Good-night.' I waited for another beer to take effect, then levered myself up from my chair too, staggered across the room and fell on the sofa. I was still wondering what Gina would think if she found me here with my shoes on her sofa cushions with their linen covers when my eyes closed, and it was about five seconds before I fell asleep. And about ten seconds before an alarm clock made my head burst. Tinkle tinkle, tinkle tinkle, tinkle tinkle... Another ten seconds before I realized that the racketeer's mobile was ringing in my breast pocket. I pressed buttons at random, hoped the right one was among them, and cleared my throat. The right one *was* among them, and I heard a voice. At the same moment everything I'd tried to work out about the origin of the blackmailers over the last few hours was turned on its head by the Frankfurt accent.

'Hey, where's you lot, then? Here's me sitting around like a fool, can't come off duty, time I went to bed. You in the disco or what? If the boss hears... where are you? Can't hear a thing...'

I tried clearing my throat again.

'You being funny? Tell me where you are, I'll tell you how long it'll take to get home. And if you don't I'm shutting up shop and going to bed, get it?'

'Yup.'

'Whaddya mean, "yup"?'

'Yup, I get it.'

I waited for him to go on grousing and with luck give me some idea where it was that his mates were supposed to come home to. But something about my answer must have sounded wrong, because all I heard was a sudden sharp intake of breath and then he ended the call. I stared at the mobile. A Hessian Mafia! No wonder the black-mailers had preferred not to talk. Who'd have taken them seriously?

I put the mobile back in my breast pocket and looked up at the ceiling. The night was actually ending on a note of relief. No language I didn't understand, no bosses I'd have to look for far afield. Just a cosy little connection probably thought up in the back room of a bar where they were putting back the local cider, the boss a meat importer or used-car dealer or the owner of some fair-ground booth, the rest of them unemployed scaffolders and drunks who took the tickets in porn cinemas. 'Hey, how's about a little Mafia op?' And I imagined myself marching into the office with its rubber tree and chrome furniture and Pirelli calendar and saying: 'No, I don't want to buy a piece of old junk sprayed metallic silver, I've come to take you in. You got me into shooting a man, and you barbecued someone I know. Now we'll see if your place burns as well as his!' And then I'd unscrew the petrol can, and the fatso in the double-breasted suit would beg for mercy, and I'd go *ping*, and I'd go *zack*, and I'd… well before I could wonder what I'd actually do in the end I'd fallen asleep again. And even the fact that the caller, who was obviously some kind of caretaker on the phone switchboard for the gang, had known nothing about either the dead men or the fire didn't get through to me that morning.

Chapter 3

The first thing I noticed when I woke up was the smell. A mixture of skin cream and lubricating oil and something chemical like sprayed grapefruit, but without any grapefruit aroma. Then a hand shook my shoulder, and I opened my eyes. Blinking, I saw a head with a furry animal sitting on it. When the picture cleared the animal turned into a complicated hairstyle piled high and held in place with a dozen clasps. Only then did I recognise Gina. Her lips were bright blood-red, and she was wearing a blue pinstriped suit and a blouse with buttons that looked as each of them would pay a few months' worth of my rent, cash down. I think this was the first time since her university days I'd seen Gina in her war paint, not dressed in an overall or a man's shirt in order to scrape away at ancient potsherds.

At the time, over ten years ago when Slibulsky first met Gina, she was working as a teacher in a school of dance and etiquette to finance her archaeological studies. With the knowledge she'd had to acquire in childhood, as the daughter of a tax inspector's wife who liked to make herself out Madame Monte Carlo rather than plain Frau Scheppes from Bornheim, Gina herself was now teaching the sprogs of Frankfurt proprietors of delicatessen shops and ladies' fashion boutiques how to waltz and drop a curtsey. She'd had to dress to suit the part. After that job ended, leaving Gina free to be much more casual about her appearance, I sometimes wondered whether the short grey skirts and bright red high-heeled shoes of those days had perhaps not been the least important consideration when Slibulsky plied her with several litres of champagne one evening.

Her Punch-and-Judy face with its pointed chin and long, aquiline nose was beaming at me. She looked outrageously healthy and wide awake. 'Hi, good morning. Had a heavy night of it?'

I wiped my mouth, cleared my throat, and accustomed myself to the fact that even now Gina could look very unlike a woman who organized pottery courses. 'Fairly heavy. What's the time?'

'Twelve-thirty. Slibulsky's been gone quite some time. Had a meeting with his salesmen.'

She'd done something or other to her eyes too, or around them. They weren't really that big and that dark. Or had I just never noticed because her hair was usually hanging over her face?

'He says to tell you you'd better leave the car in the garage for now, and you should look at the sweets.'

'What sweets?'

'You're asking me that? What car?'

Oh yes, I remembered, the evening's compensation: tell Kayankaya to leave the car in our garage, and you don't need to know it belongs to a bunch of brutal gangsters, my love, let's just pray you don't take it into your head to drive that upmarket set of wheels round town.

'Anyway,' Gina went on, 'the cleaning lady comes in half an hour's time and I have a date at the museum. If you don't mind a hoover zooming round you, stay put, otherwise I can take you into town with me.'

I looked down at myself: jacket, trousers, shoes, disgusting stains everywhere. 'OK,' I said. 'I'll be with you.'

'I need another ten minutes. There's coffee in the kitchen if you'd like some.'

While Gina disappeared into the next room I heaved myself up from the sofa, staggered into the kitchen, washed my face over the sink, got myself a cup of coffee and sat down with it by the open window, which was next to a chestnut tree. The window looked out on the yard, and silence reigned apart from the chirping of some sparrows hopping about in the branches and the sound of Gina's distant footsteps as she walked over the wooden floors. I drank some coffee, put the cup down, and pushed it away from me. I sat there for a while, slumped like a sack of flour, just staring ahead of me. So this was how it felt when you'd shot someone the night before, and a fairly close acquaintance had burned to death: you looked for a comfortable place to sit and wonder why people who can afford a cleaning lady would drink horrible filter coffee kept lukewarm for hours in a coffee machine. I made myself think of the moment when we'd come rushing out of that cupboard and fired. But everything that had happened yesterday seemed to me as improbable as a story babbled by some drunk in a bar the night before, and as if I, also drunk, had been trying very hard to believe his story. Perhaps that would change when I read about Romario's charred body in the evening papers. Or when the first thugs turned up in my office because the gang had been asking questions, and had found out who had been going in and out of the Saudade unusually often over the last few days. No one's movements went unobserved in the station district, certainly not if you were known to be something like a cop. Or would they simply blow my office up just like that? I mean, what was there to talk about?

'Got a hangover?' asked Gina as she came through the door. And with her came that strange, penetrating aroma.

'Don't know yet,' I replied, watching her go over to the coffee machine and pour herself a cup. She leaned against the fridge, cup in hand, and examined me in a friendly manner.

'Apart from that, are you doing all right?' We hadn't seen each other for over a month.

'Hm… not as well as you, I guess. You're looking great.'

She smiled at me. 'Thanks.' Then she suddenly looked at her coffee, drank some, and kept her eyes down. A brief answer. So brief that there was a silence after it. Other archaeologists might have said: yes, I'm feeling great because I've been appointed curator of the museum, or because I've found Genghis Khan's toothglass. She just said thanks, and it was as if she'd slammed a door in my face.

'As a matter of fact,' I went on, when the silence threatened to become awkward, 'if this date at the museum's an important one, I'd better tell you your clothes smell, and not just of anti-moth spray. It's like you'd sprayed them against rats, wolves and burglars too.'

'Anti-moth spray?' She looked at me in astonishment. Then she lowered her cup and looked down at herself, as if to make sure she was still wearing what she'd put on earlier. 'But I bought this only last week.'

'Ah. Well, they must have treated it with something when they were making it. Sorry, but it smells horrible.'

She lowered her head and hauled part of her collar up

to her nose. 'I can't smell anything… only my perfume.'

'Perfume?'

'Yes, perfume! Issey Miyake, if you really want to know!'

'I don't believe it.' And I really didn't. Some old archaeological joke, maybe: What's that stink in your lab? – Oh, it's what Cleopatra smelled like when she'd been rubbing in fermented goat shit for her spots!

Gina shook her head. 'Good heavens, Kayankaya! Get yourself a girlfriend! Next you'll be asking what those two bumps swelling out in front of me are.'

I opened my mouth – and shut it again. Well, well. Slibulsky didn't think it necessary to tell his partner about the gangsters' car worth a hundred thousand marks in the garage, but he was obviously happy to discuss my private life with her. I imagined them discussing my solo existence anxiously in the evening over stinking cheese and open sandwiches: poor thing, all alone in his flat – Pass the butter, please, darling – It's really depressing – Well, he can't be the easiest person to live with – Leave it, dear, I'll wash the dishes – Oh, Gina…

As we were driving towards the city centre in Gina's Fiat a little later, she said, 'And if we're talking about smells…'

'Yes, I know.' I dismissed this comment. Even as I got into the small, cramped car I'd realised that I was the last person who ought to bring the subject up this afternoon.

Gina dropped me off at my flat, kissed me on the cheek and invited me to come to dinner some time soon. When the Fiat had disappeared round the corner, I looked up at my windows on the first floor. One of them was open, and I wondered if I'd left it that way.

There was a greengrocer's shop on the ground floor of the dirty white sixties block. Its owner was also caretaker of the flats. He had stood for election to the council as a Republican a few years ago, and for a while he was mad keen on getting me out of the building. I had only to flush the loo at four in the morning to have him complain that I was disturbing the other tenants. But then German reunification came, and after a euphoria lasting just under two months and consisting mostly of his getting drunk and bawling out the national anthem every other evening, meanwhile complaining of me more than ever, his ideas of the enemy suddenly underwent a change. All at once *the Ossies* were the enemy. Not that the greengrocer ever saw Ossies anywhere but on TV, but for some reason he began hating them like poison all the same. I'd never forget the morning when he came rushing out of his shop towards me with a half-rotten apple in his hand, shouting, 'Look at that, will you? Just arrived! Imported from the east! Huh! Living it up on my solidarity tax!' Staggered to find that for the first time I wasn't the object of his displeasure, I looked at the apple and said, as if in a trance, 'Well, fancy that!' Whereupon he lost no time in putting our relationship on a new footing, leaned towards me with a conspiratorial nod, and warned me, 'We're going to get some surprises, you bet your life. Oh yes, we're going to get some surprises.'

He actually said *we*! And until now he'd used all forms of the pronouns *we* and *you* to me in a way that made it perfectly clear this wasn't just a case of a caretaker arguing with a tenant, it was a clash between nations if not whole races, it was cultural warfare of worldwide significance over disturbing the neighbours after ten in the evening. And now the two of us were shoulder to shoulder in the little lifeboat of civilisation, so to speak, surrounded by hordes of Ossies! OK, so in his view he was the only one paying solidarity tax. Perhaps he thought I paid my taxes in Istanbul.

Anyway, since that morning we'd exchanged the time of day, and when his wife died a little later and he began taking Russian tarts to his flat in the evenings, his attitude to me became almost warm. Mainly, no doubt, out of shame because in this modern building I could regularly follow the course of his Deutschmark romances through the thin ceiling of his flat. In addition, I thought, his simple view of the world and the existence of a common border between Turkey and Georgia – which still meant Russia to us children of the Cold War – gave him a vague feeling that he had, so to speak, married into my family.

Anyway this afternoon, I entered the greengrocer's shop calling out a cheerful, 'Hi!'

'Oh… hi.'

He quickly put his newspaper down. He'd probably been studying the tarts' ads. It was Friday, he'd be getting one tomorrow. These days I took care not to come home too early on a Saturday evening. I usually went to see Deborah.

He came out from behind his counter, a weedy little man, patted his thin yellow hair into place and approached me with his now usual expression of inspecting something about me or behind me with interest. Whatever else had changed since that morning with the imported fruit from the east, we never looked in each other's eyes. Like it or not they were, so to speak, the display windows of our armouries, which were still stuffed full of insults, wariness and mutual distrust. And because we knew or guessed that but didn't want to think about it, because it really was much pleasanter to exchange a word or so on the stairs than snap at each other, we'd discovered a whole series of attitudes, little habits and manoeuvres that allowed our eyes to keep from meeting.

'...Everyone already in short sleeves for weeks! And it's only May!' said the greengrocer, as he looked at my arms and then glanced over my shoulder and straight at the door, crying, 'But look at that, there's a storm coming up! A bit of rain will be good for us!'

So I turned and looked at the doorway too, and we'd done it: we were standing side by side, and there was scarcely anything in the brief conversation that followed to make us look away from the view of parked cars and a pile of empty fruit crates. When it was raining the green-grocer would use his wet shoes as an excuse to look first down and then anywhere else, in late summer he never took his eyes of the wasps zooming around his fruit, and in the morning he had to see precisely how the sugar dissolved in his coffee. All I could usually think of was scratching my lowered head; apart from that, I went along with whatever scenario he set up.

After I'd briefly given him my views on the weather I asked if he'd heard noises of any kind coming from my flat towards dawn.

'Ho, living it up last night, eh?' He waved it away. 'That's no problem. I was awake anyway.'

'What makes you think I was living it up?'

'Well...' He coughed, amused. 'If a person can't get his

own key in the lock of his own door, he's usually been having a good time for the last few hours, right? I mean, it's obvious. Well, you'd want to be living it up here and now. It's your kind of climate out there, right?'

'Hm, yes. Did I manage to get the door open?'

For a moment it seemed he was about to turn his head and look at me in surprise. But then, looking at the fruit crates, he asked, 'Well, did you wake up in the stairwell?'

'I woke up with friends. And I've been at their place until now.'

'Really? Well, that's certainly odd. I'm sure I heard someone at your door around six this morning.'

'Did you hear whoever it was in the flat too?'

'Well, now you mention it… that's right, no footsteps, though normally…'

Of course he was longing to know what it was all about, but he didn't like to ask. Since he'd taken to bringing tarts home he thought highly of the principle of privacy.

'I'll just go and take a look,' I decided, and before he could reply I'd said goodbye, looking vaguely in the direction of the vegetable display, and I was out of the door.

The lock looked perfectly normal. Whoever had tried breaking into my flat had gone about it without using violence. I put the key in it. Turned the key twice to unlock the door, as usual. I pushed the door open and looked at the small, square entrance hall, with its coat-rack and empty bottles. I stood there for a while in the doorway, listening. Finally I went in, examined the whole place, two rooms, kitchen and bathroom, and remembered leaving the window open because of a smell of sewage coming up through the sink plughole in the kitchen. Would gangsters planning to get into my flat try a couple of keys just in case they happened to fit, and then give up and go away again?

I closed the door, made coffee, and sat down with a cup by the phone. First I tried reaching Slibulsky. For one thing to find out how he was feeling, for another to ask why I was supposed to look at some kind of sweets. But the phone in his office was answered by one of the ice-cream vendors, who said Slibulsky was out stocking up on cardboard beakers. Then I rang the number of Romario's flat. Perhaps he had a girlfriend, or a visitor from Brazil, or someone else he'd been keeping a secret from us and who was now waiting unsuspectingly at the window, staring at the firewall opposite and starting to get angry. Or who was just being questioned by the police, had no idea what they were talking about, and needed help. Or who knew just what they were talking about and needed help all the more. But no one picked up the phone. I smoked, and wondered who I knew who was so close to Romario that he or she ought to be told about yesterday's events. I could only think of the cleaning lady who flicked a duster round the restaurant twice a week. A sprightly old Portuguese woman whose name and address I didn't know.

After a second cup of coffee I took the racketeer's phone out of my breast pocket and looked first for stored numbers, which it didn't have, and then for the redial button. Who would the gang members have called last? My Hessian friend of last night? Some boss or other? The lady who ran courses for mutes on how to use the phone? If speaking had really been impossible for them, of course the Hessian would have suspected something straight away.

Perhaps he'd been trained to expect whistling or tapping. On the other hand he'd asked where they were, and it seemed to me that conveying an address by whistling was a trick it would be almost impossible to learn.

I tried to concentrate and pressed the button. A six-digit number beginning with an eight came up on the display. An Offenbach number. When it began ringing I quickly thought up a couple of things to say: whoever answered had won a car in the new phone-number lottery, for instance, and where could we meet to deal with the formalities? But no one did answer, and after the phone had rung twenty times I switched the thing off. I'd find the address that the number belonged to on the computer in my office. Until then I must content myself with the redial button.

I picked up my own phone again and called a cop who could hardly refuse my request. He was head of the Frankfurt immigration police squad, he had a family, and he'd once been filmed on video playing around with underage boys. I knew about the pictures.

'Höttges here.'

'Good day, Herr Höttges. Kayankaya speaking.'

Silence at the other end... a long, indrawn breath... footsteps... a door closing, then a voice hissing in my ear. 'We agreed you wouldn't call me at the office!'

'But if I call you at home it's usually your fourteen-year-old son who picks up the phone, and that always sets off certain associations in my mind.'

Another deep breath, another silence. 'What do you want?'

'I need the name of someone who owns a BMW.' I gave him the registration number. 'And I also want all the information there is about new Mafia-style gangs in the station district.'

He hesitated. 'I'd have to ask around. As you know, it's the immigration police I'm with.'

'Then ask around. And don't try to fob me off with rubbish. I want the names of the gang bosses, their addresses, roughly the number of members and so on – by tomorrow afternoon.'

'But I can't get hold of the information just like that, most of it's secret.'

'You'll find it. After all, not everything can stay secret: videotapes, Mafia organisations – it all has to come out sometime...'

Even as I spoke he rang off. But I knew he'd work his socks off to get me the information I wanted by tomorrow. This had been going on for over eight years. In fact I'd deduced the existence of the videotapes only incidentally, during a case of forged passports and refugees, and they'd probably been binned long ago. But for one thing, Höttges didn't know that, and for another the whole business wasn't just obscene, these things always are, it was obscene with metaphorical knobs on, you might say. A mere rumour, carefully dropped into the ear of certain newspaper and TV editors, would probably have been enough to get the head of the Frankfurt immigration police hunted first out of his job, then out of his family, and finally, when his photo had been in the press, out of town. Höttges, who as regional dogsbody was responsible to the Minister of the Interior for letting practically no one who lived outside the area that could receive Radio Luxembourg into the city, and throwing out as many as possible of those who had made their way in all the same

– unless they had an income of over a few thousand net, of course – Höttges had been messing around with Arab boys of fifteen at the time. You could just imagine the headlines. *Head of deportation fits rent boys in'*, or *Gay Commissioner responsible for residence permits – kids had to line up for him.* The fact that the boys and their pimp had of course set the whole thing up and had fleeced Höttges mercilessly themselves wouldn't be any excuse for him in the eyes of either the public or his family. On the contrary, to the public he would look not just a pervert but also a fool. To me, Höttges was a real stroke of luck. As a source of information and a direct means of leverage in police HQ, he must have helped me to earn one-third of my fees over the last few years.

I pressed the redial button on the mobile again, counted up to the twentieth ring tone once more, undressed and got under the shower. When I was in my dressing-gown, sitting in front of some crispbread and a can of sardines, the first thunder rolled over the city. Soon after that Slibulsky rang. We told each other how we were, and he said that apart from the fact that he'd had hardly three hours' sleep, and he'd been racing around town since ten in the morning after stuff of some kind, he wasn't too bad. It was only when he shook hands with one of his ice-cream vendors, and the man's hand was wet with sweat, that he'd felt sick for a moment at the thought of packing those bodies up, he said.

'I'm eating sardines out of the can at this moment and feeling glad they don't have their heads on,' I said, contributing my mite to the conversation. 'Normally I prefer them whole.'

'Hm,' said Slibulsky. 'Looks like we'll survive it. Do you still want to find out who that couple were?'

'Of course.'

'Did Gina tell you to take a look at the sweets?'

'She did. But she didn't know what sweets, or where they were.'

'The sweets in the BMW, of course.'

'What's so special about the sweets?'

'They're not a brand I know.'

'Fancy that.'

'Oh, come on, Kayankaya, you know I started sucking sweets when I stopped smoking. And I've tried every brand and every variety in Germany – but I don't know *these*. So when you find out where the sweets come from... get the idea?'

'I get it. Doesn't it happen to say where they're from on the packet?'

'That's the funny thing. It says they're made in Germany.'

'What's so funny about that?'

'Because they're *not* from here. Or maybe for export only, but I don't believe that either. I think it's like with my Italian ice cream that doesn't come from Italy. But who wants ice cream from Ginnheim?'

'Germany, home from home for confectionery?'

'Makes no difference. If you want to sell something in a place where Germany has a good reputation, even if it's bananas you're selling, you stick a label on your stuff saying it comes from the German provinces.'

'Bananas grown in the German provinces – OK. But where would Germany have this wonderful reputation?'

'How do I know? Maybe Paraguay? You're the detective. If you want to take a look at them, I'll be home from eight onwards.'

We rang off, and I went on eating sardines. The storm was beginning outside, thunder rolling and lightning flashing, the first drops were falling, and soon there was a waterfall cascading down outside my windows. When the storm moved away an hour later it left a grey, dripping dishcloth above the city.

Around five I rang the only client I had at the time. A woman academic, an expert on Islam, whose German shepherd dog had gone missing. I told her I'd spent all day visiting animal rescue centres in Kelkheim and Hattersheim, no luck, but I'd go on searching tomorrow, and I was sure I'd soon be bringing Susi home. I'd been telling her that for a week, and so far there'd been cheques and no complaints. That was the way I liked my clients, very rich and very crazy.

Then I put on a raincoat for the first time in weeks and set off for the station.

Chapter 4

Around five in the morning fire broke out in an old four-storey building near Frankfurt Central Station. The building, which consisted of a restaurant and offices, burned down to its foundations. The fire-fighters succeeded in keeping the blaze away from the nearby blocks of flats. Normally there was no one in the building at night, and so far there seem to have been no victims. However, it will take days from the arrival of the fire service on the scene to clear the rubble and make sure that the only damage was to property. No information about the cause of the fire is yet available...

I put the damp evening paper into the litter bin and got on the tram going towards Slibulsky's flat. I'd been walking around the station district for four hours, my feet were sore, my shoulders were wet, and a mixture of tea, coffee, beer and cider was glugging about inside me. I had been in countless bars and restaurants and visited several stalls selling snacks, asking the owners, waiters and vendors whether they had ever heard of the Army of Reason. About a third of them seemed genuinely surprised, and usually wanted to know if this was some damnfool anti-liquor campaign. Another third clammed up, left me sitting or standing where I was, and didn't even come back for me to settle my bill. The rest had relieved me of about

58

five hundred marks with variants on the question of how much the information was worth. What I had discovered was as follows: the Army of Reason had been in the protection money racket for about two weeks, operating with a brutality uncompromising even by the standards of the station district. They always turned up two at a time, they didn't say a word, their faces were powdered or heavily made up, they communicated by means of scribbled notes couched in high-flown language, and at the slightest sign of resistance they drew pistols or knives. A kebab vendor and a waiter, both of them among those who immediately turned away from me when I mentioned the Army, had obviously shown such resistance. Like Romario, they had their right hands bandaged.

Of those who did talk to me none of them had the faintest idea who the Army were, where they came from, or who was behind them. It was as if they'd dropped from another planet into the station district and wanted to rake in as much as they could, as quickly as they could, of the stuff that the local inhabitants called money, because obviously you could never have enough of it. The Army seemed to have none of the usual interest of protection racketeers in keeping their sources going. They asked every victim for a sum which they obviously thought could be raised in cash very quickly, never mind whether that made the business go broke or not. They demanded thirty thousand from a restaurant with a wine list and white tablecloths, four thousand from a sausage stall. So although the Army had announced that the contributions would be made monthly, they were probably one-off payments. The most obvious reason for that seemed to be a desire to avoid warfare with the gangs who really ruled the quarter. Get in fast and get out fast, before the local gangland bosses could react.

For about a year the streets and businesses of the station district had been neatly divided up between a German boss, an Albanian boss and a Turkish boss, and everyone in the vicinity, not least the police, was happy with this carefully negotiated settlement. Life was almost as peaceful as it had been nine years ago when the Schmitz brothers were undisputed kings of the station district, and a bent Christian Democrat city council had left the brothers to their own devices. At the time the brothers allowed or banned just about everything that made money in the area, from registered brothels to illegal underground casinos. They made sure that business ran reasonably smoothly, sometimes with diplomatic skill, sometimes with troops of heavies, and took their cut of every mark earned, a percentage precisely calculated to keep those who paid them from ever seriously thinking of questioning the system. They had even succeeded in banishing the drugs trade and drugs consumption that had been getting increasingly nasty since the seventies to places on the outskirts of the district. That way respectable fathers of families and business travellers could look for their pleasures without being constantly reminded, by the delirious walking dead, that the glittering night-life of champagne, lucky breaks and ladies in suspender belts was largely based on veins covered in needle marks. On the whole, then, everything ran as well under the Schmitz brothers as it can in a red-light district: the police knew where to turn after a shoot-out, bar owners and brothel managers knew they could tell anyone but the Schmitz brothers to go take a running jump, the fixers knew where to slip away to, and people like me knew where to get a beer at three in the morning. But then the good folk of Frankfurt elected a Social Democrat council, the regular flow of money from the brothers into the Town Hall came to light, and that was the end of their little kingdom. The brothers disappeared first from the city and then from the country, leaving behind seven streets among the high-rise banking buildings and the Central Station that were soon, like a mountain of gold with no one to guard it, beaming out their radiance to the most remote corners of Europe. Before a month was up the first gangs invaded, killed a few bar owners to earn themselves respect, and thought they could rule the district with an iron hand. But that took more than spreading fear. The brothers had managed to give their subjects a sense of mutual profit, they were seen as guarantors of peace and a regular income, and they were relatively reliable. Those who kicked up a fuss got slapped down, the industrious got an extra thousand in their bank accounts. In addition, the brothers bought their suits off the peg and knew practically everyone in the district by his first name. The new masters with their made-to-measure suits and diamond rings just about knew the name of the city they were in, took percentages when and how they liked, and if they were in a bad mood disposed of the first handy victim to come along. Agreements were worth nothing, and all you could rely on was trouble. The gangs who moved in behind them sometimes had it easier. Once upon a time, if gangsters of some kind had appeared in the district intending a takeover, the Schmitz brothers knew about it within hours and could count on a large body of supporters. Now no one warned the gang-land bosses, let alone helped them. Far from it: everyone was happy to see them chucked out. And so it went on for seven years. More and more often, increasingly isolated bosses had to vacate the place faster and faster. They came from Germany, Austria, Italy, Albania, Romania, Turkey, Yugoslavia, Russia, Belarus, and a handful of South American countries. You had the feeling that a kind of criminal Olympic Games was going on in the Frankfurt station district. Taking part was what mattered. Some of them stayed in charge for such a short time that they hardly covered their travel expenses. It was said that one grocer, uninformed about the latest coup, had called 'Adios', with friendly intent, after a group of hardboiled thugs, only to have his shop wrecked by the insulted Latvians.

And now, after a year of relative peace, it looked like trouble again. I knew from the restaurant managers and waiters who had spoken to me that all the gangland bosses of the district had been informed about the Army's venture into extortion, and were planning to join forces against them. For the last two days a watch had been kept round the clock on all the major street corners. So far, however, the Army members had turned up and disappeared again at such speed that the guards posted hardly had time to flip their mobiles open. So from tomorrow there was always to be cars with drivers ready to block each of the main streets leading out of the district. Within a few minutes a kind of roving commando troop was then to storm in and dispose of the silent wearers of those sharp suits.

Or that was the idea, anyway. In view of last night and the lightning speed with which the Army people had reached for their pistols, I was pretty sure that a calculation involving several minutes' leeway was a miscalculation. I knew the boss of the Albanian gang in the station district, and I had his secret phone number. I could have called him and told him how much notice the Army of Reason, in my experience, took of cars blocking their way. Either they'd simply break through or there'd be a bloodbath. But I also knew the Albanian's employees, and while I rather liked the man himself, because for a gangland boss he could keep his mouth shut and use his brain surprisingly often, I had no wish at all to tangle with his thugs. Not yet, anyway. First I had to find out who or what this Army was – and who it was I'd shot last night.

It was just before nine when Slibulsky opened the door to me in his dressing gown. Muttering that he was totally done in after last night and then a day of chasing around, he dragged himself back to the bedroom and got into bed. All around him were piles of open biscuit packets, chocolate bars and bags of jelly babies. There was basketball on TV. 'The sweets are in the kitchen.'

I fetched the opened bag of sweets, sat down on the bed beside him and unwrapped one. *Orchard Fruits from Germany, Blackcurrant Flavour*, green wording on a black, red and gold background.

'Looks like an ad for the German armed forces. Maybe you'd have felt embarrassed to go to the cash desk with them?'

Slibulsky gave me a glazed look, stuffed a biscuit in his mouth and said, munching, 'If they're good I don't mind if it says Christian Democrats on them. And I'd certainly have noticed sweets that I'd feel embarrassed to take to the cash desk.'

'Maybe they're new?'

'Look at the bag. Does it give the manufacturer's name?'

I looked at both sides of the bag. It was clear plastic, nothing printed on it.

'You think this kind of thing can be sold in Germany like planks of wood? It has to say what's in it, where it comes from and all that.'

'Hm.'

Of course I was glad that Slibulsky was trying to help me, even though he thought I'd better keep out of the whole business. And possibly there really was a chance that these sweets might help me to find out about the origin of the Army. Perhaps they were just the kind of clue that seems small and uninteresting at first but leads to results in the end. Although however much further the sweets might get me, just now running around town holding them under everyone's nose in the hope that some time someone would say, 'Sure, I know those!' wasn't the way I envisaged my plans to combat the Army of Reason over the next few days. I wanted to kick up a mighty fuss: blackmail Höttges, throw my money around in the station district, and later maybe get in touch with the Albanian. Yes, I wanted to know who it was I'd killed, but I wanted to know soon, so that I could soon forget about it again too.

I put a handful of the sweets in my jacket pocket and stood up.

'I'll show them around. Let's be in touch by phone tomorrow.'

'Any news of Tango Man?'

'They're still clearing away the rubble.'

'Mmm,' said Slibulsky. 'Look after yourself.'

Out in the street I wondered for a moment whether to go back to the station district with the vague idea of finding something out today. But then my feet protested, and so did my still-glugging stomach, and I decided to call it a day. I went for a meal and then fell into a taxi.

Chapter 5

The building where I lived had a small open cubby hole at the end of the corridor on each storey where you could keep bicycles and sledges. When I was outside the door of my flat, taking the key out of my pocket, I heard a rustling in the cubby hole. I turned and looked at the dark, door-sized gap in the wall. I'd been imagining something of this nature ever since the afternoon. Outside my office, or in a quiet side street, or here. When nothing else happened I asked, 'Romario?'

The rustling came again. Then a shoe with a platform sole emerged into the light, followed by a long, thin picture of misery. His clothes were crumpled and hung off him as if they'd been stuck to the wrong parts of his body, his hair, usually accurately sprayed into shape, was flying about in all directions, and the left-hand side of his head had pale crumbs all over it.

A feeble wave with his sound hand. 'Hi. I was waiting for you.'

'So I see. Forgotten how to use a phone?'

'I've been trying all day! But either you weren't in, or it was engaged...' He passed his tongue over his lips, cast an anxious glance at the stairs, and hesitantly came towards me. 'I'll explain it all to you, but couldn't we...?'

He indicated my door. I looked at him without enthusiasm. I didn't want anything explained to me, I wanted to go to bed and watch sport on TV, like Slibulsky. I felt like asking Romario whether he couldn't stay in the bicycle cubby hole until tomorrow morning. 'What are those crumbs on your head?'

Surprised, he put his hand to his cheek and then looked at it. 'Oh, those.' He ran a hand through his hair and over his face. 'I had some savoury breadsticks with me, so when I got tired in there I must have put my head on the packet.' He attempted a smile. 'I brushed them all off. Don't worry, I won't mess your flat up.'

'You set my mind at rest.'

After I'd closed the door behind us and propelled Romario in the direction of the kitchen, I asked, 'When did it dawn on you what a bloody stupid idea it was to set the Saudade on fire?'

'But... but I didn't set anything on fire!'

'Oh, come on, Romario! First thing this morning the boss of the gang, or the coordinator or whatever he is, called those guys' mobile and asked where they were. Which means he didn't know they were dead, so he didn't send anyone to get revenge for them and smash up your place. What's more, you got out alive. Which you'd hardly have done if the Army of Reason had been involved.'

He shifted restlessly on the spot, making a big deal of holding his bandaged hand as if to say that his quota of rough treatment had been met one hundred per cent. And he kept glancing at the kitchen chairs, but didn't quite like to sit down uninvited. 'Maybe someone quite different torched the place. Someone from the offices upstairs, or the owner of the building to get the insurance. Or it was an accident, or...'

I dismissed all this. 'Insurance, yes, but that was your idea. You were drunk, you realised you were never going to get your place clean after people had been bleeding all over it, and suddenly you had this brilliant idea for getting rid of the extortionists and cashing in yourself in one go. Perhaps you'd had something of the sort in your head for quite a while. I mean, the Saudade wasn't exactly a gold-mine.'

'The Saudade was like my...'

'Yes, yes, like your girlfriend. But rather an expensive girlfriend for some time. That doesn't matter to me. Two things do, though: first, I hate fires and I hate arsonists, specially when they're lighting their fires in the middle of town among blocks of flats and gas mains. Second, when we saw the Saudade blazing away ahead of us I though you were in it, and it was my fault. That would have been the third death down to me, and it was a horrible thought. Literally sickening. It was only when the caretaker here said some idiot had been trying to get into my flat with the wrong keys that it dawned on me you must have sur-vived.'

Romario had bowed his head and was now trying to glance up at me with the expression of a frightened rabbit, but as he was a good twenty centimetres taller than me he looked more like an alarmed stag, with antlers of lacquered hair sticking out all whichways.

'I didn't know where to go. I was afraid to go to my flat, I'm in the phone book, and those murderers were probably waiting for me there. And then...' He raised his head and looked at me as if to say: very well, this is the truth, here you are and I hope it makes you happy, but don't forget what a great guy I must be to tell you even when it does me no credit. In fact what he said was, 'And then the fire spread so fast that I had to leave my wallet in the Saudade. My ID, money, credit cards – all gone. I couldn't even take a hotel room.'

'Why didn't you go to the bank?'

'My branch is just round the corner from the Saudade, and I really didn't want to show my face there.'

'All right.' I pointed to the chairs. 'Sit down. Want a drink?'

'Yes, please. Thanks.' Slowly and ponderously as an old man, he lowered himself to one of the chairs, his bandaged hand still prominently displayed in what he assumed was the centre of my field of vision. 'Would you have anything to eat too? I haven't eaten a thing all day except those salty breadsticks.'

I muttered a yes, put vodka and glasses on the table and slammed down a can of sardines, a can opener, and the packet of crispbread I'd started in front of him. 'Sorry, but that's all I have.'

'It'll be fine,' he replied, looking at the sardine can as if he'd seldom thought anything less fine in his life. I poured vodka, we drank, Romario said, 'Ugh!' and added, 'Oh wow, on an empty stomach!' and then we both relished a couple of full minutes in which he tried to open the can with his elbows and one hand. When I finally reached over and removed the lid for him he thanked me effusively, and I came very close to throwing the can in his face, opener and all.

'So now what?'

'Well…' Romario drizzled the last remains of oil from the can on a piece of crispbread and stuffed it into his mouth. When he'd finished munching, he said, 'I've been thinking I could go underground until I see how things work out...'

He looked at me expectantly. I looked expressionlessly back.

'So well, I was thinking, well, it only crossed my mind, and only if you didn't object, whether... well, whether I could maybe stay with you for a few days.'

I examined him for a while, wondering whether he might for some strange reason enjoy my company, or if he was just so washed up and on his own that he'd put up with any amount of harassment for a place on a sofa. I poured myself more vodka and lit a cigarette. 'Why on earth didn't you just fly off for a few weeks in the south, like we agreed...' It wasn't a question, it was a sigh. To my surprise I got an answer.

'But I couldn't!' said Romario, and even for this occasion, which wasn't exactly short on desperation, he made an unusually desperate face.

'What do you mean, you couldn't?'

'I...' He looked at the floor. 'I can't fly anywhere. Except Brazil, but I don't have the money for that. You're right, the Saudade wasn't making much these days, and well, let's face it, I'm skint. I could just about have paid for a ticket, but then getting there and not even being able to invite the family and my old friends out for a meal – I can't face that.'

'Brazil's not the only place in the world. We could have scraped up a few marks for a package trip to Mallorca.'

He raised his head, his face suddenly twisted with rage. 'I told you, I can't fly anywhere, just like that! I'd need a visa, and a visa takes time, and in the end I guess I wouldn't get one either!'

'Hold on… you don't mean you only have a residence permit, do you?'

'That's what I mean, yes.'

'Oh no. But you were always saying how you'd been to the Côte d'Azur and so on in summer.'

For a moment his gaze bored into me as if he were assessing the chances of suing me for mental cruelty. But then he looked down at the floor again, his shoulders, a moment ago energetically braced, drooped, and he said in an exhausted tone, 'That's what I *said*, yup.'

'And where were you really?'

'In my flat.' The words were coming out in robotic tones now. 'Sometimes I took a tent and went to camp by the artificial lake for a few days.'

'Tell me,' I said, grinding out my cigarette and leaning over the table, 'this isn't some sob story you're pitching me, is it?'

Without looking up, he shook his head. 'Can I have a little more to drink?'

'Help yourself.'

He poured some more, drank, and put the glass down. Suddenly he seemed curiously calm. As if he were under hypnosis. Hands flat on the arms of the chair, fixed gaze on the table in front of him, he explained, 'I've lived and worked here and everything for over twenty years. Every year I have to go to the Aliens' Registration Office and get my residence permit extended by the guys there. Some of them haven't been in this world as long as I've been in Frankfurt, and they don't much mind whether they're here or in Bielefeld. I do mind. I earned my first money in Frankfurt, I rented my first flat of my own here, I was really in love for the first time here. There's not much left of any of that, but the city reminds me you can start up somewhere and succeed. And never mind how things are going, it gives me pride. I've learned its language, I can tell Heinninger beer from Binding, I know where to get the cheapest car tyres, and I know more bars than any native of the city.'

He paused, reached for the bottle and poured us some more. Everything about him seemed calm, except that the neck of the bottle clicked against the rims of our glasses a little too often and a little too fast.

'But like I said, every year I have to go and beg to be allowed to stay another year. Every year I have to prove I have work and a place to live and I'm not costing anyone money. And then I sit in that waiting-room with all the other poor fools who've cleaned their shoes and put on clean shirts so as to make a good impression on Herr Müller or Herr Meier, and they're all sweating and smoking and some of them have to sit on the floor because there's not enough chairs, and after three or four hours when your turn finally comes you're just a crumpled, stinking Thing and you'd almost agree with Herr Müller or Herr Meier if he looked at you as if to say, what's a pathetic creature like you doing in our lovely country?'

He stopped and looked absently at his hands, lying there on the arms of the chair and playing dead.

'I mean, it's one day a year when they make it very clear that this is no place for you. Or two days if there's some piece of paper missing and Herr Müller or Herr Meier wants to harass you. And of course those are the days when you're moving house or starting a new job or opening a business or, like I said, you want to go away. But all the other days in the year I'm the kind that gets stopped in the street by people asking me where which underground train goes or where to find the nearest post office. And I'd like you personally, and all of you, everyone to think of me that way.' He looked up. 'Other days I've managed to complain about the weather in Frankfurt without anyone giving me that stupid line about why don't I go back to sunny Brazil if I don't like it here? But would they still have not asked it if they knew how I've had to crawl to people with rubber stamps sitting at desks for the last twenty years, and that this is probably never going to end.'

I looked at his grey, unshaven face and slowly shook my head. I'd have been sorry for anyone else. Not because circumstances or the laws were the way they were and gave people problems – any kind of circumstances and laws did that, and at some point I'd realised that sympathy in that context was just a relatively respectable way of folding your hands and doing nothing. But when someone made life-determining rules for himself in secret and stuck to them, never even wanting to know that no one cared in the least whether he kept them or broke them, then I really did feel for him.

Or I normally would, anyway. Obviously Romario had used up any such feelings that I had in reserve for him last night, leaving nothing.

I lit my next cigarette and poured more vodka. 'I've no idea who'd have asked you what. But most people really don't mind whether you have to crawl or not. Anyway, I could have got you your papers within a week.'

'What?' he exclaimed, and at last life returned to Tango Man. His eyes cleared, his gaze was turned on me both hopefully and incredulously, and in a surprisingly sharp tone that wasn't going to tolerate any trickery, however kindly intended, he added, 'What do you mean?'

'I know someone who can do it for you. All official. I'll call him tomorrow.'

For a moment he seemed to be wondering where the snag was. Then he said, 'Kemal, that would be really...' And he looked as if he was going to embrace me.

I hastily dismissed his gratitude. 'That's OK. It won't cost me anything. In fact it'll be fun.'

'Fun?'

I nodded, put back the last of my vodka and got to my feet. 'Nothing to do with you.' I looked into his wide, shining eyes, and shuddered at the thought of Romario keeping this expression on his face from now until he got his papers. A grateful Romario was almost more unbearable than an ungrateful one. And anyway I knew that as soon as the visa was in his hands the familiar chicken-livered swaggerer would be back. Perhaps he wouldn't fancy its colour, or he'd have preferred his height to have been given as a couple of centimetres taller.

'I have to go to bed now. You can sleep on the sofa tonight. And find yourself somewhere else in the morning.'

'Yes, sure,' he agreed eagerly, getting to his feet too. 'Anything you like. I really don't want to be a burden to you.'

'Well, that's great. And where there's a will, luckily, we all know there's a way.'

Romario stared at me, then laughed with some difficulty and winked as if to say: I know you, Kayankaya, old fellow, tough outside, soft at heart.

Everything suggested that he would often get lost along the way.

Chapter 6

'When was the car reported stolen?' I asked.

Höttges's heavy breathing mingled with the noise of traffic. He was ringing from a phone box. Paper rustled, then he said, 'Yesterday. But the owner said he'd been away for the last four days, so it could have been stolen as long ago as last Monday.'

'What's his name?'

'Dr Michael Ahrens.'

I made a note of it. Coughing and hawking sounds were coming from my bathroom.

'Addresses: work, private…'

He gave me street names and phone numbers. As I wrote them down under the man's name, the noises from the bathroom grew louder, more full-bodied, and merged at increasing speed, until you might have thought a herd of elephants had sought out my bathtub especially to throw up in it.

'OK. What about new Mafia gangs in the station district?'

'None. Just the usual Albanians and Turks.'

'How about Röder? Has he gone?'

Röder was the boss of the German gang, and of course he hadn't gone. But while every Russian pickpocket was instantly regarded as evidence of organised criminality, many people still thought of German gangs which had tight leadership as nothing but a bunch of cartoon burglars in big peaked caps with sacks full of candlesticks slung over their shoulders. Even a pro like Höttges, who should have known better, avoided linking the terms Mafia and Germans in any but a mutually hostile connection.

'No. Röder's still around.'

'Albanians, Turks and Germans, then.'

Höttges did not reply. Instead I heard the flushing of the toilet from the bathroom, accompanied by something that sounded like a stuttering foghorn.

'You've never heard of an outfit calling itself the Army of Reason?'

'No. Like I said, only the usual.'

'OK. Thanks very much. And I have a small request. An acquaintance of mine would like to get German citizenship.'

I briefly explained what he needed to know, made an appointment for Romario, and the phone call finished. The shower was turned on in the bathroom. My shower. My soap. My back-brush. I wondered if it wouldn't have been a better idea to ask Höttges to cancel Romario's residence permit today, once and for all. A single poncy black hair in the plughole of my bathtub, and Romario would be sorry! Just as I was thinking that, he began singing in the shower. That well-known folksong *No Fairer Land*. What the hell was his idea? Rehearsing for a thank-you performance when he'd been given his citizenship papers? Or was this simply the stuff he usually warbled under the shower anyway? Perhaps he sang the national anthem while he was washing up, perhaps as a future German citizen he was planning to vote CDU? I imagined him standing outside his new restaurant the Germania in a year's time and, when asked what he liked best about Germany, saying, 'The clean streets.' And perhaps just then I'd come staggering out of one of the bars opposite and drop an empty cigarette packet on the pavement, and he'd point at me and explain: now there's an example of unwillingness to integrate, and I think a man who's lived the life I've lived has the right to say we're not putting up with this kind of thing.

I stood up and marched to the bathroom door.

'Romario!'

'Yoo-hoo!' the happy echo came back.

'Shut up!'

The splashing died down a bit. 'What?'

'Stop singing! Shut up!'

'Yes, up with singing! I always sing under the shower! When I came to Frankfurt I went to evening classes on German songs, did you know? We like German music a lot in Brazil, and I just love singing.'

I stared at my bathroom door.

'It gives quite a different feel to the start of the day!'

'Romario!'

'Yoo-hoo!'

'I don't want you giving quite a different feel to the start of the day here.'

A short pause. 'Didn't quite catch that!'

'Stop singing like that!'

'Oh, too loud, is it? No problem!'

The volume, I thought as I went back into the kitchen, that's all our CDU voter understands!

I made a fresh pot of coffee, listened in case any more of the heritage of German song was coming out of the bathroom along with the splashing of the water, finally closed the door so that I wouldn't have to hear the water either, lit myself a cigarette and sat down at the table with a cup of coffee. I picked up the racketeer's mobile and pressed the redial button for the umpteenth time. It was almost a shock when someone actually answered.

'The Adria Grill, good morning,' announced a friendly male voice.

'Good morning... er... did you say the Adria Grill?'

'Yes, how can I help you?'

'Er... a friend of mine recommended your restaurant, but he didn't know the address, and...'

'Are you applying to join?'

'To join? Well, perhaps... I was thinking of it. I mean, it all depends on...'

'To find out details you'll need to come Tuesday to Thursday about nine.'

'About nine. Wonderful. If you could give me the address now...'

He gave it to me. A street in Offenbach.

'Are you open today?'

'Every day from six in the evening, except Mondays. But like I said: no more recruitment until next Tuesday.'

'I see. Tell me, what kind of thing can I apply to do if I join?'

'Depends on your abilities. We've had trained tank drivers and even pilots, but normally you'd be assigned to one of the ground troops.'

'Aha. Sounds good.'

'Yes, great stuff. And so important.'

'So reasonable, too.'

'You said it.'

'Right, see you next Tuesday, then.'

'We'll be glad to meet you.'

I thanked him and flipped the mobile shut. Obviously the term Army didn't just arise from megalomania.

There followed half an hour when Romario kept coming into the kitchen, asking in short order for shaving gear, aftershave, and clean underclothes. I handed all that over in the hope that then he'd feel spruce and well enough to go out into the wide world and find himself another place to sleep.

'Do you know a restaurant in Offenbach called the Adria Grill?'

The bathroom door was open. I've no idea what he was doing in front of the mirror, but when he answered his voice sounded kind of squeezed.

'Yup, I know it.'

'What's it like?'

'Yugoslavian – or whatever that's called now. Anyway, it used to have a sign saying *Yugoslavian and International Specialities*. I think then it was Croatian and International Specialities for a while, and when I last drove by it just said *International Specialities*. It depended on how the war was going and where people's sympathies were.'

'What takes you to Offenbach so often?'

'A girlfriend of mine lives two blocks past the restaurant.'

'Ah. Does she have a large flat?'

He didn't answer at once. Only when he came into the kitchen, his face plastered with scraps of loo paper drenched in blood, did he say, 'She's married. I can only get to see her for an hour or so in the afternoon sometimes.' And when he saw my expression of slight distaste, he remarked, 'I've nothing against your razor blades, but I might as well try shaving with a chisel.'

'Hm. Sorry about that.' I smiled at him. 'But luckily all this will soon be over. From tomorrow you'll have the best razor blades you could wish for, you'll be able to sing under the shower as loud as you like and get yourself some breakfast.' I shrugged apologetically. 'Afraid I don't even have any more coffee today. I've already drunk the last of it.'

He stopped, his mouth opened, and for a moment I was afraid something awkward was coming. But then he just nodded, turned, and went into the living room.

I heard him tidy up the sofa, folding his bedclothes – with one hand, as he did not forget to remind me by dint of theatrical groaning and the whispered words, clearly audible in the kitchen, 'Damn thumbs!'. The hell with him.

Ten minutes later I gave him the spare key to my flat, and said that if he really couldn't find anywhere else to stay he could stay another night – if it was a real emergency. Looking injured, he replied that he didn't want to accept my offer, but next moment, and with a much less injured look, he was enumerating circumstances that might force him to accept it after all. The hell with me! I picked up my jacket and left the flat.

Chapter 7

Dr Michael Ahrens was the owner of a packet-soup and instant-pudding factory. The factory consisted of a huge metal shed, a four-storey brick building, and a hoarding measuring eight by eight metres from which the doctor, showing me all his teeth, announced: *My Good Name Guarantees Good Food – Ahrens Soups, Pleasure On Your Plate.* He had thick grey hair, blow-dried a little too stylishly, a suntanned face and a white shirt unbuttoned to just above his chest hair. However, his eyes looked at me over the top of a plain, narrow pair of glasses as gravely as if he were delivering the Eleventh Commandment. When he had that picture taken the good doctor had obviously been unable to decide whether he'd rather sell a lot of soup or screw a lot of women.

I turned away from the hoarding and walked to the brick building through the rain, which had been falling since morning. Just behind the front door there was a reception desk and switchboard behind glass. A young woman sat in front of a console with several receivers and any number of switches and little lights, chewing gum and reading the paper. I knocked on the pane between us, which was closed, and she reluctantly looked up.

'Yes, what is it?' she said. The pane stayed shut.

'Is that your style at Ahrens Soups? Shouting at your best customers through the glass?'

At first she looked even more reluctant, but then she seemed to think better of it, plastered a smile on her lips and rose to her feet. As she pushed the pane aside, she explained, 'Sorry, I didn't catch what you said. It's difficult to hear through the glass…'

Interesting tactics, I thought, and replied, 'I said don't bother, just stay put, I don't mind shouting.'

'Hm.' She said nothing, looked me challengingly in the eye, and for a moment her smile seemed genuine. 'So how can I help you?'

'Orhan Yaprak, import-export. I have an appointment with Dr Ahrens.'

'You do?' She looked at an engagements notepad beside her. 'I don't have that down. Did you speak to Dr Ahrens personally?'

'My secretary did.'

'Your secretary…' She looked at the notepad again. 'Well, there must have been some kind of mix-up.'

'Why don't you just call Dr Ahrens and ask if he has a few minutes to spare? It's very urgent business, and if his firm isn't in a position to deliver two million packet soups within a very short time there won't be a deal anyway.'

Her mouth dropped open. Then she repeated, 'Two million packet soups?'

'That's right. Earthquake in Kazakhstan yesterday evening. Humanitarian aid. The German government will be paying, of course.'

'Yesterday evening…' She narrowed her eyes slightly and examined me again as if I'd only just come through the door. 'So just when did your secretary call?'

'I'll give you one guess.'

'I'm no good at guessing, but I've sitting here since

eight taking all calls, and there wasn't one from any secretary with Thingummyjig Import-Export.'

'Thingummyjig Import-Export! You certainly go to endless trouble to please your customers here. What's the matter, sweetheart? Is this the Federal Chancellery? Or is the doctor just blow-drying his hair? I didn't eavesdrop on my secretary while she was phoning, but it could be she didn't get through at once and said to herself, like some others I could mention: well, then I can just go on chewing my gum in peace for a while and finish reading my horoscope.'

As I delivered this speech she had formed her lips into a pout and begun to inspect her turquoise fingernails, looking bored. Perhaps I wasn't the first to complain of customer relations at Ahrens Soups, or perhaps she'd given in her notice to leave at the end of the month. Or then again, perhaps she was just an easy going girl.

After a pause she asked, with a sigh, 'Finished?' and looked up from her nails. 'Then I can call Dr Ahrens, but you'd better tell him all that stuff about the earthquake yourself.' With these words she turned away, picked up one of the receivers and pressed a button.

'Dr Ahrens? There's someone here who wants to speak to you… no idea, he wants to tell you personally… says it won't take long… yes, I'll tell him.'

She put the receiver down and gave me a sweet smile. 'You can go up to see him in ten minutes' time. While you're waiting, why not think up some fairy tale to tell the boss? In the Federal Chancellery?'

I nodded. 'Must have been the poster outside. I thought someone who has his own photo blown up to twenty square metres and hangs it in front of my nose must be suffering from something that prevents him from talking to anyone but the real bigwigs.'

'Hm,' she said evidently agreeing. 'But...' and she looked me appraisingly in the eye, '...but that doesn't make him stupid.'

I nodded again. 'That's what I thought. In personnel matters, all the same, I can see he's just fantastic.'

This time the smile came very slowly. First she moved her lower jaw sceptically to both sides, then tiny lines formed around her eyes, her lips opened and her eyes began to flicker. Either that or my own eyes were beginning to flicker.

She pointed down the corridor. 'There's a lift over there. Fourth floor, you'll find his door. You can't miss it.'

I thanked her and went on looking at her for a little longer, and her eyes flickered again.

At the end of the usual grotty neon-lit office corridor, floor covered with plastic and doors with the paint flaking off them, was something that at first sight looked like a piece of scenery for a tale from the *Arabian Nights*. A dark brown double door four metres wide, with a pattern of gold and silver suns, moons and stars adorning its frame. The handle was a recumbent angel, and more angels were playing ring-a-ring-a-roses as they danced around Dr Ahrens's nameplate. Two white marble columns flanked the door, a red rug in front of it bore the design of a mermaid embroidered in silver, and lamps imitating burning torches hung on the walls to left and right.

As far as I could tell the gold, silver and marble were genuine. At my second knock there was a curt, 'Come!' I pressed the angel down and went in.

My initial surprise shouldn't really have been a surprise at all. But at the back of my mind, obviously, I had been thinking up some kind of explanation for the design of that door. It was left over from a birthday party, perhaps the man's wife had esoteric tastes and it was a present from her, or a sample of some crazy interior designer's work. In fact the door was only the relatively modest entrance to Sheikh Soup's domain. A fantasy desert measuring about two hundred square metres opened up before me: bright golden-yellow walls sprinkled with every imaginable shade of red, ceiling covered with undulating sky-blue velvet, sand-coloured fitted carpet with imitation zebra and tiger skins lying on it. The walls on the exterior of the building were all glazed: windows with the glass held in place at five-metre intervals by flat black metal structures cut to the shape of palms and cacti, their fronds, stems and spines apparently growing into the panes. In one corner fur-covered seats were placed around a shallow, leather-clad drum. In another was a huge cinnamon-red bed with a pile of cushions in the shapes and colours of outsize coconuts and bananas. And above it all an arrangement of lights showing all the signs of the Zodiac hovered below the sky-blue velvet, spanning the entire ceiling.

I suppose I hadn't moved from the spot for quite some time when a voice from the middle of this vast hall asked, 'Yes, what is it?'

I closed the door behind me and set out on my way to a desk adorned with carved lions' heads.

The second surprise was Dr Ahrens. His hair wasn't grey but black, he didn't wear glasses, and he looked at least twenty years younger than on the hoarding. They'd really worked hard on him to make him reasonably like someone who might be supposed to be in the packet-soup business. The way he looked sitting in front of me now, he could have made ads for steroids. Everything he wore was a tight fit: black stretch T-shirt over his bouncer's torso, gold chain around his bull neck, even the strap of his enormous sports watch seemed about to break apart. Either some of his muscle had been airbrushed out of the photo, or they'd put his head on top of someone else's body.

The third surprise was that a man who furnished his pad as if he liked nothing better than listening to flute music all day long, while murmuring prayers to the sun and nibbling dried fruit, had the kind of aura that made you wish you were wearing a warm jacket in his presence.

'What's this all about?' he asked, and his hard blue eyes stared keenly at me. He was jiggling a pen up and down impatiently in his hand.

'Hello, Dr Ahrens, nice of you to see me.'

He didn't say anything to that, just pushed his lips out expectantly – indeed, as expectantly as if he were giving me exactly two seconds.

I made an airy gesture. 'Pretty place you have here.'

No reaction. He went on staring at me. Obviously this was his usual approach: look at his interlocutor like a beast of prey and wait for him to make the first move. So I made it.

'Tell me, is this some kind of nature therapy or do you have a touch of schizophrenia?' I winked at him cheerfully. 'You're really a big game hunter, or Moses, or something like that?'

The pen in his hand stopped moving up and down, and his gaze became if possible keener still.

'Well, never mind that. The main thing is, you feel good in here, and it doesn't bother you if people tap their foreheads behind your back. I'm just wondering how it goes down with your business contacts. Do they insist on having a medical doctor present when they're signing contracts?' And without waiting for him to answer, I pointed to a bamboo chair. 'May I sit down? It was a long way to your desk.'

I'd cornered him now. He really had to do something: either go for my throat, or call for the works security men, or give a couple of explanations. Sitting there listening to me saying what a nutcase he was wouldn't do, anyway.

The longer the silence lasted, the more physical violence seemed to be ruled out. Perhaps he thought it beneath his dignity. And he seemed to me vain enough to be actually interested in my opinion of him. Sure enough, he finally said in a tone suggesting that it was all the same to him, but he didn't mind a quick explanation, 'All this stuff is for the women. They like that kind of thing, and I like women. OK?'

'Fancy that. And it works?'

He made a casual gesture at the room.

'Star signs, exotic countries, arts and crafts stuff, all looking as if it cost a lot – what do *you* think works with women? Sharing a pizza?' He waited a moment to see if I had anything to say about that before leaning over the desk, his large brown hand stretched in my direction, moving his fingers up and down like a cop wanting to see your ID. 'So now hurry up and tell me what you're doing here.'

'How about if I sit down?'

He seemed to consider this idea briefly, and then jerked

his chin in the direction of the bamboo chair. I strolled the few metres over to it, moved the chair slightly, sat down carefully as if to test the sturdiness of its thin struts, crossed my legs, looked around the vast hall again, and finally said in casual tones, 'I kind of wonder why someone who takes such trouble furnishing his office doesn't even have a little tiger stuck to the dashboard of his car. Or one of those humorous coconut cushions on the back seat. Do you never take the ladies home afterwards? Must be quite a contrast for them, out of here and into a BMW that looks like it just rolled off the production line. Maybe there's one of them you'd like to see again, she'd notice the moment she got in that car how phoney this pad of yours is.'

As a surprise it wasn't a thunderclap, but it did at least get some reaction out of him at last. He frowned and folded his arms, and his biceps, steely from the weights room at the gym, began twitching in a quiet, unpleasant rhythm.

'And incidentally,' I went on, 'it occurs to me to wonder on what occasion the BMW was really stolen? Even more interesting, when and how did the thief get hold of your keys? I'm assuming that even someone as comfortably off as you are doesn't leave a brand new car worth umpteen thousand marks outside a bar with its engine running.'

No doubt about it, something was going on underneath his blow-dried hairdo. I leaned back comfortably in the chair, looked at him in a friendly way and let him take his time. When the silence began to put him at a clear disadvantage, he said, 'I get it,' and suddenly a nasty little smile came to his lips. 'You stole the car and you want to sell it back to me.'

For a split second I wondered if I was on entirely the wrong track, but I knew that now I couldn't back out anyway. I sighed and said, sounding bored, 'Come on, Ahrens, don't try that old trick on me. Why not tell me where you were for those four days when the BMW went missing?'

It really had been just a trick. The anger that now spread over his face couldn't possibly be because I was taking the mickey out of him. I'd been doing that for the last ten minutes, and so far he hadn't been particularly impressed. But he had just come down to my level, so to speak, and instead of simply throwing me out he'd looked for what he thought was a way out of the situation I'd set up. For a moment he had been the one sitting in front of the desk, and I'd been behind it, and that moment was now pumping the blood into his face.

'Who are you?' he asked as his body tensed in a way that told me I wasn't going to spend much more time in his office today.

'That doesn't matter.'

'And who are you working for?'

'Only myself at the moment.'

'Ha,' he said, and it sounded like the maximum penalty imposed by the law. As he spoke, he pushed himself away from the table, chair and all, and rested his hands on the arms of the chair. 'And what's a wanker like you doing, making his way in here and telling me some kind of crap about my car?'

'I know where it is, and I thought you might be interested to know how it got there.' I stopped, adjusted my shirt slightly, and looked out through the wall of windows at industrial yards and heavy goods vehicles. A staring match to see who would look away first was not my kind of thing, but I could do well in a who-keeps-his-mouth-shut-longest competition.

'So how *did* it get there?'

'A bunch calling themselves the Army of Reason was driving around in it extorting protection money. But two of the extortionists had to leave the car the day before yesterday. And now I have it.'

'Ah.' He opened his mouth in the grimace of a teenage lout and jutted his chin in my direction. 'So why don't *I* have it? It's my car! It was stolen from the yard out there. What do I have to do with this Army of whatever it was?'

'Reason. Perfectly simple, just Reason.'

'Interesting name.'

'Oh, not all that interesting.'

'Why not?' he asked, and for a moment he looked genuinely curious. My God, like something out of the psychology supplement to a magazine. And good heavens, how quickly I'd got where I wanted. Or so I thought, anyway.

'You know, what I don't understand…' I leaned forward. 'It was all so elaborately done. The disguise, the powder, the mute trick, the name – how could you be stupid enough not to change the car number plates?'

He was in the act of getting out of his chair to do who knew what – probably come round from behind his desk and squash me flat between two fingers. But suddenly he stopped, his shoulders dropped back into place, and his face assumed an expression as if a very attractive idea had just dawned on him.

'Suppose there's something in the nonsense you're babbling,' he said, and there was almost a smile on his lips, 'then why don't you go to the cops with it? Why come to me? What do you really want?' And when I didn't answer right away he thrust his head towards me, and a really hearty smile came over it. 'You surely weren't thinking of blackmailing me? Oh, wow, you have no idea at all!' He smiled a little more, then leaned back in his chair and inspected me with satisfaction.

'I want to know who the two men driving the car the night before last were.'

'What?'

'The two extortionists after that protection money. Where they came from, how they lived, what they were planning to do.'

The satisfaction left his face. '*Were* planning to do?'

'Were.'

For the first time I realised how quiet it was in his desert kingdom. The engines of the HGVs and forklift trucks in the yards outside must be making a lot of noise. But there was nothing to be heard except quiet clicking as Ahrens undid the metal strap of his watch and did it up again.

Finally he said, 'Piss off.'

It was clear he wasn't going to say it again, and I'd be lucky if I got away unscathed. I rose and set off for the door. Before I pressed the handle down I turned once more. 'I mean it. I want to know who those two were. Perhaps that'll be enough for me and then I'll leave you alone. But not without knowing that.' I tapped my forehead. 'See you soon. And don't think any of this set-up made any lasting impression on me.'

I slowly closed the door behind me, and then I moved fast. I raced past the lift door and went down the stairs as quietly as I could. No one came to meet me, and I heard no voices or other sounds on any of the office floors. I went the last few steps to the ground floor on tiptoe, peered around the corner, and saw to my relief that there was no one waiting for me outside the lift. Perhaps Ahrens was telling himself a little bastard like me couldn't harm him. Or perhaps he simply had no one available just now to wait for me there.

I went down the corridor to the telephone switchboard and leaned against the narrow counter. Miss Chewing-Gum looked up from a swimwear magazine.

'Your boss is really weird. Ever been on safari with him?'

She raised her eyebrows, not as if she were surprised, looked searchingly at me, and finally shook her head. 'Wouldn't be much of a safari. Nothing to be seen but a fat pig.'

I couldn't help grinning, and for a brief, careless moment I enjoyed the sight of her thin, perky face with a layer of freshly applied, impossible turquoise lipstick echoing her fingernails. Too late, I saw the alarm in her eyes. When I followed the direction of her gaze and turned, a small, fat man was standing very close to me.

'So how you doing, mate?' he asked, pulling his thick lips into something that was probably supposed to be a smile. 'I hear you found the boss's car, right? I want the keys, so let's have 'em, OK?' he said, and I was just thinking, I know that voice, and wondering why he was holding his hand behind his back in such an odd way, when he made a movement that was remarkably fast for someone of his girth, and my face exploded.

★

Someone was tugging at my shirt. At the same moment the pain in my head started up a rockers' party with everyone dancing and stamping, beer bottles clashing, brain cells scrapping with each other. Something wet and sticky splashed over my face, I flinched back and opened my eyes. Through a red haze, I saw Miss Chewing-Gum bending over me with a bottle of Fanta.

'Come on, get up!' she whispered. 'You have to get out of here!'

I held out my hand, and she pulled at it until I was more or less sitting up and could see all the blood around me.

'Go on, hurry! He's only gone to get someone to take you down to the cellar.'

To the cellar. I managed to concentrate for a moment and imagine what the fat man would do to me in some dark hole if he was prepared to hit me so hard in broad daylight and in the presence of a witness that I felt I was now minus practically everything you can see on a passport photo. With all the strength I could muster, and Miss Chewing-Gum's assistance, I managed to get to my feet. My face was dripping like lettuce that's just been washed.

'Hit me!'

'What?'

'I'm supposed to be watching to make sure you don't get away, and I can do without trouble, so go on, hit me!'

I tried to raise my arm, but the rockers instantly opened up a new dance floor in my shoulder, and it dropped back to my side.

'Oh, for God's sake!' she hissed, took my hand, raised it in the air, making me cry out again, and smashed it down on her turquoise mouth. No idea if it was my blood or hers, but anyway she stayed behind, smeared with red, as I staggered out of the door into the yard. The rain beat in my face, it was cold and windy, the twenty metres to the street seemed endless, and my head felt like one huge open wound. I felt like flinging myself down on the tarmac and howling. The last thing I saw when I reached the street and turned once more was Dr Ahrens smiling as he promised *Pleasure On My Plate*, and in return I promised him all the tortures in the world.

Chapter 8

'Oh no!'

Romario jumped up from the armchair, took my arm and helped me to lie down on the sofa.

'What... what happened?'

'Found the Army of Reason.' My voice sounded as if I were talking underwater. 'Get me a bottle of vodka and call the emergency doctor.'

When the doctor closed his bag about an hour later, he said, 'That needs to be X-rayed. You'd better go straight to the hospital. I can call you a cab if you like.'

'Anything broken?'

He shrugged. 'Can't tell because of the swelling. How did you come by that?'

'Sheer stupidity.'

'Looks as though someone hit you in the face by mistake with his garden hoe or something.'

'With a knuckleduster, and not by mistake.'

'Ah.' He cleared his throat. 'Well, if you want to rest for a while before you go to the hospital, put some ice on it.'

The doctor left, and I sent Romario to the supermarket round the corner for supplies of alcohol and an Ahrens packet soup. Then I went to sleep. When I woke up two hours later, Romario was sitting beside me holding a tea-towel full of ice to my cheek.

'How's it feel?' he asked.

I was going to say something, but I couldn't get anything out, and made a so-so gesture with my hand.

'Soon as you feel strong enough to stand up I'll call a taxi and we'll go to the hospital. By the way, they didn't have your soup. But maybe you shouldn't eat anything just now anyway. Wait and see what the X-ray shows. In case they have to operate, I mean.'

I watched him trying, with an expression of concern, to hold the tea towel full of ice so that it cooled my face but didn't press against it. After a while I fell asleep again.

It was just after ten when we came back from the hospital. Nothing broken but a good deal of damage done, whatever the doctor meant by that. They'd bandaged my head, injected a painkiller, and I was to spend the next few days in bed. While I settled down on the sofa with the remote control and a mineral water, Romario went into the kitchen and cooked up some stuff he'd bought at an all-night convenience store on our way back. Fumes of burnt butter floated out of the kitchen door. I leaned back and switched the TV on.

After we'd eaten, and after I'd wondered yet again why Romario had ever chosen the profession of chef, I told him about my morning visit to Dr Ahrens. He sat in front of me the way I imagine one of my unknown grannies would have sat in front of me in such a situation: hands clamped between his knees, nodding vigorously at the exciting moments of my tale, and for all his sympathy constantly casting critical glances at my plate, which was still half full.

'Which means,' I concluded, 'that you'll have to stay awake tonight.'

Romario hesitated. Now that it had all been told and

cleared up he seemed to be thinking of his usual daily life again, and regular sleep at civilised times played a not unimportant part in it. 'Why?'

'Because Ahrens could find out who I am, and then he'll be marching in here.'

'Hm,' said Romario sceptically. 'So then what? Do I march out to meet him?'

'Then you wake me up. I have my shotgun and pistols, and before they even get in here half the neighbourhood will have called the police.'

He began stacking the dishes with his one good hand. 'How did you know Ahrens had anything to do with it?'

'I didn't know. I went off there to poke around a bit, and suddenly it all came clear, just like that.'

He took the dishes into the kitchen and clattered around there for a while. Then he came back with two dishes of ice cream, gave me one of them, sat down in the armchair again and began slowly spooning up the other.

'OK, Romario, I get the idea. You want to say something, so go ahead and say it.'

'Well, look at it like this… when it all started up last week I thought, this is just a normal protection-money racket, same as usual. And I'm not a coward, you can believe me there. Out of eight goes at extortion since the Schmitzes left, I've dealt with five…'

As far as I knew Romario was not in fact a coward, which always surprised me slightly. I'd seen him deal with two thugs who were trying to take him apart in front of his assembled customers. He had reminded me of those well-brought-up young ladies who, setting out in a mood of mingled adventurousness, naiveté and arrogance to explore the world beyond places with guest loos and country houses with underfloor heating, find themselves in very tricky situations without being aware of it, so that perhaps for that very reason almost nothing bad ever happens to them. Anyway, Romario treated the thugs like idiots who'd do better to stop and think how, if they kept getting in his way while the restaurant was at its busiest, he was ever going to make the money they were demanding from him. After half an hour, and when Romario had wrecked their digestive systems with two free Lambruscos, they went away with their nerves in shreds.

'...So I figured, with a pistol and some shooting lessons, I could handle whatever came. You can get rid of most of them, but if someone won't be got rid of and if you can afford it, well, you pay up. I mean, it was just the enormous amount this weird Army was asking made me ask you for help. But now I'm thinking – always assuming the insurance people don't make difficulties – it'd be better if I do pay. And then you can give them the car back, and we'll forget the whole thing.'

'Oh yes? And do I give the dead bodies back too?'

'You just explain to this Ahrens how it happened – self-defence. They understand such things in those circles.'

'But I don't move in those circles. And you're forgetting about my face. How about that?'

Romario shrugged slightly and hummed and hawed. Perhaps he thought a smashed-in face didn't alter my appearance too drastically. I also suspected that it was just because of my face he was trying to persuade me to drop the whole thing. Up to now his plan had been to get the insurance money, go underground for a while, and try his luck again somewhere else once the situation had calmed down. The fact that I wasn't letting it go, and he was in it with me whether he liked it or not, meant that his plan was in danger, and so, not least, was his own face. In particular his own face. A reverse projection of that kind was the only way I could account for the touching and apparently completely unselfish nursing care he had lavished on me all afternoon.

At that moment the phone rang. Grateful for the interruption, Romario jumped up and brought it over to me. Then he disappeared into the kitchen. I took the receiver off and said, 'Hello.'

'Hey, Kayankaya,' an obviously elated Slibulsky shouted in my ear, 'you sound as if you'd found those bloody Army characters and they'd chucked a concrete bar in your face by way of hello.' He laughed cheerfully, and after my rather stuffy evening in the company of Granny Romario it was like a breath of fresh air. 'What's up? Been screwing Deborah under a ventilator and caught a cold?'

'I did find those bloody Army characters, and they did indeed chuck a concrete bar in my face by way of hello.'

'What? No joking?'

I told him briefly what had happened, and how I was beginning to feel a bit better after the injection.

'Your face is bandaged up?'

'That's right.'

'When does the bandage come off?'

'No idea.'

'Are you fairly recognisable all the same?'

'What are you getting at? Is this a confession that you feel deprived if you don't get to see my face every few days?'

'Gina's giving a dinner party next Friday, the whole works, candles and tablecloth and all. She's been appointed head of a department at the museum. So a lot of her women friends and colleagues are coming. Very elegant ladies, some of them. But if all they can see is your pot belly, those aren't exactly the best conditions for a first meeting.'

'You'll find this hard to believe, but at the moment...'

'I know, I know: the Army and your conscience and no spare time and so on and so forth... Look, if you're reasonably presentable next Friday and you don't drop in, we have a real problem. OK?'

'OK.'

'Heard anything of Tango Man?'

'You could certainly say so. A performance of *No Fairer Land* under the shower this morning, and at the moment he's polishing my kitchen to a high gloss.'

'Still not joking?'

'No. He's alive. And how.'

'Well, tell me about it some other time. I have to go back to my vendors. We're having a little party – three years of Gelati Slibulsky, who'd have thought it?'

'Congratulations. By the way, I think you were right about those sweets. There's something funny about them.'

'Aha,' he said, satisfied, and we said goodbye until next Friday at the latest.

In the kitchen Romario was busy scouring lime marks off my sink with a sponge pad. He had taken off his shoes and socks and unbuttoned his shirt. Another day or so and he'd probably be running about my place naked – singing, cleaning, shedding pubic hair.

He smiled at me over his shoulder and said, 'Just making myself a bit useful.'

'But only a very little bit. Listen, Romario: I'm carrying on with this case, and I don't want anyone around here who isn't happy with that.'

He turned, shoulders drooping, scouring pad in his hand. 'I was only making a suggestion. And I did it mainly for your sake because they beat you up. What was it the doctor said? "You were lucky". Well, if that's luck…'

Water was dripping from the sponge pad on to his bare feet. Didn't he notice? Or was he just pretending not to notice so as to show how upset he was? When Romario presented a picture of misery I was never quite sure where the picture stopped and the misery began.

I took what cash I had out of my trouser pockets, two hundred-mark notes and a few tens, put it on the kitchen table, and said, 'Find yourself a hotel for tonight, and let me know tomorrow where you're going to be for the next few days. Sorry, but that's how it is.'

Of course, it wasn't that simple. Reproaches, climb-downs, offers, a couple of new bids for sympathy, and any number of variations on the familiar subject of his poor hand, but finally he had to see that there was no negotiating with me this evening. When he closed the door behind him a little later with elaborate care − see what a quiet, harmless creature you're turning out into the street so heartlessly − I even thought for a moment I could breathe through my swollen nose again. Then I took a few precautions: I put some empty bottles just inside the door as an alarm system, laid out all my weapons beside the bed, got my bulletproof vest out of the wardrobe and hung it on the window catch. Then I took the TV set into the bedroom, swallowed painkillers, and lay down to watch a French film in which a man being attacked pleaded with the thief, 'It's not my money.' To which the thief impatiently replied, 'I'm not stealing it for myself either.' As the final credits were rolling I turned off the TV and the light. It was Saturday evening. A song by Heino was coming up from the greengrocer's flat: 'Come into my wigwam, wigwam…' Did he think it was good music to go with sex? I heard his entire programme: dog-like panting, corks popping, the disc from the beginning again, singing along to it, more panting. Around two the front door of the building closed, and finally it was quiet.

Chapter 9

I spent the next two days in bed. No one disturbed my orgy of television, baked beans and chocolate ice cream. Outside it was drizzling, and according to the weather forecast it was going to stay that way for the rest of the week. The cool, damp weather was just right for someone with a swollen face. I got a fright only once, when the racketeer's mobile alarmed me. A text message said the mobile was going out of circulation at once.

On Tuesday afternoon I felt reasonably all right again, and called the Albanian. We'd met at a billiards tournament five months before, and then drank a couple of aniseed schnapps together. Soon after that I discovered by chance that his two daughters went to the same expensive boarding school as the son of Slibulsky's tax adviser. From what the tax adviser said, the Albanian's daughters weren't having a great time there. Their class teacher obviously thought it educationally valuable to connect their poor school work with their ethnic origin, doing so at regular intervals and in front of the other pupils. Apart from the fact that they had both been born in Frankfurt, and spent more holidays in Florida than Albania, you might have expected that for school fees of two thousand marks a month each, plus extras, you could at least expect teachers who don't trumpet their own backwoods prejudices. Normally I wouldn't have thought anything of it – injustice in institutions for the rich elite was not among the things that bothered me. In this case, however, I had an opportunity to improve my relationship with the Albanian. After I'd been through interrogations first by a bodyguard and then by a private secretary about the reason for my call, their boss finally came to the phone. I told him about his daughters' problems, and judging by what he said this was the first time he'd heard about them. The girls were presumably embarrassed to tell him. As so often when such things happen, it's the wrong people who feel ashamed. I took care to give the impression that I would continue to keep him up to date with his children's school lives, and finally he thanked me warmly and actually gave me the number of his mobile. That number could be worth gold in my job. I never knew exactly what happened to the class teacher who also taught the girls German and sports, but a little later he had to give up teaching sports.

I exchanged a few remarks with the Albanian about his daughters, whose marks had improved to a remarkable degree over the last couple of months. Then I told him in rough outline, without mentioning names and places, what I knew about the Army. Not only could he keep his mouth shut surprisingly often for a gangster boss, he could certainly never be called talkative in general either. If he wasn't discussing his daughters, phoning him was rather like playing tennis up against a wall. His tone of voice changed too. Warm and melodious a moment ago, it now sounded like a warped wooden door being moved back and forth by a slight wind.

'I need a few more days to find out what its structure is like, who does what where and how much longer this outfit is expected to operate, but then we could strike.'

'Pick the time and we will.'

'It's a small factory. We'd need about forty men to surround it.'

'Forty.'

'But we don't want a bloodbath. You'll get my information only if you can promise me your people will keep a grip on themselves. We want to stop the Army operating, that's all.'

'That's all, then.'

'And the boss is my affair.'

'And the boss is your affair.'

'OK, then, I'll be in touch within the next few days.'

'Within the next few days,' he replied, but as I was about to ring off I sensed him suddenly hesitating, as if he had to venture into unknown terrain. I kept the receiver to my ear until he finally asked, 'Who are you working for?'

'Myself.'

'Unpaid?'

'Yes.'

'Why?'

'The Army made me do something I didn't like at all, and I can't leave it at that.'

'Hm,' he said, and after a pause, 'If you try taking me for any kind of ride, I'm finished with you. Is that clear?'

'That's clear.'

'Well then, good luck.'

I rang off and remembered how I'd lost to him in the semi-finals of the tournament. A fair opponent, no fooling about, no tricks. The problem was his retinue of henchmen who always had their hands on either their guns or their pricks in their trouser pockets, and were constantly on the point of taking out one or the other to let fly with it. But he'd promised they would do no more than I wanted, and a boss like the Albanian really couldn't afford to break his promises. That kind of thing got around, and it was bad for business. Or so I hoped, anyway.

I looked at the time. One-thirty, a good time to have had an accident at work and come off my first shift of the day, trudging round dogs' homes.

'Hello, Frau Beierle.'

'Herr Kayankaya – dear me, you sound as if you have a bad cold!'

'Well, I had a little accident. Just now, in Oberursel, I thought I'd found Susi at last, and I went into the pen. But it was a different dog, one that likes jumping at people's faces. And well, it broke my nose.'

'Oh, my God!'

'It's not too bad, but I have to go to the doctor now, and maybe I can get back to searching for Susi at the end of the week.'

'Of course, of course! You must look after yourself. Take your time. Injuries to the head should never be taken lightly.'

'I'm just sorry for Susi. Now she'll have to be shut up longer in one of those awful pens.'

'Oh, Susi will be all right. It's really amazing how many animal rescue centres there are around Frankfurt.'

'Yes, amazing.'

'Because people are so cruel, specially in this town. Or that's my opinion, anyway.'

'An interesting opinion. Although after today's incident I have to say,' I added, chuckling hard, 'the animals in this town can be quite cruel too.'

'Of course, you poor thing! I mustn't keep you here talking. You go off to the doctor, and then go to bed.'

'Thank you for being so understanding, Frau Beierle.'

'Oh, never mind that. And if you need anything, just call me.'

We said goodbye, and I wondered when the day would come on which she realised that her bow-wow was probably never going to come back with my assistance. And I also wondered how much longer I wanted to play the pop-eyed Turk for her benefit. Because of course the Islamic scholar had picked me from the yellow pages on account of my name, and of course when we first met she had explained to me at length what the Turks were like, myself included. Industrious, proud, strong on family values, keeping up old traditions, the secret rulers of Asia – in short, I was a whole great nation in myself. Not for the first time, I was fascinated to discover what having a good education and a university degree did *not* mean. But as I'd been out of a job for weeks, and as my normal daily retainer fee had automatically doubled the moment I set foot in her villa with its large garden, I didn't shake her belief that she had practically invented the Ottomans. Only when she played me some appalling music, and I could see from her face that she was obviously expecting me to drum along with it or do a little dance, did I suggest that even in a people who appeared to be of one and the same origin, individual tastes might differ. Whereupon she said I didn't really know what I liked any more, Western values and the Western lifestyle had distorted my true identity. To keep her sweet, I did her a small favour when we came to the business part of the deal: I tripled my retainer, just like that, and let her haggle until she beat me down to double the retainer, as if I usually did that kind of thing. Her small, knowing smile as she wrote me her cheque seemed to be saying: you see, that's how the Orientals live. Once I had the Army business behind me and set out looking for Susi again, supposing I actually found her I'd have to find out how the Orientals felt about rewards. Perhaps there was some nice fifteenth-century proverb: find my watchdog and I will shower you with gold.

I made fresh coffee, drank a cup, dressed, cleared away the bottles from inside the door, and went to the supermarket. The manager there told me that the Ahrens company had stopped delivering three months ago for unknown reasons. When I asked whether Ahrens Soups had sold well, he said, 'No worse than other products of the same kind.'

On the way home I bought all the newspapers with local Frankfurt sections, and thought of the deserted corridors and offices in Ahrens's admin building. Obviously the place was closed, and not just on Saturdays. But then why did it employ a receptionist? In addition one who thought so little of the way the wind was blowing there that she'd help an enemy of her boss to get away?

At home I leafed through the local sections, and found the reports I had been more or less expecting.

Serious accident in Kaiserstrasse. In circumstances that are still not clear, a car burned out on Saturday night near the station. Both male passengers died in the fire… Shoot-out in the station district. Four shots woke residents of Windmühlstrasse on Sunday at four in the morning… and so on… *one dead… hit and run accident, driver failed to stop.*

Not far from the station a grey Mercedes rammed a car parked by the roadside on Sunday evening, and then drove off, according to eyewitness accounts, in the direction of Sachsenhausen. Those in the car got off with only a scare.

If the Army went on like this, even an authoritarian like the Albanian wouldn't be able to keep his men from taking a proper revenge for long.

I spent the rest of the afternoon reading the sports sections and having a nap. Around seven I dressed and undid the bandage. The swelling around my nose had gone down, leaving a blue and yellow bruise behind. It wasn't pretty, but wouldn't make people turn and run. I put a pistol in my pocket and set off in my Opel for Offenbach.

Chapter 10

If Marilyn Monroe had gone through life in the company of a small, thin, spotty sister who wore braces on her teeth, you could have said Offenbach beside Frankfurt looked like the Monroe sisters side by side. Although there were hardly five kilometres between their boundaries, up to now I'd been there at most four or five times, and after my first visit I'd always needed extremely compelling inducements to go again. Unless you knew better, you drove into the town, down a street a hundred metres wide and lined by grey office blocks, until you were right out of it again, and glad to see a few faces appear on the advertisement hoardings on both sides of the road from time to time. I've no idea what the people of Offenbach did with themselves all day, but at least they carefully avoided their drive-through main road with its resemblance to an airport runway. The only evidence of any human life outside the eight-hour working day was the existence of the snack bars that had sprung up here and there in front of office façades, and the logos winking from dark corners and pointing the way to fitness centres and gambling salons. You felt this was the way a main thoroughfare would look after a deadly epidemic.

If you knew your way around a bit, there came a point where you turned off right to the town centre and came to a square about the size of a football field, its most impressive building apparently inspired by the need to give the bunker architecture of World War Two a chance in civil life. It was a huge, higgledy-piggledy, unplastered pile of concrete forcing its way up like a grey monster amidst the silvery department stores and brightly coloured shopping malls. Although signs promised you that the monster contained a pizzeria, ice cream parlour and supermarket, and in spite of the trouble taken to provide for something like an inviting atmosphere with outdoor flights of steps, airy passageways and terraces, you couldn't shake off the feeling that the moment you set foot in the place you'd be arrested, shot, and processed into something. Or anyway, I couldn't shake off the feeling. The typical citizen of Offenbach, at least if he liked doing drugs, hanging about aimlessly and supplying his environment with boom-boom music from a portable cassette recorders, just loved to linger outside and inside the building. And the citizen of Offenbach who was so tight that he pissed and threw up against the nearest wall instead of looking for a public toilet liked the building too. But the one who, of course, thought particularly highly of it was the citizen of Offenbach who had just failed his final school exams and was now in a hurry to become an established part of the great wide world of hanging about and throwing up.

The problem with the town, for anyone who didn't know it, was that there was almost no means of finding your way anywhere except down the plague-stricken avenue and past the monster building. Once you'd done that Offenbach turned out not much uglier than Darmstadt or Hanau. The usual pedestrian zone, the usual box-like sixties buildings, the usual crimes freely and publicly committed in the name of municipal architecture. But the first impression stuck, affecting everything else. I had once found myself in Offenbach standing outside a perfectly normal little department store and thinking: good heavens, this has to be the ugliest little department store in the world.

So I drove past the monster, left the square behind, stopped by the side of the road and, opening my window, asked a young man who looked local for the street where the Adria Grill stood. He plucked his sparse moustache for a while and frowned all over his retreating forehead before he began to tell me. He took his time about it, and managed to make turning right twice and left once sound a very complicated business, but finally we had it. I thanked him and followed the route he had described.

Ten minutes later I parked the car in a quiet side street. Blocks of flats, bars, a garage, a gay sex shop. I walked a little way until I was outside the glass door with the words *Adria Grill* on it. The doorway and window were draped inside with crochet wall-hangings. The menu was up in a glass case by the door. It was Yugoslavian and International Specialities cuisine as found chiefly in Germany, so far as I knew: fifteen meat dishes with chips, five salads, two desserts and fifteen varieties of schnapps. The fact that this cuisine was now very seldom called after Yugoslavia, but after one of the tracts of land that had seceded from Yugoslavia over the past few years with strong support from the German Foreign Ministry, was indicated by the cocktail menu with little Croatian and German flags stuck on it: for five marks ninety-five you could drink a Genscher Sunrise.

As I entered the restaurant about fifteen men fell silent and turned their heads my way. They were sitting and standing more or less separately at tables and the bar, but they were all one party taking up the whole room. Most of them were around fifty and looked as if they always had been, as if they'd always been hanging around in bars and only went out now and then to get cheap suits and hair-cuts. The exceptions were two young men in their mid-twenties sitting in the darkest and most remote corner, with shaved heads and wearing flashy sports jackets. They all had beer glasses in front of them, and as I went up to the bar and wished the landlord 'Good evening', they all remained silent. Perhaps the swelling on my face was more impressive than it had seemed to me in the mirror at home. I hoped they'd decide to regard me as someone who'd had bad luck, not a thug.

'Evening. What'll it be?' The landlord, a massive man with a round, comfortable face, looked at me in a free and easy but friendly way.

'A beer, please.'

He turned to the beer tap, and I looked around the room with an innocent expression, as if I noticed neither the silence nor the glances bent on me.

A few dusty fishing nets and two faded posters of Dubrovnik hung on the walls by way of decoration. Otherwise the place had bare wooden tables, stained beige linoleum on the floor, a jukebox flashing only faintly under layers of dirt, and pale green fabric lampshades in which bulbs too strong for them had burnt an irregular pattern of small, black-rimmed holes. The only relatively new and well-cared-for item was a large photograph in a frame with a removable back; it was enthroned behind the bar on top of the shelves of schnapps bottles. The photo showed a grey-haired man in a white admiral's uniform with plenty of gold buttons and coloured braid, kissing another man on the cheek. All that could be seen of the other man was the back of his head.

The landlord brought me the beer. 'Cheers.'

After I had smoked two cigarettes, ordered another beer, and looked ahead of me with determined naiveté, the guests got talking again one by one. Five minutes later loud, confused voices filled the room. Some of the men were speaking Croatian, many German, mostly in Hessian dialect. Their subjects of conversation were prices, the weather, sport, women. One of them fed some coins into the jukebox, and soon Bonnie Tyler was drowning them all out with *Total Eclipse of the Heart*.

I drank my second beer and ordered a third. When the landlord pushed the glass over to me, I beckoned him closer. He propped his round elbows on the bar and turned his ear my way.

'If you don't mind a direct question...'

He nodded and winked encouragingly at me. He probably thought, after my looking-like-a-sheep act, I wanted to ask the way to the toilet or something equally delicate.

'...have you ever heard of the Army of Reason?'

For a moment his eyes seemed to stop looking at me but without actually closing, the way hands can suddenly stop in mid-gesticulation. Then he turned away in a leisurely fashion, as if at the end of a fairly long conversation between two guests about the meaning of life, went back to the tap and continued serving drinks. If he looked my way I was just a piece of furniture. If I'd left without paying he probably wouldn't even have glanced up.

I stood around for a while, thinking. The first guests began ordering food, and I watched as the landlord leaned through an open hatch beside the bar, passed on orders and received plates. As far as I could see, there were two men working in the kitchen. The chef and a young assistant. I took a pen out of my pocket and wrote, on a beer mat: Two members of the Army of Reason rang this place on Thursday. I want to know who they were. I'm not leaving until I do.

Next time the landlord, loaded down with plates, tried pushing his way past me I got in his way and put the beer mat in his shirt pocket.

'I'm waiting five minutes. If you still haven't spoken to me then, you'll be doing lousy business here this evening.'

He walked on without reacting. But soon after that the chef's assistant appeared in the room, took over at the tap, and the landlord beckoned me over to the end of the bar.

'I got no idea what yer talking about. I'm running a bar, I am, not a war.'

'But you made off fast enough when I mentioned the Army.'

'Hey, look at you! If a man what got a mug like that talks garbage, am I a shrink?'

I looked at his round face. Nothing about it indicated that he was lying. He was the image of a fat, comfortable man who didn't like trouble in his life. And he managed to run this scruffy place so that a lot of people felt happy here and the takings were probably in tune. If one of his guests was the member of a gang extorting protection money, he wouldn't want to know. However, he would take messages on the phone, pass them on, and keep his thoughts to himself. And he would act the simple clown for someone like me trying to worm those thoughts out of him.

I pointed to the framed photograph. 'Who's that?'

His gaze followed the direction of my finger, and when he looked at me again I saw something unpleasant in his eyes for the first time. Irritated, he said, ''S'our president, innit?'

'Mine too? Never saw him look like that.'

''S'posing you ain't noticed, this here's a Croatian restaurant. Thass my homeland, is Croatia, thass where my heart beats.'

'Ah.'

'So whass your line, eh? Asking questions, like?' The amiable fat man was increasingly coming to resemble a fat slob with a fanatical light in his eyes.

'Private eye,' I said, and went on, without letting him get a word in, 'You said you're running a bar here, not a war. And you said your heart beats in Croatia. What's that funny uniform your President's wearing?'

First he said nothing, then he raised his voice. 'Funny?' And as there had been no music playing for some time now, the babble of voices died down too.

'Whassa big idea? Funny!'

I looked from the presidential photo to the now red-faced landlord and back again. I myself didn't know exactly what my idea was. But after more than a week I was at last beginning to get some idea of what kind of outfit the Army of Reason, with its silly name, might be. 'Reason' had come of the tosh Dr Ahrens talked, I felt sure of that. He had liked that word too much, whether because he linked it to some deeper meaning, or because he just thought it sounded interesting. But 'Army', I thought, was from somewhere else. For instance a place where war was thought a matter of honour and uniforms were smart. The word Army might be intended to make people think that instead of an average gang this bunch were something higher, something pure, serving a good cause. And perhaps they even were in a way serving what they called a good cause. They wouldn't be the first gang to try sanitising their obscene business by using zero point such and such a percentage of the takings to throw a few crusts to the poor.

'OK, not funny. But a uniform. Does he like that sort of costume stuff, or is it the official dress of a Croatian president?'

By now there were no more clattering forks or clinking bottles to be heard, and the landlord and I were centre stage. I wondered how long, if the argument became more animated, our audience would confine themselves to watching and listening. And I estimated how many seconds it would take me to get out of the door.

After the landlord had stared at me for some time as if I wanted to steal his President's gold buttons and use them as bog fittings, he pulled himself together and said, as calmly as he could. 'Reckon we done enough talking. The beer's on me. Push off.'

I shook my head. As I did so it seemed to me as if something was moving in the darkest part of the back of the room. I took a few steps back towards the door until I had a view of all the customers. There were no more real clues for me to pick up here; I had only to look into those stony faces to see that. Whether they'd understood what I was riling the landlord about or not – this was their landlord, their drinking-hole, and I was in the way. But perhaps I could kick up enough fuss for one or other of them to let something slip by mistake.

I couldn't. Before my general announcement to the whole company – 'There's a gang of racketeers in Frankfurt at the moment calling itself the Army of Reason…' – had died away, the door behind me opened, and several hands grabbed me at the same moment, knocked me off my feet and rammed me head first into the bar. There was a mighty crash, and everything went dark before my eyes for a few seconds. When it was light again, and I felt my arms twisted behind my back, the first thing I thought of was my pistol. It was about ten thousand kilometres away in my trouser pocket. The second thing I thought of was the way something had been moving at the back of the room. They must have gone out through another door and round outside the place. The third thing I realised, with relief, was that my nose had escaped the impact. Finally I recognised the flashy sports jackets to left and right of me.

'Whaddya want we do with this bastard, then?'

They were addressing the landlord. Berliners, judging by their accent. Did the Berliners have a finger in every pie now? I turned my head until I could look into the sodden eyes of one of the baldies. 'That dulcet tone of voice, that elegant phrasing, anyone can see we have visitors from the capital.'

'Shut your gob!' he snarled, kicking me in the back of the knees.

'How about we see who he is?' said the landlord, sounding as friendly and casual again as he had when I arrived. I had definitely underestimated him.

While the two shaven-headed men went through my pockets, some of the guests left the restaurant in silence. The rest watched the show with interest. Some lit cigarettes, others sipped their beer. The only one in the room who seemed unhappy with the situation but couldn't escape it was the chef's assistant. Out of the corner of my eye, I saw him fidgeting nervously with beer mats and turning his head aside at frequent intervals.

'The bastard's got a gun!' cried one of the Berliners, cracking his heel into the backs of my knees again. Obviously he was used to knowing where and how to lash out. Another couple of kicks and I might even had been wishing he'd hit me in the face for a change.

He held my pistol in front of my face. 'Whaddya call this, then? Come on, whaddya call this?'

'Pistol, a pistol.'

'Got it!' cried his friend, proudly waving my wallet. While the knee expert held me down, the man who was so triumphant over finding a wallet in the inside pocket of a jacket was looking at my papers.

'Kemal Ka… ka… What sort of a name's that? Kaka… Krap, I call it. Kemal Krap!' He laughed, held my ID out to his mate, and they both laughed. 'Kemal Krap! Hey, that's good!'

'Why make it so complicated, lads? Why Kemal? Why not just Krap Krap?'

'Keep your mouth shut, I said.'

This time his kick made my legs crumple, and for a moment I was hanging in the air by my arms, which were still twisted behind my back. When I screamed they dropped me, kicked me in the side so that I landed on my back, and the knee expert put his foot on my throat. My pistol was dangling in the air above me from his hand.

'One more crappy remark like that and I finish this off.'

I briefly closed my eyes to show that I'd got the message. Meanwhile more guests were leaving the place. Were they thinking that the show was getting stronger all the time, and what was about to happen now was too unappetising for them? I turned my eyes to the tap. The chef's assistant had stopped playing with beer mats, and was staring straight ahead of him, gritting his teeth. If this went on he was my only hope. I unobtrusively moved my arms. As far as I could tell from the feel of it, I'd only imagined them cracking.

'You a Turk, then?'

'I'm a Frankfurter.'

'I said no crappy talk!'

The pressure on my throat was increased.

'I thought the landlord wanted to know who I was,' I gasped, 'not just theories.'

Knee Expert frowned. 'Whassat in aid of?'

Before I could answer, his friend pushed into my line of vision. 'We got Turks back home too…' He grinned down at me. 'Been fighting them bastards two years.' He spread the fingers of one hand and waggled them up and down. 'Count 'em, you! That's how many I done in. One more won't make no difference.'

'Yes, I hear that kind of thing goes on in Berlin.'

'Berlin? You daft or what? Nope, in *our* country! Get an education, you layabout! Whaddya think them shitty Muslims are to us? Kemal Kraps, the whole bunch.'

'I see.' I tried to look expressionless. 'What a wonderful education in foreign languages you get in your native land! Amazing!'

'You watch yer step,' said the landlord, coming into the small circle of space above me. 'You ain't bin acting none so friendly here. You insult our President, you made fun of our country. Dunno why, we're peaceful folk, we never done you no harm. Fact is, I wouldn't mind teaching you a lesson – but forget it. You clear out now, and you hear this: show yer face in here again and you'll be thinking of today real sad, remembering how pretty it once wuz. Get it?'

'And how.'

The landlord was still looking into my eyes rather as if he was not too happy with the decision to let me go, but in the end he nodded to the Berliners and disappeared behind the bar. Knee Specialist looked disappointed.

'This beggar's a lucky beggar too,' he said, and couldn't refrain from letting me feel once more how quickly my larynx would be crushed if he wanted. Finally he took his foot away.

It was some time before I could get to my feet and follow him to the bar. As if the last ten minutes hadn't happened, he was standing there casually watching the chef's assistant draw him a beer.

'My pistol, please.'

He slowly turned his head and looked surprised. 'What pistol?' And to his mate, standing next to him, 'Imagining things, ain't he? Potheads, all these guys.'

'They ain't allowed no beer, see? Knifing folk, screwing bints, all that shitty drugs stuff, they can have that. But there ain't nothing for Allah in a beer.'

They looked at me with relish.

I leaned both arms on a bar stool to take the weight off my knees and looked down at the floor, exhausted. While that foot had been on my throat, there'd been no room left for pain. Now it was quickly taking over all the parts of me that had been abused over the last ten minutes. I sighed. 'The gun's registered. If I lose it I have to report the loss and say where and when it happened. A lie risks me my job, and I'm not telling any lies for you. So either you finish me off now after all, or you give me my pistol, or this place will be full of cops tomorrow.'

I looked at the floor again, fumbled for a cigarette in my pocket, lit, and waited for whatever they decided. By now everything was hurting so much that I felt almost indifferent to it. Only I didn't want to look at them any more. Except when I shot them.

'Take the magazine out, give him his gun, then maybe he'll go.'

Soon after that something fell into my jacket pocket. Without even turning round again, I staggered out of the door.

Chapter 11

I was sitting in the car on the other side of the road from the Adria Grill waiting – smoking, listening to the radio, dozing. My face throbbed, my shoulders were burning, and when I moved my knees something in them seemed on the point of breaking. I dropped off to sleep from time to time, waking with a start from fevered dreams a moment later. Mostly the dreams were about fighting. Once companies of men dressed in costume with bright plumes and golden shirts of mail like something out of a historical film were clashing, stabbing and hacking each other to pieces with spears and swords. There was blood everywhere, and severed heads lying about, and techno music boomed out from the surrounding forest. Two eyes were blazing in the middle of this bloodbath and wouldn't stop looking at me, although the body they belonged to was dead. I was the only one who had a gun, but it wouldn't do what I wanted. When I put the safety catch on it fired wildly all over the place, and when I took the safety catch off and pressed the trigger there was just a click. Then the techno music got louder and louder, changed to a deafening rattle, and I woke up. The rattle came from the radio. The tuning of the channel had slipped.

Just before one in the morning the light behind the crochet drapes finally went out. I rubbed my forehead, lit a cigarette, and checked yet again that I'd loaded the pistol with the spare magazine.

Ten minutes later the landlord and his two employees came out into the street. The landlord locked up, nodded to the others, and they all set off in different directions. I forgot my knees and my shoulders, got out of the car, closed its door quietly, and followed the chef's assistant. I got him in a dark side alley. I quietly made my way to within ten metres and then ran at him. At about the same moment as he spun round in alarm the muzzle of my pistol pressed against his chest.

'Don't make a sound!'

I grabbed him by the collar and dragged him into the entrance of the nearest building. His slight body was trembling like an animal's. Only now did I realise how young he must be. Twenty at the most.

'Don't worry, nothing's going to happen to you.'

'Please...' he begged, gasping for breath. 'Please... I'm not one of them!'

'I know. Take it easy.' I patted him on the shoulder. 'I only want you to explain a few things to me.'

'But I don't know anything. I'm only his nephew. I'm working there to earn money. I don't have anything to do with that lot.'

He was talking so fast that I could barely understand him. He never took his eyes off the pistol, but at the same time turned his head as far away from it as possible.

'Listen: I'll put it away if you promise not to try anything silly.'

'What?' He wasn't listening to me.

'The pistol. Look...' I put it in my jacket pocket. 'Better now?'

He stared at the opening of the pocket for a moment

longer before looking hesitantly at my face, as if expecting to see a monster. 'What... what do you want?'

'I want you to tell me what you've heard at work, or
from your uncle, about the Army of Reason.'

'Army of Reason?'

'Could be you've never heard the name mentioned. It's
a gang that started extorting protection money in Frankfurt about two weeks ago. I assume the Adria Grill is the
place where they meet, if only for a beer.'

At the words 'extorting protection money' he jumped,
and I saw him checking up on opportunities for escape
out of the corner of his eyes. I stood a little more four-
square in front of him and shook my head. 'Don't even
think of it. If you help me we'll never see each other
again, and no one will know that you talked to me. If you
don't, I'll tell your uncle that you phoned me and tried to
sell me information.'

'Are you crazy?' It burst out of him before he turned
his eyes away and stared at the ground, lips compressed. I
waited. Standing there in front of me now without a
kitchen apron on, he looked like a youth from another
period. He wore pointed shoes with leopard-skin trim, a
pair of suit trousers much too large for him, a white shirt
with a starched collar, and he had a crew cut. Perhaps his
favourite band was The Who, and either that was usual in
Offenbach or he had a good chance of leading a revival in
three or four years' time.

'I... look, I'm going to university in the autumn, I
wanted to work through the summer so as not to have to
take a job during my first year. I never specially liked my
uncle – why am I saying specially? Not at all. But I could-
n't find anything better... I had no idea what I was get-

ting into. Imagine it, you just want to earn some cash, and suddenly you're right in a…'

He stopped and stared ahead of him again. I lit myself a cigarette and registered the adrenalin closing down for the night in my body, while pain took over again. After a while he raised his eyes and pointed cautiously to my jacket pocket with one finger.

'They took the bullets out, didn't they?'

'I had a spare magazine in the car.'

'Oh.' He made a face as if thinking of something really disgusting to eat. '…Would you have shot me?'

'Let's say at least I wouldn't have let you get away.'

He thought about it for a moment, and then nodded. 'They really took you apart.'

'Yes, and it hurts, and I want to go to bed. Tell me about the protection money gang.'

'OK,' he sighed. 'But you'll have to…'

'I won't have to do anything,' I snorted. Only just now he'd been close to shitting himself, and now he was a little too inclined to have a cosy chat for my liking. 'You either trust me or you don't. I'll wait another five minutes. If I haven't heard anything that interests me by then, I shall get your uncle out of bed this very night, and you can start thinking of some place to go and study abroad.'

It took him a little more swallowing, marking time on the spot and looking at the ground, but finally, head bowed, he talked. He turned out to be a bright, inquisitive lad, and half an hour later he'd answered a great many more questions than I had meant to ask.

The Adria Grill functioned as a meeting place for Croatian nationalists who liked to have a drink together, and also for German Nazi and Ustasha fans who were seeking salvation as mercenaries in the Bosnian war. True, the war was officially over, but there were still paramilitary bands of all political colours as fond as ever of murdering each other in the name of a Greater Croatia, Greater Bosnia or Greater Serbia – for a good fat fee. Checking up on the mercenaries and dispatching them was organised by a tall, thin man who was always very smartly dressed, but whose name was never mentioned. He turned up in a Mercedes three times a week and held audience for one or two hours in the back room of the Adria Grill. He hadn't turned up this evening, and Zvonko – that was the boy's name – had seen his uncle go to the phone several times after I was flung out to call this man, but without success.

'Was he there last Thursday?'

'Thursday… yes, of course, that was the evening when the palefaces didn't turn up. That's what I call them to myself. Their faces are powdered and they wear blond wigs. They first turned up two weeks ago, and at the start I thought they were cranks of some kind, a cult or something. How would I know? Suppose Jesus is blond and loves Croatia. You wouldn't believe what weird characters come into that place. Sometimes I think Yugoslavia and the war was like winning the lottery for all the weirdoes who have some kind of obsession going that won't get them anywhere here. I heard one of the interviews. The man kept saying how he couldn't stand his wife any more, that was all he talked about. And he went off there, and the first thing he did was probably to shoot ten Bosnian women between thirty and forty. And then he said Croatia was a wonderful country because of its literature and music. I mean, sometimes it's quite funny.'

'What happened next with the palefaces?'

'After that they turned up almost every evening. Like the tall man. A week ago I saw them giving him money for the first time. After that I looked out for them, and they always bring something. If the tall man isn't there they give it to my uncle. But only for safe keeping. He's not a big wheel. He makes himself out important, but...'

I let him whinge on about his uncle for a bit, and then I asked if he knew where the money came from. He did, and that wasn't all. Most of the 'palefaces' were Bosnian refugees blackmailed into working for the gang. If they objected, they were threatened with the deaths of friends or relations who had stayed behind in Bosnia. The job would be done, as Zvonko put it, by 'German lovers of Croatian literature'. He'd once overheard the tall man explaining to a tearful paleface that after his wilful behaviour they'd be obliged to do something about it.

'...My Croatian isn't perfect, but that's roughly what he said. And suppose it was only your brother but you still have a wife and children there? I expect you'd be a hundred per cent in favour of working for them then.'

I thought of the brutality with which the racketeers went to work, and realised that if someone like Romario didn't pay up, the gang would be more or less literally holding a gun to their families' heads.

'And what specially amuses the tall man and the others when they're sitting over a schnapps later is that of course the palefaces are from all the so-called ethnic groups: Serbs, Muslims, Croatians, gypsies. One of their favourite sayings is, "We're sending all Yugoslavia out on the streets for us."'

'How can they know for certain which refugee has family where?'

'They have lists, no idea where they get them. Anyway, you can bet the tall man is only quite small fry in the organisation. The bosses will be in Croatia, and then there's a kind of German who talks big. He came twice, acting the way my Granny said German tourists used to.'

'A man with uncomfortable blue eyes?'

'That's right. Always looks as if he didn't know whether he wants to screw someone or kill them. The day before yesterday he came in and bawled out the tall man in front of everyone as if he was the last one hiring out the deckchairs. I don't know exactly what it was about, I was in the kitchen. But I think there's going to be some kind of important meeting in the next few days.'

'Of the bosses?'

He shrugged. 'My uncle ordered about a ton of fillet steak for the weekend. That won't be for the few regulars who drink at his place.'

I thought of the Albanian. It was only in my fury with Ahrens's Hessian who broke my nose that I'd dragged him into this too hastily. I couldn't possibly hand him people who'd been blackmailed into being gangsters and would probably be very glad to stop at once. But I had to give him something. I couldn't offer the Albanian a deal and then say a couple of days later: sorry, I made a mistake. At least, not if I wanted to go on earning money as a private detective in the same town in the future. A meeting of Croatian bosses would be just the thing. If it took place. And if I could find out when.

'Do you know why they powder their faces and wear wigs and never say a word when they're extorting money?'

'Orders from the top. But I can't see why either. I only

once heard one of them who'd taken off his wig because of the heat being bawled out in the back room. That get-up must matter a lot to the bosses.'

Finally I asked him about the two palefaces who hadn't turned up last Thursday, but he couldn't tell me any more except that no one had mentioned them since. Then we'd both obviously had enough for one night. I offered him a cigarette, and we sat smoking, exhausted.

After a while he asked, 'I don't have to worry about you landing me in trouble, do I?'

'Not in the least. But all the same, you'd do better to look for a different job. It could get pretty hot there soon.'

'You must be joking. How many jobs do you think there are around here for me?'

I took a pen and a scrap of paper out of my pocket and wrote down Slibulsky's name and business phone number for him. 'Ice-cream vendor. As far as I know it pays very well. Call this number first thing tomorrow and say you were sent by me, Kayankaya.'

I gave him the note. He glanced at it, and hesitantly put it in his pocket. 'Thanks.'

'It's for me to thank you. And if your uncle or his friends make trouble for you, call me. The faster you get out of there the better.' I shook hands with him. 'See you at Slibulsky's.'

He nodded, and then he suddenly seemed to have to pull himself together so as not to laugh out loud. He was probably only now beginning to believe that this man with the bashed-up face and the pistol in his jacket pocket really wasn't going to do anything more to him tonight.

Ten minutes later I was racing away from Marilyn Monroe's sister at full speed, and if my shoulders hadn't

131

been in such a bad way I might have stuck two fingers out
of the side window by way of goodbye.

I left the car in the no-parking zone and dragged myself
into the Mister Happy. It was just after three, and generally only the video recorder was working at that time.
While the inmates dozed on plushy pink sofas, or sat
over coffee and crossword puzzles hoping for a last customer, the troops were slogging it out on a large screen,
naked, against scenery like a furniture warehouse. Soft,
continuous moaning mingled with equally soft piano
music.

I crossed the room, greeting girls to left and right, and
found Deborah in the kitchen, as I'd expected. She was
eating ham sandwiches and leafing through mail-order
catalogues with a colleague.

'Hey, baby, what happened to you?'

Whatever had happened to me, at least it was no reason
for her to spread a bit more mustard on her sandwich and
take a hearty bite. She added, with her mouth full, 'You
don't look too good.'

Deborah a.k.a. Helga was a small, plump twenty-year-
old from a village in north Germany. She had an 'Italian
style' perm, nail lacquer in Malibu, Cherry Red and
Flamingo, tracksuits with as many zip fasteners as possible,
and when she went out she wore a cap saying *Foxy Kitten*.
From what she said she didn't mind her job, and sometimes even enjoyed it. All the same, she was saving hard to
open an espresso and sandwich bar in her home village a
couple of years from now. What she definitely enjoyed, all
the time, was eating. And I really liked her for that. She ate
like a cow: slowly, with relish, never letting anything dis-

turb her. Watching her eat had an effect on me like doing yoga.

'I'm OK,' I said, as she fished a gherkin out of a jar and waved it about to dry it. 'Do you have anything else to do?'

'Huh, there's been nothing going on here for hours. I'm just having a bite to eat and then I'm turning in. You can go upstairs if you like.'

'I could do with a dunking in your whirlpool bath.'

'Ha!' She stabbed the air with the gherkin. 'That comes extra!' And laughing, she nudged her colleague in the ribs. The colleague, a tough dimwit, grinned derisively.

I had once helped Deborah out of a rather sticky situation with her pimp, we had come closer to each other with Willy DeVille's *Heaven Stood Still*, and since then we'd had a tacit agreement: I could have her spoil me once a week, and in return I'd be available for any further fix she might be in. The point was that there hadn't been one, and there wasn't going to be one for the foreseeable future. The Mister Happy was as civilised and homely as a village bakery in a French film. I should know; I'd been acquainted with the madam for years, and had found Deborah the job here. Signs that she herself was seeing less and less point in our arrangement had been increasing recently, and although she laughed now, I was sure that at the back of her mind a fierce little calculating devil was registering another two hundred marks unearned.

'Come on, baby, just joking. Of course you can go in the pool. But you'll have to rinse it out first. No one cleaned it after the last guy, and he was all hairy.'

'Oh. Hm.'

'See you.' She threw me an airy kiss. 'And I'll see that

you feel as good as new tomorrow.'

She did, too. When Deborah was well-fed and in a good mood there were few who could tell her anything about how to do that. For an evening's good screw to make up for things, I reflected, I wasn't as badly off as Slibulsky thought.

Chapter 12

Perhaps I didn't feel exactly new, but after a night of extensive massage and breakfast in bed in the morning I was in surprisingly good form except for the variegated colours of my face. Deborah kissed me goodbye, and as I went out to my car and removed the parking ticket from under the windscreen wiper I thought almost lovingly of how, before I'd even had a chance to look at the breakfast tray, she'd asked if I didn't want my egg.

I drove home, showered, put on clean clothes and went round the corner to drink coffee and read the newspaper in a café. I'd really intended to drive out to Ahrens's factory next and wait until my rescuer from the switchboard knocked off work. Presumably she knew when the bosses would be meeting. But the newspaper spared me the trouble. In the local section I found a headline saying *Frankfurt Expects Visit From Croatian Interior Minister Plus Economic Delegation*. Along with all kinds of guff about the traditional friendship between Croats and Germans, and a welcome given by German credit institutions to the 'rising young country', the article went into detail about cooperation between Croatian and German firms. Ahrens won praise for his packet-soup outfit as one of the first Frankfurt companies to have been active in Croatia after the war.

I put the paper down and thought about Slibulsky's sweets. Probably they were exactly the kind of thing that

Ahrens's activities consisted of. So there actually was work being done in his factory. In addition, the article seemed to me to answer the question of why the racketeers had to disguise themselves and mustn't utter a word betraying any accent: the revelation that a Croatian-led Mafia was chopping fingers off German bar-owners would hardly have had a favourable effect on the granting of credit. Which meant that the bosses of the Army of Reason were far enough up in the Croatian power structure for their personal interests to coincide to some extent with the national interest.

That is, if part of the credit didn't find its way straight into their pockets. As far as I knew, the Croatian president didn't exactly have a reputation as a staunch opponent of corruption and the Mafiosi. He probably didn't care about having such a reputation either. I'd once seen a picture of his yacht. Along with his uniform in the photo yesterday evening, it gave an impression rather as if the mayor of Frankfurt's wife went about her daily business in a swimming pool filled with champagne.

The Interior Minister's visit was going to be next Saturday. That left me three more days. I paid my bill and went home. From there I called an acquaintance who knew his way around the refugee hostels. He gave me the name of one where most of the inmates came from Bosnia.

It had begun raining again, and the square outside the place, which had once been a youth hostel, was full of mud and puddles. I wove my way past them to the entrance, found myself in a dark corridor smelling of food and disinfectant, read a series of notices hanging from the ceiling – *Dining-Room, Showers, Sick-Bay* – and followed the arrow on the one that said *Secretarial Office*. On the walls to left and right hung posters produced by the Evangelical church showing young people, black and white, moving down streets and stairways and through meadows together, under brightly coloured slogans saying things like *Wow, man, loving your neighbour is great!* and *I'm all for multi-ethnicity!* In between, dingy notes were pinned up telling you not to smoke in the corridors, not to make a noise, and not to assemble, eat or drink there. As far as I could see these instructions were being obeyed to the letter. No one came to meet me, and only the distant sound of children's voices and the clatter of crockery indicated that the place was inhabited at all.

The door of the secretarial office was at the end of the corridor, which was getting darker and darker. I knocked, and thought I heard a couple of harsh, commanding sounds through the wood before a cheerful, 'Yoo-hoo!' rang out. When I opened the door bright light shone in my face. Before I could make anything out someone called, 'Come in, do just come along in!' as if I'd arrived intending to see somebody turning cartwheels.

I closed the door behind me and blinked at a row of neon lights. As my eyes got used to the dazzle I saw the usual shabby grey-green office furnishings paid for decades ago out of the public purse, the usual private touches consisting of holiday postcards pinned to the wall and amusing newspaper cuttings, and the usual photographic landscape calendar. Behind the desk sat someone not quite so usual in this setting, a woman of about forty-five, with a girl of around fourteen on a chair in front of her.

The woman was tanned deep brown, in ultra-fit condition without a trace of extra fat, and judging by the way she was smiling at me with two incredibly white, immaculate rows of teeth, apparently in the best of good humour. She was wearing a short-sleeved blouse in a jungle-animal print that showed off her muscular arms, earrings with little heads of Charlie Chaplin dangling from them, a necklace with a small Buddha pendant, and her hair was in a long, thick, blonde braid that she had flirtatiously brought round over her shoulder to hang in front of her. Presumably she felt that the last word about what she'd do with her life hadn't yet been spoken. She fitted into the grey-green secretarial office of this refugee hostel about as well as into a bowling alley.

The girl, on the other hand, could have come straight out of an ad appealing for donations to the Red Cross. A thin, emaciated body in worn jeans and a dirty T-shirt, arms covered with scratches and bruises, and a chin with a thick, blood-encrusted scab on it. She was looking sceptically at me from dark eyes which, for her age, were impressively ringed with dark circles. Her gaze seemed to be asking whether she was the reason why I was here, and if so, whether I intended to do something just bad or very bad indeed to her. Perhaps she was older than fourteen; it was hard to say in her condition. But anyway I had thrown nearly everyone from sexual maturity up to the age of twenty five into the same pot. Sometimes the pot was labelled *Child*, at other times something else.

'Hello-o-o,' fluted the woman, turning as emphatically and exclusively in my direction as if she'd like to turn the girl into a flowerpot or something else that wouldn't attract my attention. Perhaps she was ashamed of this dirty heap of misery in her office, or of her astral body beside the skeleton. Or perhaps it was simply her normal behaviour when a man and a girl were in the same room with her.

'Hello to you too,' I replied. 'Kayankaya, private detective.'

She gave a slight start, and her eyes narrowed as if I had blown air into her face. 'Private detective,' she repeated, trying to maintain her cheery tone. 'So... er, how can I help you?'

I really wanted to ask her to send the girl out of the room for a little while, but decided not to. It would only have warned her that I was here about something worse than stolen bicycles.

'I'd like to talk to you about a gang extorting protection money who are probably forcing inmates of this hostel to work for them.'

On the way here I'd been prepared for one of those difficult and usually fruitless afternoons when large numbers of people kept suggesting more or less clearly how great it would be if I finally stopped asking questions and went away. I was all the more surprised to find I'd obviously scored a direct hit in double-quick time. Her lower jaw dropped foolishly, her eyelids began to twitch, and the heads of Charlie Chaplin shook like a have-a-go-free notice on an ancient pinball machine. I watched her struggling to regain her composure. The she suddenly broke into hearty laughter.

'And there was I thinking I was dealing with a madman! Private detective! Whoever heard of such a thing these days?' She laughed again. 'You were only joking, right? Well, you certainly took me in. You must be the electrician, aren't you? It's the lighting in the corridor. Wait a moment and I'll show you. Leila...' As she waved towards the door, she turned to the girl. 'Go upstairs, please, dear. We'll go on talking later.'

Either she had realised pretty quickly how little she wanted someone listening in on any conversation with me, or I had hit even harder than I'd guessed. Perhaps my mere appearance in the secretarial office at this moment was a direct hit in itself.

But however that might be, her little performance wasn't running too badly so far – and if the girl had got up and gone out she could have carried on with it, acting slightly stupid, talking about corridor lighting, claiming not to know anything, believe me or not as you like, goodbye.

However, the girl didn't get up and didn't look as if she could be easily persuaded to do so. Hands clutching the arms of her chair, she thrust her lips out defiantly and stared, unmoved, at the woman behind the desk.

'Leila!' The mouth was still smiling, but the voice had taken on a barracking tone. That didn't seem to bother Leila. To make it perfectly clear that she was not going to obey, she slipped off her plastic flip-flops and stuck her feet behind the chair-legs. Apart from that she didn't move.

The woman tried hard to indicate, by rolling her eyes with amusement, how widespread and really rather sweet such teenage obstinacy was, but how trying too. Of course there was no reason for it at all, we grown-ups were of the same mind there…

'Leila, if you don't go I'll have to call Gregor, and he'll take you to your room, chair and all.' She leaned forward and smiled at the girl, closing her eyes so much that I couldn't see them. 'Do you really want to deprive me of

140

my chair? I have to discuss the corridor lighting with this man, and I'd like to ask him to sit down. I'm sure you can understand that.'

Leila slowly opened her mouth, wiggled the tip of her tongue between her teeth a bit, and looked at the woman as if she were a conjuror whose tricks have all failed, but who's still passing round the hat. Then she said calmly, 'I heard, old cunt,' and pointed her finger to her ear. 'Private detective. Corridor lighting shit!'

You could have charged entrance money for the ensuing pause. While it was as much as the woman could to do keep her facial muscles under control, Leila scratched her head and looked straight in front of her, frowning, as if wondering whether she was sitting here with an old cunt for any good reason.

'Would you believe it?' the woman finally managed to say. 'Here we are, caring for them day and night, and what thanks do we get?'

'Does caring for them day and night mean talking such garbage?'

'…I beg your pardon?'

'You heard. Why were you suddenly so keen to have the girl out of the way once I mentioned extortionists and protection money?'

'It's no such thing! I…' She pursed her lips and looked across her desktop as if an answer might be lying around somewhere there. 'I don't like discussing such things in front of children. I'm sure you can understand that. Quite apart from the fact that your suspicion is, of course, wildly far-fetched.'

'Fetch far?' asked Leila, who was following our conversation with interest.

Before I could reply to her the woman interrupted. 'That's enough of that! Go away, Leila, or I'm calling Gregor!'

'Gre-gor!' Leila imitated her, but the the next moment she shut her mouth and looked like she was scared by her own words. It was to be assumed that Gregor's name put a lid on audacity.

'Just as you like!'

As the woman reached for the phone, tapped in a number and waited, face averted, for someone to answer, I tried to think what I was going to do if Gregor did drag Leila off, chair and all. And I wondered how ruthless I wanted to be. By now I was convinced that either Leila knew something I wasn't supposed to find out, or I knew something that she wasn't supposed to find out. Either way, I couldn't ask her about it in front of this woman. The mere fact that I was here, seeing the woman try to get Leila away from me almost without bothering to pretend about it, could get her into all sorts of trouble. Depending on how high one assessed the chances that I saw her as a source of information or a witness. For the girl's sake, I thought, it would be best if I left.

Meanwhile Leila was acting the defiant child again. She went on wiggling her tongue between her teeth, stretched out a dirty foot now and then, circled it in the air and examined it critically. All the same, you could sense that the increasingly probable arrival of Gregor scared her. She looked briefly at me a few times. Perhaps she was hoping I'd stay.

'Gregor?… Please would you come down quickly… Yes, a little problem… Leila… Uh-huh, see you in a minute.'

After she had put the receiver down she sat deep in thought for a few seconds, and then looked up with a fleeting smile as if to say: sorry about that interruption, now, where were we? She did not in fact say anything, just kept on smiling. Obviously that was how she meant to occupy the time until Gregor arrived.

'Frau... er?'

'Schmidtbauer.'

'Well, Frau Schmidtbauer, you have now done all you can to make it clear that there's something shady going on here. Either you talk to me about it, or I stay in this place and rummage around until I've found out about it. The difference is that if you talk to me, I can turn a blind eye. If you don't, and if you have a skeleton in the cupboard and I discover it, I'll inform on you.'

Her smile became a little more fleeting, but nothing else happened.

'Think about it. It doesn't look to me as if you're much more than the receptionist here. You know what goes on, and presumably there's a few marks left on your desk now and then to induce you to keep your mouth shut. How much is the money worth? A new blouse, a good meal in a smart restaurant? I'll bet it's not enough for you to travel somewhere you'll be safe from the police. If what I suspect is right, there'll be charges of organised crime, blackmail, and possibly aiding and abetting murder. And even if you're convicted only of knowing about the crime, you'll get a long enough sentence to remove you from circulation for the part of your life that matters. There'll be nothing left later but a little sport for senior citizens, and reincarnation if you're lucky.'

No reaction. She smiled and went on holding out. But

the hunted look in her eyes told me that she'd soften up once we were alone. So I dismissed all my theories of the last ten minutes and just hoped Leila was only a girl sitting in the wrong room at the wrong time, and Gregor was a nice lad with frizzy hair and comfortable shoes doing civilian service instead of the draft, who'd behaved perfectly in persuading Leila to go with him.

These hopes lasted just a few seconds. Then the door was flung open and Popeye on coke burst in. Muscular in a T-shirt, tracksuit bottoms, trainers like small, brightly coloured cruise missiles, shaved head, a chin fit to knock doors down, and eyes with their pupils moving as if they had to register the tempo of three hundred herds of white elephants charging his way. He measured something above two metres, and to see from one end of his shoulders to the other I had to turn my head back and forth slightly, as if watching tennis. Then I recognised the showy sports watch. Perhaps it was chance, but Ahrens wore the same model.

Without taking any notice of me or Frau Schmidtbauer, he made for Leila, snarling, 'You lousy little beast! What's the idea this time? Didn't I tell you…'

Whatever he had told her, it was drowned out by Leila's shrill scream as he closed his great paws round her arms and pulled her out of the chair. Leila's legs flailed in the air as she tried to kick him. At the same time she never stopped screaming, and the small secretarial office became an acoustic torture chamber. Popeye was bellowing, 'You shut up!' Frau Schmidtbauer was crying, 'Don't grab her so hard!' And I drew my pistol.

'Hey, you!' I shouted, trying to drown out the others. 'Gregor!'

He turned, with the girl wedged under his arm. It took him a moment to realise what it was gleaming in my hand, and then he looked incredulous. Leila struggled and screamed a little longer, until she too looked at me and immediately fell silent.

'Put the child down again,' I said, waving the pistol.

Gregor looked even more incredulous. In the process the pupils of his eyes grew ever larger and ever emptier, and I had the feeling I was facing a horror dummy. The kind of thing that could be used at cinema entrances to advertise films like *The Massacre Man* or *The Devil's Dinner.*

He turned his head to the desk. 'Who's this arsehole?'

Frau Schmidtbauer bit her lower lip, looked at my pistol, and didn't seem to think Gregor's choice of words very sensible. 'Er,' she said, shrugging her shoulders.

I said, 'This arsehole is the character who'll shoot holes in your knees if you don't let go of the child.'

It was as if something inside him exploded. His head whipped round, and with his teeth bared and his eyes popping he clamped Leila to his chest and held her out in my direction. 'Oh, so that's your idea? You think you'll shoot holes in me?' he roared, chin jutting. 'Go on, then! But you'll have to shoot through the girl first. Didn't think of that, eh? Shoot holes in me! I could kill you with one hand.'

'With your little toe for all I care. But we're not here for a fight, and I don't want to shoot you in the chest either. Just in the kneecaps. You'd need to be holding a wall in front of you to stop me doing that.'

'Please, Gregor!' begged Frau Schmidtbauer, and at the same moment she started crying.

Gregor was now snorting like a horse. He began

145

twitching and sweating, looking around him as if his good friend coke had left him in mid-flight, and now he was sailing alone through some kind of cosmos that was a total mystery to him.

'The child,' I said, trying again, but he wasn't listening any more. He looked at the floor, froze for a moment as if hypnotising himself, his snorting and twitching died down, and whereas he had just been gleaming with sweat it now looked as if he had a layer of grey dust on his skin. Nothing indicated the presence of a brain any more. It was pure reflex when he assumed a close-combat position. Then he bent his knees, braced his shoulders back like someone putting the shot, and tensed his biceps. A slippery film formed between the pistol and my hand.

When Leila came flying towards me, I shoved her to my left and under the desk, threw myself to the right, saw two metres of cokehead above me, and fired my pistol. Gregor, hit in the legs, bellowed, froze briefly in a kind of jazz-dance distortion, grabbed his thighs and collapsed. At the same moment Frau Schmidtbauer started screaming.

I lay gasping for air and trying to steady my trembling arm. Gregor's body, barely three metres away from me, wasn't moving any more. He had obviously fainted. Dark patches were spreading over his tracksuit bottoms. I'd emptied my entire magazine into his legs and the wall behind them. Even sober, Gregor probably wouldn't have allowed me to keep cool. Pumped full of drugs he'd looked to me, for a moment, like the last person I would ever meet on earth. Still, I hadn't aimed any higher.

Frau Schmidtbauer kept on and on screaming. Finally I struggled to my feet, went over to her and slapped her face until she covered it with her hands and began whimpering quietly. Then I bent to look under the desk. Arms around her knees, T-shirt torn, feet bare, Leila was cowering in the furthest corner with her eyes and mouth tight closed, and tears running down her cheeks.

I straightened up and looked for the cigarettes in my jacket pocket. The girl was beginning to get on my nerves now too. Why didn't she run away? Why, whatever she was threatened with and whatever happened, did she stick around in the secretarial office, a horrible place in every respect? Whether Leila knew anything or not, I was beginning to think I'd have had a really successful afternoon without her: half an hour at the most to crack Frau Schmidtbauer, about another twenty minutes for her to spill all the details of the link between this hostel and the Army, and last, with a little luck, information about two brief lives which for one reason or another were unpleasant enough for no one to mourn their end much. Even now I had a chance. A little poking about in Gregor's wounds, and Frau Schmidtbauer would probably have given me all she knew in writing. But this way... I could neither haul Leila out from under the desk and put her outside the door, nor use the methods of a military junta in front of her. The question was, what could I do instead? I smoked, and thought about it.

'...oh, baby, your life's up the spout, you just don't know it yet,' came a grating voice from the floor. Gregor seemed to be coming round. 'I'll finish you, you bastard... I'll smash you up but I won't let you die... I'll crush your balls until you're throwing up your own shit... and you'll bleed so much you'll wish so much you'd never put your bloody wog face out of your bloody wog mother ...'

He went on like this until I went over and kicked him

in the head. He gurgled something else, and then we had peace and quiet again.

'Right,' I said, turning to Frau Schmidtbauer, 'now tell me how we get out of here.'

But Frau Schmidtbauer didn't want to tell me anything. She wanted to weep and wail and call me names in a stifled voice. 'You murderer! You've killed him! You're a murderer!'

'Nonsense. He can take it. The question is how much you can take. I am now going to call the police and tell them the story of a crazed cokehead – if you'll back me up. If not I'll have to try the truth on them: how your hostel is pretty well under the command of a German-Croatian Mafia, and you and Gregor here are more or less running it for them.'

'…you murderer!'

'Oh, do stop that. He'll be beating someone up again in three weeks' time. At the latest. Unless you go on howling like that much longer, and then maybe there's a chance he'll bleed to death.'

'You… you…'

'If you're going to say "murderer" again I'll murder *you*.'

'You… you're brutal, cruel…'

'OK, let's tell them the truth.'

I went over to the phone, raised the receiver and dialled. Before it began to ring a thin arm shot past me and a small hand, with bitten nails painted pink, came down on the cradle. 'No!'

I turned and looked into Leila's tearful face.

'Please!' Her eyes, which had little burst veins in them, looked pleadingly at me.

'You don't want me to call the police?'

She shook her head.

'Why not?'

Before she could open her mouth someone who had apparently just come into the secretarial office snapped, 'Because her tart of a mother's involved! That's why, you great child-lover!'

I turned and looked at Frau Schmidtbauer, astonished. In spite of everything that had happened I could hardly believe the voice that had greeted me so merrily, barely half an hour ago, came from the same human being as the one that now sounded as if hatred was its principal register.

With a triumphant grin, she defiantly pushed her face, now visibly flushed in spite of the sun tan, towards me. 'Didn't think of that one, did you? Her mother's the worst of the lot! And this little witch is just as depraved! See how she's wrapped you round her little finger!'

Worst of the lot? Depraved little witch? Was she simply making up some kind of fantasy, just so long as she thought it sounded tough and might induce me to leave?

I shook my head slightly. 'What is it you people here have about mothers? Are we in some kind of ghetto movie, or in Italy, or what?'

'But I'm telling you the truth! Her mother's a tart! I could tell you stuff to make your hair stand on end...'

Suddenly I guessed something. I'd only ever heard anyone crack up as furiously as this when there was jealousy involved, and the more furious Frau Schmidtbauer grew, the further she leaned towards me and the more garishly did the colours of the jungle-animal print of her blouse hit me in the eye. I thought of Gregor's watch, and how there might be reasons other than a few marks of hush money why someone like Frau Schmidtbauer, who said things like, 'I could tell you stuff to make your hair stand on end', would let herself act as general dogsbody to a Mafia gang.

'…a filthy creature, a…'

'Tell me, how about Dr Ahrens – does he just have animal skins lying on his floor or does he fuck like an animal too?'

For the second time during our short acquaintance I managed to get her making that foolish face, lower jaw dropping and eyelids twitching.

'What… what are you talking about? I don't know what…'

I smiled magnanimously. 'That's OK. Why not? He's a smart guy, is Ahrens – smart office, smart car… all the same, in your place I wouldn't shoot my mouth off quite so loud about tarts and depravity.'

'What on earth are you thinking of?'

'Not a lot at this moment. I'm going out with Leila for a little while, and meanwhile you can see to the monster there. It's probably in all our interests not to kick up a big fuss about this. Call Ahrens and ask him for a doctor who'll take the bullets out without asking too many questions. I'm sure he knows one. And then I want a private conversation with you later. If you disappear, or summon reinforcements, or do anything else to stop us having that conversation you'll be in jail this evening. The same applies if you bring Ahrens or Gregor into it against Leila. She was here today only by chance and she has nothing to do with it – whether her mother's what you say she is or not.'

She briefly opened her mouth to say something, thought better of it, nodded slightly, looked at the phone and picked up the receiver. When I closed the door behind Leila and myself I could hear her clearing her throat, and then fluting again, as if restored to her old self, 'Oh, my dear, I'm glad to catch you. I have to speak to Dr Ahrens. It's urgent…'

Apparently she took my threat seriously. I briefly imagined Höttges's face if I'd actually thought of asking him to have a woman with absolutely nothing against her arrested. I'd have had to think up something special to persuade him. Perhaps a projection of the film featuring him on the façade of police headquarters, for instance. Or a Zeppelin circling above Frankfurt by night, with a huge monitor hanging from it showing details of his little rendezvous all the way to Offenbach.

'Let's go somewhere we can be alone and keep an eye on the square outside this building.'

'Keep an eye there?'

'Go somewhere we can see it.'

Leila pointed down the dark corridor. 'Visitors' room.'

If the place where we found ourselves a little later was really meant to be a visitors' room, they seemed to think here that 'visitors' was just a synonym for a robber band. And one that must have mastered the trick of finding a market somewhere in the world for the sale of rusty metal chairs with their foam rubber upholstery spilling out, and tables that were obviously used mainly for stubbing out cigarettes, knife-throwing, and inscriptions in thick felt pen saying 'Fuck the cunt'. All the furniture – which besides the tables and chairs consisted of a standard lamp without a bulb in it and an empty bookshelf – was screwed to the floor with strong angle-irons. There was nothing you could have moved in any way at all. When I tried opening a window to get rid of the stink of disinfectant, Leila waved my attempt aside.

'No try.'

'No try?'

'Hostel manager say.'

'No try what? Getting a breath of fresh air?'

Leila shrugged. 'Don't know. Steal windows?'

'Steal windows,' I repeated, and looked at the cracked, battered plastic frame, which was painted a bilious yellow.

'Well, let's keep this short.' I looked at Leila. She was leaning against the wall a few metres away from me, her arms folded, and once again looking as unmoved as before the appearance of Gregor. Yet she seemed to know as little as I did what we were really doing here. I had got her out of the secretary's office so that I could go back on my own and deal with Frau Schmidtbauer, and she had probably come with me only to make sure I wasn't going to call the police after all. After Frau Schmidtbauer's outburst I though I knew enough about Leila's part in the affair. A short conversation to persuade her to trust me, and then I hoped she'd finally disappear.

'Your mother works for Ahrens and that's why you don't want me to call the police, right?'

She nodded.

'And she doesn't really want to work for Ahrens at all, but he blackmails her into it, the way he blackmails other people here in the hostel.'

She nodded again.

'OK, then there's no problem. I was never really going

to call the police, I just meant it as a threat.'

I waited for some sign that she understood and now we could go our separate ways. Instead she dug her hands into her trouser pockets and began walking slowly up and down the room. As she did so she kept casting brief, appraising glances at me, as if I'd made her some offer that wasn't entirely on the level. In fact it was now that I finally realised how little she could still be called a child. In the secretarial office I had noticed only the rings round her eyes, the scab, the shoulder-length, greasy mop of hair and her loud mouth. Now I looked at her properly for the first time. Her face reminded me of one of those little bistro tables when you are having lunch for two there. Eyes, nose and mouth all seemed to be pushing each other over the edge. Not that her face itself was particularly thin, but everything else was so particularly large and pronounced, like a series of slightly outsized features of classical beauty. Dark, huge, almost protuberant eyes, a slightly aquiline, strong nose, and lips like pink air cushions. In addition she moved like those long-legged girls of whom you can never be sure whether they know what they can do to a man just by taking a short, meaningless walk across the room.

All things considered, it was suddenly clear to me that possibly I wasn't the first old fogy to have helped her out of a tricky situation or done her some other favour, and perhaps other men had then insisted on being shown gratitude in a room as remote as this one.

'Hey, Leila, what's the matter?' I asked, overdoing the loud voice. 'Stop marching around like that! We've dis-cussed everything we have to discuss. Go to your room and wait for your mother to come back. I promise, she won't have to work for Ahrens any more after next week.

She stopped. 'Private detective?'

'Me? Yes, you know that.'

'How much?'

'How much what?'

'How much you cost?'

'How much do I cost…?' What was all this? You could-n't say Leila had no talent for dragging things out at length.

'Yes… How much the day? You look for my mother. I can pay.'

As I was still wondering whether I really had to take this pocket-money fantasy seriously, doors slammed somewhere. I turned to the window. The first thing that occurred to me was that not trying to steal the windows meant, in my case, being slow to hear cars coming. The black Mercedes was right in front of the hostel entrance. At the same moment I lost any hope that it could be a doctor sent by Ahrens, or someone else parking his car as if God had created that vehicle on the first day and then created everything else for it to park in. The two figures moving weightily from the Mercedes to the door and nodding at each other, as if anticipating something partic-ularly tasty to eat, were my two charmers from Berlin: the knee expert and his mate who was so proud of the number of people he'd done in.

I leaped back from the window, grabbed Leila's arm and pulled her to the door in a single fluid movement. 'Get out of here at once!' I hissed at her. 'There are some guys coming who…'

'Can't stay.'

'What?'

'Can't stay here. Gregor know we…' she flapped her hand back and forth between us. 'He know we talked. I…' and her hand fluttered in the direction of the ceiling. 'He kill me.'

'Now listen, Leila…'

'No now listen! You look for my mother! With me! You private detective! I can pay!'

For a moment we stared at each other as furiously as if, for two pins, we'd have got in ahead of Knee Expert and his corpse-counting friend, who were presumably here to silence us as far as possible, by doing ourselves in instead. Then I heard those long, confident everybody-listen strides that Berliners have coming down the corridor, pulled Leila away from the door and signed to her to keep quiet.

When the steps moved on I whispered, 'OK, I'll take you with me – for now, anyway. We'll go out to my car, very calmly. We won't run, and we…'

'My money! I can pay!'

'Oh, God, I've heard you say you can pay quite often enough!' I snapped, hoping to make a few things painfully clear when I added, 'But you can't pay me! Forget it! I cost more than a few lollipops or collectable stickers!'

'Collectable? Stickers…?'

There was a rather foolish pause. Of course, I could have said to myself, from her broken German, that she didn't know what collectable stickers were. But something in her eyes told me that at least she could guess the probable nature of collectable stickers, and her astonishment was solely to do with the likely fact that while a girl her age might collect all sorts of things, stickers were not among them.

'I…' she said, pointing at her chest, 'can…' she added, aware that she was repeating herself and enjoying it, '…pay! I have money. Much money! And I…' here she pointed to her chest again, and I was beginning to feel as if I were standing in a corner with the Albanian or some Mediterranean gangster boss, '…want you find my mother.'

The boss was waiting for a nod, so I nodded. 'OK,' I sighed. 'Where's the money?'

'In my room. I get it. Videos too.'

'Videos?'

'So you know what my mother look like,' she explained impatiently. 'You private detective or…'

Or what? I thought I heard a half-swallowed A and R, and perhaps even the hiss of an S. Before long I'd be entirely in agreement with Gregor's way of dealing with this girl.

'Hurry up, then! I'll wait exactly five minutes and then I'm going whether you're back or not!'

'What you mean, whether back or not?' she asked, her hands fluttering back and forth as usual. 'I talking to Schmidtbauer about my mother! Then you break into office, make trouble with Gregor. Now you say: whether back or not! Am I stupid fucking sow or what?'

Fucking sow…? For God's sake, who taught them German around here? I opened my mouth, but I couldn't think of anything to say. I just put up with the look she gave me as she left the room: you got me into this, you can get me out again or you'll be sorry – and then, finally, she was outside.

I lit a cigarette and breathed out smoke. My new client. We'd see if she was going to let me help her with the investigations now and then.

Next moment what I'd been fearing for some time happened. Doors began slamming, footsteps echoed down the corridor, I heard shouting. 'Can't be far away!' 'I'll do that bastard!' 'Hey, Krap, here we come!'

And they were indeed coming right towards me. I couldn't get out into the corridor now, and there was no other way I could leave the visitors' room. Or no quiet and reasonably elegant way. After I had briefly and unsuccessfully tried wrenching one of the chairs from its angle-irons to throw it through the window, and myself after it, I jettisoned the chair idea. The window sill was about a metre from the muddy forecourt of the hostel. I put my jacket over my head, with ends of its sleeves covering my hands, listened once more for a moment to the steps that were still approaching, took a run and jumped through the glass, one shoulder hitting it first.

About three seconds, an enormous crashing and clattering, and one belly–flop landing later I raised my face from the mud, heard a shout of, 'Hey, there he goes!' in the building, and worked my way round on my front to shelter behind the boot of the Mercedes.

'Look at that, then!'

'Krap's James Bond, who'd've guessed?'

'James Bond don't leave no tracks like a baby crawling. Hey, Krap! Don't get our car all dirty!'

'Come on out, let's talk sensibly!'

I peered round one tyre and saw the two of them looking my way through the empty window frame, which was rimmed with jagged shards of glass. Their right hands, and what they were holding in them, stayed below the level of the sill.

I had to find out if a peaceful settlement was at all

possible. Perhaps Ahrens really had sent them with instructions to negotiate or to bribe me. Perhaps he was finally getting sick and tired of shoot-outs. So I took off my muddy jacket, now spiked with splintered glass, and held it briefly out from behind the tyre. A peaceful settlement was not possible. Next moment what had recently been a garment on my back was a pile of rags riddled with holes lying in front of me in the mud, graphic evidence of what our lads understood by 'talking sensibly'.

I turned my head and saw what I already knew: I couldn't get away from the shelter of the car. They could see the whole forecourt from the window, there was no cover except for the Mercedes, and after my panic-stricken burst of fire at Gregor's legs I had no ammunition left to shoot back with. Although they didn't know that yet, and they obviously hesitated to harm the gleaming, brand-new metal of their vehicle

I crawled round to the side of the car facing away from their window, and saw that the driver's door was half open. They'd been in such a hurry and they liked to put on such airs that I hoped the key might be in the ignition. As I crawled on I called, 'I thought you wanted to talk? Doesn't look like talking to me! Apart from the fact that that was my favourite jacket – and always assuming you know what a jacket is.'

'Oh wow, man, is Krap ever witty!'

I reached the open driver's door and saw the picture of the Croatian president welded into a key tag hanging from the driving column.

The car was about three metres from the entrance to the hostel. The swing door and thus the corridor beyond it looked to me a little wider than the bonnet of the car.

'Seemed like it was just some old rag!'

There were barely ten metres between the visitors' room and the swing door. That would take them three or four seconds, less if they ran. Or they might jump out of the window – in which case all I could do was throw mud at them.

'Hey, lads, what next?'

'I said we talk sensibly, OK?'

'What about?' I peered cautiously across the driver's seat. The car was an automatic.

'About what's next.'

I thought I heard a suppressed splutter of laughter. They thought themselves such a superior force, and indeed they were. If I'd suddenly begun weeping or praying, they'd only have seen it as further confirmation of their superiority. That was my chance.

'You mean that?'

'Sure we do.'

'I'd like to talk sensibly to Ahrens.'

'Ahrens? Why not? We can drive you there.'

That suppressed splutter again.

'But we have to agree on something first.'

'Oh yeah? What?'

'Everything's nice and peaceful from now on.'

'Why, sure. Word of honour.'

'OK… then I suggest we meet here outside the entrance, unarmed.'

A pause, one of them cleared his throat, then my partner in the negotiations spoke up again. 'Why not just come out from behind the car? Like we said, it'll all be peaceful now.'

'Well, let's say as evidence of your goodwill. Down here

we'll be on the same level, and I can see if you've really put your pistols away.' I stopped for a moment, and then went on in an increasingly defensive tone, making it sound as if I was making a great effort to stay cool. 'I mean, boys, believe me, I'm sick to the teeth with all this violence! Normally I just go looking for dogs and husbands and so on. Honest, I'd like to be well out of this. So what I think is, it'd be best for us to look each other in the face here, and then sit down around a table with Ahrens like grown-ups and discuss the rest of it. I could have one or two other things to tell you that I'm sure would interest Ahrens. About the Albanian and what the police are planning. We Turks have a proverb: if you soil a stranger's carpet, you must shear your own sheep for him. Understand?'

'Sure. Sounds real good. How about your gun?'

'But I said I want to negotiate.'

'Sure, shear your carpet and all that, but…'

'If you agree to my proposition, I'll throw my pistol down outside the front door – call it the first step in negotiations. Then I could only run away from you. How's that for an offer?'

'Not bad! Go on, then!'

There was such outrageous amusement in his voice that it wasn't hard to imagine them splitting their sides with laughter. Just so long as they didn't jump out of the window…

'OK!' I raised my hand with the pistol in it above the roof of the car, and still it wasn't shot away at once. 'I trust you!'

'Sure thing, Krap! Trust means a whole lot!'

I straightened up, levelling the empty pistol, and we

looked into each other's eyes across the car and a few metres of muddy forecourt. They were both making the grim faces of people who are trying not to fall about laughing at a funeral.

I pointed my pistol at the swing door and smiled with restraint. 'See you, then. Nice and peaceful, right?'

They nodded, and their eyes looked down at me, sparkling with anticipation of a wonderful bloodbath. If only they came to the door…

I swung my arm back a little way and threw the pistol down on the mud between the Mercedes and the entrance. Then I looked back at the window, and my blood was roaring in my ears. They were still there, looking back. For a moment I thought it was all over. They were young, fast and strong, and presumably had enough ammunition to turn me into something like my jacket ten times over. I felt old and fat, and I had nothing.

We stood there like that for two or three seconds, and if they'd simply climbed out on the window sill and jumped down, I probably wouldn't even have tried to run for it. The attempt would have been plain ridiculous. But suddenly, as if years later, one of the two made a brief gesture in my direction, grinned again as if he couldn't understand such stupidity, and next moment they had both disappeared from the window frame.

Ten metres, three to four seconds. Less if they ran. I flung myself behind the wheel of the car, turned the key in the ignition, and shifted the automatic gear-change to *Drive*. When the engine came on so did the stereo system, with Janet Jackson belting a song out from six or eight loudspeakers. Once I saw the shaved heads appear in the corridor behind the glass of the swing doors, I stepped on the gas. The car leaped, and our lads opened their mouths wide. Of course they hadn't put their pistols away, but before they could raise them to the right height the Mercedes was crashing through the door. All they could do was retreat, fast. So far everything was going smoothly. Only the walls of the corridor appeared to be a problem for a split second. About three metres beyond the swing door they narrowed, and the car wouldn't really fit between them any more. But the walls were plaster, the Mercedes was a Mercedes, and I had no choice anyway. As I drove the car down the corridor with a grating sound, chasing our lads before me, plaster panels and polystyrene linings were scraped off to left and right. Meanwhile Janet Jackson was singing, 'Whoops now', and as far as I was concerned we could have gone on like this indefinitely. Once or twice the pair of them swerved towards doors on both sides of the corridor, but in the kind of hostel where the dilapidated chairs were screwed to the floor of course nothing was left unlocked. As a bonus, they dropped their pistols when they grabbed at the door handles.

The corridor of the former youth hostel ran all the way through the building. It was seventy or eighty metres long, and it ended in a blank wall. The last possible way out was the door of the secretarial office. Our lads didn't know where the corridor came to an end, and because of the poor lighting they couldn't see it in time. When they realised what was waiting for them, it was too late for the secretarial office door. There were about ten metres of empty space left before they literally started climbing the walls. They dug their fingernails into the plaster and hopped up and down. After I'd passed the office door myself, I trod on the brake and managed to get the front bumper to a distance of about 0.0 millimetres from their legs. I just had time to see them failing to free themselves from the trap before a cloud of plaster dust fell on us. I took the key out of the ignition, leaned back in the driver's seat and kicked the windscreen out. A moment later, when I was standing on the bonnet of the car and the dust was settling, I saw the horrified Frau Schmidt-bauer looking out over what had once been the wall of her office, but was now lying in the corridor.

'Hi!' I called wittily, and waved to her. 'I did tell you not to summon reinforcements.'

She looked at me, shook her head as if to dispel a hallucination, and disappeared behind the heap of rubble. The sound of cries and running footsteps came from the stairwell. I turned to the lads. Covered with white dust, shoulders stooped, faces distorted by fear, they looked up at me as if I were some barbarian king famous for cutting off his prisoners' ears.

'Well, lads? Good show, eh?'

They didn't reply. Only now did I notice that it probably wasn't just fear distorting their faces. A distance of 0.0 millimetres between the bumper and their legs had been a fair estimate, but in fact it was a few centimetres less. Those legs had an unusual bend in them, and they were standing so still that every movement must be extremely painful. My friend who liked counting his victims seemed to be in a particularly bad way. Though that could also have been because one of the Evangelical posters had caught on his jacket, and with the declaration *I'm all for multi-ethnicity!* all over his chest he looked as if a few kids from a Rudolf Steiner school had been playing a Nazi practical joke on him.

I threw them the car key. 'Park it somewhere else. I don't think this is a great place for it.' I winked at them. 'Fun and games with Krap.' Then I tapped my forehead by way of goodbye, turned, climbed over the roof of the car and jumped down on the floor. Gregor was sitting on a chair in the secretary's office, legs up on the desk and a puddle of blood under him, and behind him Frau Schmidtbauer was phoning. He was very pale in the face, but otherwise looked in pretty good shape, considering. It was probably because of my muddy, dusty appearance that, as I passed, we looked at each other like two people trying to work out where they'd met before. A few metres further on, the first baffled hostel inmates came towards me, looking curiously around them. They were soon followed by a man in a suit, sweating heavily, gasping hysterically and now and then exclaiming things like, 'No!' 'Heavens!' 'Catastrophic!' Probably the hostel manager. When he grabbed my sleeve and asked, panting for breath, what all this was about, I shrugged. 'No idea. I'm the electrician, but to be honest the openings in the walls are a bit too big now for me to do any rewiring.'

'Openings in the walls...?'

'Mmph. If you want the wiring to go under the plaster, that is. I'd rather have rewired over the plaster anyway. A bit of paint on it and hardly anyone would notice. Would have come a lot cheaper too.'

'Cheaper!' he uttered, with his eyes popping. Then he let go of my arm and hurried on.

Leila was waiting where the swing door had once been. She was wearing an expensive-looking dark brown fur jacket, green wool tights and walking boots. Two leather suitcases stood on the floor beside her.

'What happen?' she asked, half anxious, half reproachful as her eyes moved over my dirty figure.

'We found it hard to say goodbye.' I picked up her cases and nodded at the forecourt. 'Let's get out of here. And pick those pistols up.' Then we splashed through the mud and puddles to my Opel, and she contented herself with looking back two or three times at the entrance. Perhaps, apart from one of the cases in which it seemed possible that she might be carrying lead piping, she wasn't such a bad client after all.

Chapter 13

We were sitting in the car on the way to the Ostend district and my office. As my private address and my private phone number weren't in any public directory, or available online either, I assumed that if Ahrens had wanted to send me any warnings, threats or offers I'd find them at the office. After our meeting and my performance at the Adria Grill, which would certainly have been reported to him, I thought it was out of the question that he'd simply let me carry on in the same way. Now at the very latest, after extensive phone conversations with Frau Schmidtbauer, he must react somehow. I suspected he'd try bribing me and thus get his chance to finish me off.

'...my father is Croat, my mother is Srbkinja. I am born in Bosnia. My father is worker in engineering works, is not soldier. And when the war begin he is against it. He talks big: better dead than leave mother Serbia. Always talks big. So he imprisoned in Croatia or Bosnia, somewhere. My mother says, always say you Bosanka, never Srbkinja. Bosanka is like hostel manager's poor old dachshund. All people say: aah, that poor old dachshund. Srbkinja is like hostel manager's wife.'

'Hm. How long has your mother been working for Ahrens?'

'Three weeks.'

'Doing what?'

'Make money.'

'Yes, fine, but how does she make it?'

'Just how don't know. My mother not say because of my father. Fat Ahrens has finger in pie all way to Croatia.'

'And when did your mother disappear?'

'Last Sunday. That why I in Schmidtbauer office. She know where my mother is. But she don't say. Only say, coming back soon, coming back soon.'

'Did Gregor leave those bruises on your arms?'

'Yes. For shouting and so on. Since my mother gone, I sleep badly.'

'Hm.'

I wondered what Ahrens was planning to do when his lightning takeover of the protection money racket in Frankfurt came to an end. When the entire wobbly structure, maintained only by means of enormous pressure and large amounts of violence, crashed to the ground. He probably had his dated ticket to God knows what beach resort in his wallet already. And if he actually got there he'd be leaving part of the city demolished for years to come – in retrospect, the departure of the Schmitz brothers would look like any everyday business crisis by comparison. As a result of the Army's activities, all normal protection money rackets would be scandalous, and every serious extortionist would have to go about in a tank if he wanted to keep his extortion undercover. And they *would* go about in tanks, too. The business would get even more secret, even more brutal, even more excessive. Bar and restaurant owners would think back nostalgically to the days when they could relatively easily balance their protection money against their income on the black economy. And their guests would long for those boozy nights when they didn't have to fear that some idiot might come marching into the bar any time, shooting one of them down just to show that he was to be taken as seriously as the now legendary Army of Reason.

I lit a cigarette, and Leila asked if she could have one too.

'How old are you?'

'Next month fifteen.'

'Smoking's bad for you.'

I thought I could feel the airflow as her head whipped round. 'You my mother or what?'

'You wanted to come with me, and I decide who smokes in my car and who doesn't. Fourteen-year-old girls don't.'

'Huh! But fourteen-year-old girls have to breathe old detective's smoke!'

'Listen, sweetheart: call me old again and you can go back to Gregor by yourself, on foot.'

It wasn't a laugh or even a giggle, but a sound that did have something to do with amusement – derisive, deploring, almost pitying. After a pause she said, 'Like Schmidtbauer. Don't like her age either – two old cunts.'

Hit the nail on the head again. In a game of 'Who has the last word?' I'd have staked all my money on her. In a game of 'Who's good at dealing with fourteen-year-olds?' I probably wouldn't even have made the first selection stage.

Finally I handed her my cigarettes and lighter, and after we'd been smoking in silence for a while I asked, 'How many do you smoke a day?'

'Sometimes more, sometimes less. Depends how day is. Sometimes cigarette is like last bit of fun.'

'Hm, yes, same with me. Doesn't your mother object?'

'Sometimes more, sometimes less.'

'OK, let's come to an agreement…'

'Agreement? Come to where?'

'Let's do a deal.'

'OK.'

'When I'm not around you can do as you like. But in my presence you don't smoke more cigarettes than I do.'

'Presence…?'

'When we're together.'

'You smoke many?'

'Quite a lot.'

'Good. Is deal.'

At the next kiosk I stopped and bought a packet of chewing gum.

'Swindle, right?' said Leila as I got back into the car. 'Now you not smoke in presence.'

'A deal is a deal.'

'And swindle is swindle.'

'Hm.' I nodded. 'And dumb is dumb.'

'OK. Chewing gum, please.'

I hated everything about it: the taste, the sticky sound of chewing, the picture of me and Leila chewing the stuff in competition, so to speak, because of a dubious agreement. I'd just managed to shake off three killers, I was covered in mud and dust from head to foot, I had *the* criminal outfit in present-day Frankfurt after me, and I went and did a stupid thing like this. But instead of simply spitting out the unfamiliar, minty clump of gum and lighting a cigarette, I thought about ways I might extend our bargain. How may scoops of ice cream was a cigarette worth, for instance?

There wasn't much time left for such meditations. As I

was still imagining Leila making pitying noises again and explaining that if she happened to want an ice, she could buy hundreds for herself, we passed the first fire engine. Next moment I saw half my office desk lying behind a roadblock in the street.

A firefighter waved me to the side, I stopped the car and leaned across the steering wheel. On the third floor of the box-like fifties building where I'd had my office for the last six years there was a large, gaping hole measuring about four square metres. The back wall was still intact, and I noticed the round kitchen clock which one of my clients had once said was about as trendy in a detective's office as a piece of knitting.

'What that?' Leila was leaning forward too, pressing her nose against the windscreen.

'No idea.' It seemed to me she must have exhausted her capacity to absorb scenes of violence for today. At the moment she seemed quite brave, but at her age, I assumed, that could change quickly. And a hysterical girl of fourteen was the last thing I needed. 'Probably a gas explosion. I was actually going to move my office here next month.' I lit a cigarette and tossed the packet into her lap. 'I'll just go and take a look. You stay here, OK?'

'OK,' she replied, but she didn't sound really convinced. She probably wasn't going to be outmanoeuvred another time as easily as over the cigarette deal.

I got out and walked around a bit. There wasn't much to see. Firefighters, a few onlookers rubber necking, and a number of tenants of the building all talking excitedly. No one recognised me under my coating of mud and plaster dust.

Naturally the loss of my office together with a phone

and fax machine, a computer, a first-class coffee machine and a crate of schnapps wasn't good news, but it didn't particularly rile me. I'd never much liked the place, twenty square metres in size, badly heated, with woodchip wallpaper, and acoustically filled with Sting, George Michael, and umpteen rehashes of cute soul pieces played by the TV production outfit that had moved in next door. Perhaps this way I'd even get around having to pay the overdue rent. What did bother me was the way that over the last few days the Army of Reason had turned my life into something increasingly like a military confrontation. I already knew about threatening letters, home-made bombs, squads of thugs, answering machines filled up with torrents of abuse, and I'd once been sent a dead sheep slit open and wearing a Turkish fez, a very imaginative touch. But this was the first time I'd ever had my office blown up in the middle of Frankfurt in broad daylight, just to stop me pursuing a case. Of course, there was always the possibility that unknown to me, there were genuine faulty gas connections in the building. Or that the ladies of the TV Larger Than Life production company had planned a firework display in line with the company name, to celebrate the opening of a new series about dentists' daughters having problems with architects' sons, and they just happened to have put their twenty boxes of rockets down outside my door for a moment. But I didn't think I'd bet on it.

I took a last look at my kitchen clock and then went back to the car. Just before I reached it I spoke to a man who was leaning against a barrier, staring up at the wall of the building, and looked as if he'd been there for some time.

''Scuse me, can you tell me what happened up there?'

'Huh! You may well ask!' he exploded with surprising fury, but somehow with a kind of satisfaction too, and without taking his eyes off the building. He had bad teeth, bad skin, hardly any hair, a pot belly, alcohol on his breath, stained nylon clothing that didn't fit him and a gold ring in his ear. 'God knows what that bastard did in there!'

'Er… what bastard?'

'Some wog detective.'

'Wog detective?'

'Yes, well, a wog's what I'd call him. He's a Turk, he is — or was. Could be it blew him to bits. Think of it.' He cast me a brief sideways glance. 'Fellow like that. All we need now is wogs in the police… and then goodbye the Ostend!'

Slap a little plaster dust on now and then, and you got to know what the neighbours really thought of you.

'When, roughly, did it blow that bastard to bits?'

'Half an hour ago or thereabouts. I was over in Heidi's place. But I reckon blown to bits is just wishful thinking. I mean, can't see anything, can you? Blood or body parts or that.'

Heidi's Sausage Heaven was the culinary high spot of the street. Strictly speaking, if you didn't count a hamburger bar and a bakery selling sandwiches, it was the only culinary spot in the street. Hunger had driven me to Heidi's greasy plastic tables now and then, forcing me to swallow stuff that no dog would have looked at.

I acted as if I had to search around to locate the place bearing Heidi's name. *Heidi's Sausage Heaven*, I read aloud from the sign over the door. 'You'd have a good view of this place from there. Did you happen to see anyone go in before the explosion? Someone who might have set it off. Someone who doesn't belong here. Doesn't necessarily have to have been a wog.'

He let the question hang in the air for a moment before wrinkling his nose busily and nodding a couple of times in a very matter-of-fact way. Here at last was someone who knew who really mattered in the Ostend district. Wog offices flying through the air were all very well, but the important point, without a doubt, was that no stranger could pass his lookout post at Heidi's place without his noticing that stranger and identifying him as such.

'Hm, now you ask, yes, there was someone made me think, hey, what's he doing here? I know everyone around this place, see — by sight anyway. I mean, you noticed yourself — it's my knowledge of human nature, eh?' He looked me straight in the face for the first time, and while the rest of his demeanour still signalled a large amount of new-found liking for me, an expression of some doubt entered his eyes.

'What happened to you, then? You look almost like you…'

'The name's Borchardt. Explosives expert.' I offered him my hand, and he automatically shook it. 'I came straight from another bombing raid. A lot of dust there, as you can see. So how about this guy you noticed before the explosion?'

But he wasn't to be fobbed off so easily. He looked me suspiciously up and down, let his eyes dwell on my hand holding the car key, connected the Opel logo on its tag with the old wreck behind me, let go of the barrier, bent down a little way and was asking, 'Your car? Don't I know it from…?' when he caught sight of Leila.

'There's still a surprising number of these old things still on the road. Not my private car, of course. But as you see, in our work we explosive experts don't have it all neat and tidy, so the city gives us these old transport fleet rejects. It's no fun for anyone driving them, I can tell you.'

'You're an explosives expert? Police?'

'Uh-huh. Frankfurt CID.'

He straightened up, stared at me unimpressed, and jerked his thumb at the car window. 'So who's that? Frankfurt CID too?'

'She's… er… well.' I put my mouth close to his ear and lowered my voice. 'The raid I mentioned just now was on a refugee hostel – know what I mean? And that's one of the witnesses, a…' I showed him a dirty grin. 'Well, you can see her hair colour and her… er… complexion.'

He reacted as if a twenty-mark note was suddenly looking at him from a pile of dog shit in the street. First his eyes lit up and he ran his tongue over his lips, then his expression suddenly froze and darkened, until he suddenly took a step back and explained, shaking his head, 'I didn't mean it that way! You can't pin anything on me. All I said was that the guy the office up there belonged to is a show-off arsehole and definitely didn't have blue eyes, and you're still allowed to say that, right?'

'And how! Don't worry, we in the police weren't born yesterday either. We know the time of day, and we'd always rather have an honest opinion than all that do-gooding Benetton stuff. I mean…' and once again I approached his ear, 'I mean, where do Nobel prize-winners come from? That's what I always say. They don't come from Africa, do they?'

His scepticism lasted a moment longer, then he slowly

raised the corners of his mouth, and a conspiratorial gleam came into his eyes. 'You put that very nicely.'

'Well,' I said, dismissing the subject, 'a man can't help thinking. But could I ask you, all the same, to describe the person you saw from Heidi's place?'

What he described was a small, fat, white man with thick lips – Ahrens's Hessian, the one who had smashed my nose in.

I thanked my new Klu-Klux-Klan mate, gave a wave and went to the car.

As I started the engine, Leila asked, 'What did that old queen with the earring say?'

Maybe I ought to have introduced them to each other. Maybe, once a few prejudices were out of the way, they'd have got on like a house on fire.

'As I thought. A gas explosion.'

'You talk long time for as-I-thought.'

'He was a nice guy. Told me a bit about the area. After all, I'm going to be here every day after next month.'

I drove the Opel past ambulances and groups of people deep in discussion – 'Fucking bastard', 'Wog detective?' – and filtered into the rush-hour traffic.

'I don't think.'

'Hm?'

'Gas explosion, I don't think.'

'Oh, don't you?' I said in an offhand way, and gave her a smile saying: you can think anything you like, I'm not going to lose my temper. Unfortunately she didn't mind in the least how or if I smiled at her.

'First Gregor and whole hostel smashed up, then you drive off look at new office?'

'It was on my way. Why not?'

'I don't think. You covered with dirt. And you think Ahrens because of Gregor. And then we drive back just the same way.'

And you can go take a running jump, thought the latest member of the Bockenheim League to save the White Man.

Which was more likely to discourage her, yet more proof that her mother's boss was not exactly a scrupulous negotiator in his business affairs, or a detective who, she was bound to think, was lying to her?

I told her the truth. Not a trace of hysteria.

'Stupid that with office,' she said. 'But with Ahrens, that your problem. I have my problem, and I can pay. You look for my mother first is agreement.'

So far I hadn't asked her, and I didn't really want to know either, but now I did think for a moment of what she might have gone through during the Bosnian war. Perhaps by comparison she thought all this fuss about an office blown to pieces was just hysterical shit for those who lived in a land where people drove Mercedes.

'...and of course I'll keep my word. Don't worry.'

'Good. But with office, why lie?'

'Because your mother is probably with Ahrens, and I didn't want you to be afraid.'

She thought about that.

'Understand. But I not afraid. My mother is strong.'

Yes, sweetheart, but obviously not strong enough to get home to you last Sunday, and certainly not as strong as knives, knuckledusters and guns, and when Ahrens hears – as he'll have heard by now – that I took you away from the hostel with me, he doesn't have to be a genius to work out a nice little blackmail move appealing to my professional honour, and then we both have a problem. Because I'm not quite so honourable as to hand myself over in exchange for your mother, and get shot down.

Instead I said, 'I'm sure she is. I only have to look at her daughter.'

'Look at her d...?' she began, before she understood, and for the first time since my appearance in Schmidt-bauer's office her pouting lips curved into a smile. 'Yes, we all strong people.' And after a pause, sounding almost annoyingly confident, 'Will be nice when my mother back. You like her too.'

'I certainly will,' I agreed. And I registered, to my surprise, that my heart changed its rhythm and skipped a couple of beats.

Ten minutes later we drew up outside my flat, and if I had not quite admitted my fears to myself, I felt very relieved all the same at the sight of the building standing there, not shattered by any bomb. My flat might be badly heated, it might have woodchip wallpaper, and I couldn't make up my mind whether I preferred the sound of Heino or Sting coming through the walls, but by comparison with my ex-office I liked it. Slibulsky had often asked me why I didn't find myself something nicer than this two-room coffin in a new building. But I'd never yet thought of any kind of flat to suit me better than the two-room coffin. Some people liked to wear check suits, others drank Fanta with fish. And I'd once seen someone perfectly happily dancing to a German-language cover version of *Stairway to Heaven*. I'd grown up in flats in new buildings. The angular, low-ceilinged surroundings, always smelling slightly musty of glue or cleaning fluids, gave me the kind of feeling others get from the smell of Christmas baking.

When I'd showered, put clean sheets on the bed for Leila, shown her the bathroom, given her towels, and in reply to her question had told her, to her satisfaction, how many cable channels my TV set received, I ordered enough casserole, cheese and salad from a Turkish restaurant for a whole party of truck drivers. Then I poured myself a vodka, and while soft splashing and bubbling sounds came through the bathroom door I rang my caretaker-greengrocer friend.

'Oh, Herr Kayaya!' he greeted me cheerily down the phone. At first I thought I should take this as the sign of a night with a tart ahead, and because Leila was here I was almost about to ask him to turn the volume down a little today. But then I realised that we were speaking on the phone for the first time since our west-of-Thuringia-alliance pact, and that he was probably just keen on this form of communication because it could be relied on to exclude any eye contact. I was used to the innocently proffered curtailment of my name. It was among the last when-are-you-going-to-go-home tricks that he still allowed himself from time to time.

'How can I help you?'

'Well, listen, I don't like this, but I have to tell you…' I paused, and heard his breath halting slightly. 'As you know, I'm a private detective, so now and then I have to deal with people who… well, people one would rather *not* have to deal with, know what I mean?'

He hesitated before a cautious, 'Well, not really,' came over the line, and definitely any other answer would have been a joke.

'Then let me put it bluntly.' I cleared my throat. 'I'm

talking about pimps, or to be precise a pimping gang. Tough guys, Russians, Mafia members. I'm sure you've heard of the Russian Mafia.'

'Er…' He swallowed.

'For instance,' I said, helping him out, 'that massacre in the upmarket brothel a few years back, ten prostitutes dead and about a dozen of their clients, I don't recollect the exact figures – that was the Russian Mafia. Or the men who arranged the call-girl orgy last autumn and then tried to leave without paying the bill and as a result… well, it was in all the papers. Why I'm calling you now is because, in connection with an ongoing investigation, I was speaking to one of the bosses today, and when I gave him my address so that he could send me something… well, he looked really grim. He finally said, and he didn't sound good: there's a swine lives in that building beat up my best little floozy…' By now the other end of the line sounded as if I were phoning a tomb. 'Well, that's the kind of way he speaks. Anyway, then I asked him for a description of this… er, swine – I mean, it seemed just about certain he must be one of my neighbours, and naturally I wanted to warn whoever it was…' I took a deep breath and then went on firmly, 'I'm really sorry, and I'm sure there's some mistake, but the description he gave me fitted you exactly…' I stopped for a moment. 'Hello?'

I heard a distant noise, human in physical origin but sounding more mechanical. Like the final breath escaping a corpse.

'Are you still there?'

The corpse groaned. Then it said, almost in a whisper, 'It can't be true… please, believe me, I…'

'That's just how I reacted. My neighbour the greengrocer – it can't be true! I mean, we both know that *I* know, and I entirely understand – we all do as nature demands, don't we? – I understand that you have, let's say, visitors now and then.'

'Well… er…'

'You don't have to tell me anything, really you don't. And you can rely on me not to tell anyone about it, so far as that's in my power.'

'Thank you, Herr Kayankaya, oh dear, this is all very unpleasant…'

Kayankaya! And uttered with perfect fluency. I thought of the discipline it must have cost him to get my name wrong in front of me all these years.

'But it doesn't have to be. I'm sure this will all turn out to be a misunderstanding. For now, however, I'm afraid I must advise you to keep a sharp eye open for anyone approaching this building. Especially at night. As I see it, these people will either try to throw a bomb into your flat or your shop, or send a bunch of thugs. They're acting according to their lights: leave a bruise on my girl and I'll put you in a wheelchair.'

'But I didn't leave any bruises!' he burst out. 'I didn't even – I mean…' He was gasping in panic. 'Didn't even do anything unusual. Understand? Perfectly normal, and always with a condom. And sometimes we just talked!'

Yes, of course: Heino belting it out and groaning fit to shake my bed, and the two of you were just talking!

'Like I said, I'm sure it will all be cleared up. But I do insist that you must call me at once, even in the middle of the night, if any stranger tries getting into your shop or through the front door of this building. I'd say – well, my instinct tells me – the front door's more likely.'

'Wouldn't it be better to call the police?'

'You know what the police are like! By the time they arrive you'll have been beaten to a pulp long since, and the thugs will be back in Uzbekistan or somewhere. Quite apart from the questions you'd have to answer then. And the police don't do it discreetly, they bawl you out in the middle of the front hall, what filth were you up to with that poor Russian girl? I mean, think of it, maybe before supper time…'

That corpse-like noise again.

'No, no. You just call me, and I'll be down at once. I know how to deal with these people, don't you worry.'

He stammered a bit more about how he couldn't make all this out, I told him to make a large pot of strong coffee for the night ahead of him, then we rang off, and it looked as if Leila and I could sleep easy.

A little later the front door bell rang. Once I'd convinced myself by looking out of the window that I wouldn't be letting in any thick-lipped Hessian or a killer with his face powdered white, I pressed the door opener. Soon after that I was taking delivery of a bag the size of a laundry basket, full of polystyrene boxes and aluminium foil containers. I laid the sofa table, found a bottle of mineral water for Leila, poured myself more vodka, and tried working out a plan for the next few days.

The Croatian economic delegation was arriving on Saturday, and if Zvonko had been telling me the truth the Croatian head of the Army of Reason was among them. By then I had to find out where the fillet-steak banquet cooked up by Zvonko's uncle would take place. A nice cosy evening with all leading members of the Army –

there could hardly be a better moment to embark on final hostilities, along with the Albanian and his chain-wearing followers. The question was, what was I going to do for my new client until Saturday? If I wasn't to endanger the bosses' meeting, I must go underground for the next few days. I wanted Ahrens to believe that the attack on my office had sent me running from the field of battle. Which incidentally also decreased the danger of my being black-mailed into a swap: detective exchanged for detective's client's mother. For the moment, then, there was only one thing I could do for Leila: find out on the quiet whether her mother really was with Ahrens. Either of her own free will because, as Frau Schmidtbauer said, she was 'the worst of them all' and a tart who'd seized her chance to get her hands on some of Ahrens's takings, or alternatively under duress. Presumably she didn't look too different from her daughter, and perhaps Ahrens was keeping her in some cellar as his safari partner.

I drank some vodka and lit a cigarette. The idea that Leila's mother had been Ahrens's sex slave since Sunday, for some reason, appealed to me even less than such very unappealing ideas normally do. Of course she could just have been picked up by the police while travelling on public transport without a ticket. An eager-beaver cop, and as a refugee she'd have landed in jail. But suppose Ahrens really was keeping her prisoner? Was I to leave that state of affairs alone until Saturday? Because of two guys who were now worm fodder?

The bathroom door opened, and out came – what the hell was going on here? – a belly dancer. She wore a white blouse printed with glittery flowers, low-slung baggy golden-silk trousers, a kind of belt with gold coins hanging from it, and brightly embroidered slippers. The coin belt sat loosely around her bare hips, hanging down in front like a letter V. When Leila moved, it jingled, and the point of the V swung against the spot between her legs like a gentle tip-off.

What was the idea? A local history and folklore show? Carnival time? Seduction? She came into the room a little gingerly and looked expectantly at me.

'Good heavens.' I gave her a friendly smile. 'Anything planned for this evening?'

'Planned?'

'I mean, are you going out dancing, or to the funfair or something?'

She stopped and looked at me in astonishment. The way you'd look in astonishment at the feeble-minded. Then she suddenly appeared to be gazing right through me, let her shoulders droop, shuffled over to the sofa, sighed, 'Supper?' and sank into the cushions, jingling.

'Yes, that's right, supper.' Had she expected applause? Did she want to put on some sort of performance? Or did she perhaps think, on account of experiences she might have had with proselytising workers in the hostel, that you had only to wear some kind of folk costume in the land where people drove Mercedes for the natives to fall about in ecstasies at the idea of cultural exchange? It must be something like this, I imagined, when your own kids came home from school with the nutcrackers or candlesticks they'd made in handicraft lessons. Or was there something I didn't quite get here?

'Well, I for one haven't eaten since this morning, and as far as I know you haven't eaten since midday either. And after a day like this…' I nodded at her, filled our plates, and ignoring her elaborate lack of interest told her to tuck in.

Perhaps she simply wasn't hungry, or she didn't like the casserole, or girls of her age nourished themselves on lettuce leaves – oh, not too many, for goodness' sake – but anyway, eating supper turned out to be a one-sided and thus oppressive business.

'No appetite?' I asked after I'd shovelled the first few spoonfuls down myself.

Leila leaned back on the sofa, kicking off the embroidered slippers and bracing her bare feet against the table, and twirled a little green stalk of something in her fingers. Without looking up, she murmured, 'No appetite?'

'Aren't you hungry? Don't you want to eat?'

'Smell like home cooking.'

'Then you have pretty good cooking at home,' I heard myself saying, like one of those adults I sometimes saw on kids' TV programmes on mornings when I had a hangover, and who always made me wonder whether there was a soul in the world over three years old who didn't take an instant dislike to that stupidly affable tone.

Eyebrows raised pityingly, Leila gave me a brief sideways glance, then looked back at her little green stalk and audibly breathed out.

'OK, then tell me what you'd rather smell. After all, you must eat something in the next few days.'

'Why must?'

Why must...? My spoon stopped suspended in the air, halfway between plate and mouth. Defiant, cheeky, outrageous – yes, all very well, but certainly there wasn't ever a minute in my life reserved for this.

'Because people have to eat if they're not going to die

of starvation,' I grunted, putting the spoon in my mouth.

'I look nice?'

'Look nice? Yes, you do look nice. You're beautiful,' I told her, hoping to make her forget my botched reaction to her big entrance as a belly dancer. 'But if you carry on like this you'll soon be nothing but a beautiful skeleton.'

'You like better fat slut, hm?'

'Fat slut... look, who gives you lot German lessons in that hostel?'

'I self.'

'You yourself? What from? Off the walls of public toilets?'

'Porn.'

'What?'

'Boys in hostel have films and book. I have book too, *The Sperm Huntresses.*'

'Oh...' I tried to assume as down-to-earth an expression as possible. At the same time I registered that the spoon in my hand was stirring the casserole in a slightly manic way, as if of its own volition. 'Um... all that's kind of a specialised vocabulary. What about if you just want to go and buy rolls or something?'

Very slowly, she turned her head, looked at me from under drooping eyelids, and suddenly began to laugh. Loud, hearty, engaging laughter. No doubt about it, there was something here I didn't get.

When she'd finished laughing, she asked, 'We watch films?'

'Er... what kind of films?'

'Films with my mother, of course, moron.'

Moron. Was that out of the porn book too? Fuck me, moron?

Relieved by the change of subject, I pointed my spoon across the room. 'The video recorder's over there.'

At school I regularly got such bad marks in foreign languages that they were a joke – would I have paid more attention if the languages had been taught in porn? Maybe I'd be working with the United Nations now.

Laden up to her chin, Leila came back from the bedroom, made her way past me balancing about fifteen video cassettes and knelt down in front of the VCR.

'Hey, I only want to know what she looks like. I'm not planning to write a doctoral thesis on her.'

'Doctoral thesis?'

Yes, well, *The Sperm Huntresses*… 'If we're going to watch all these videos we'll be here till tomorrow evening.'

'I play just few nice ones, OK?'

'Play some where I can get a good look at your mother. What *is* all this stuff?'

'Birthday, wedding, holiday, my first school day, all that: my grandma, my grandpa, my mother in garden, my father ride bike but only on one wheel. We often go out of city. And then is wedding. I begin with wedding, OK?'

'Why the wedding?'

'Because my mother much in it. And I like it.'

'What's your mother's first name?'

'Stasha.'

For the first ten minutes almost nothing appeared on the screen but cars, and tables laid for a meal. Every guest was filmed arriving, and every guest was sitting in a car on arrival, and there were a great many guests. And a great many tables laid for them. Extensive panoramic shots followed: stone-built cottages, olive trees, wild meadows, then the farm where the wedding was being held, along with its interior courtyard and a bonfire over which three men waving at the camera and drinking to each other from bottles were turning five sheep on spits. Leila sat on the floor, leaning forward and concentrating. She had firmly taken possession of the remote control and thus any chance of fast-forwarding, and she supplied me with names and background information. She laughed at the sight of many of the faces, others made her knit her brows, and as two puppies now and then scampered across the picture she made coaxing noises as if calling to them.

'There, look!' She pointed to a little cherry tree. 'Is planted for my birthday, real birthday, now tree is tall as a house.'

'Hm, yes.' Of course it was touching to see Leila almost getting into the onscreen picture, what with the attitude she assumed and the way she looked at it. But the vodka was beginning to take effect, a cherry tree was a cherry tree, and the cameraman had either had a few drinks himself or felt called to higher things in the world of cinema. Anyway, his camera dwelt on even the cherry tree for the amazing length of the time it took to smoke half a cigarette.

'Who's the cameraman?'

'Friend of my father. But is not so good. Usually my father take pictures. Was first at home to have camcorder. He take many films. And he take photos and he paint and he make lamps, funny lamps made from old pots, and he…'

'Can ride a cycle on only one wheel.'

'Yes, too. My father is crazy man.'

The video finally moved on from the cherry tree. The bridal couple drove up in a flower-bedecked car. The party applauded, a combo began playing a mixture of village music and gypsy marches, doors were opened, two bare legs slipped out of the darkness, and there she was: slender, black-haired, very bright-eyed and looking if she had got into the wrong video. *End of the World 1992* or *Christmas with My Mother-in-Law* – that's the kind of thing her expression would have suited. Before she got right out of the car she leaned into it again, and her head jerked. Then she straightened up, brushed something off her shoulder, and turned to the waiting guests with a smile as if she had just discovered that her fiancé still had ongoing relationships with most of the female guests. Or as if someone had short-changed her on her wedding outfit; she wore only a short white dress, white sandals and a pearl necklace.

For a couple of seconds everyone hesitated. Even the combo seemed to play several bars of repeats. But finally a man stepped out of the surrounding crowd, went up to Leila's mother, hugged and kissed her, and soon I saw the backs of head after head. Half a courtyard full of guests wanted her to greet them. So far as anyone could see amidst all the separate embraces, Leila's mother wasn't exactly on the point of bubbling over with beguiling charm, but as the ritual went on her expression at least thawed sufficiently for the guests not to feel they had to apologise for being there at all.

After the backs of about fifteen heads, the cameraman changed the angle of his shot and zoomed in on her face.

It was more fragile and finely drawn but also harder than her daughter's. Thin, caramel-coloured skin, rather small, rather delicate bones, and light green eyes that seemed almost transparent. On the other hand her gaze, both cold and inquiring, and a hint of future wrinkles that wouldn't look as if they were only laughter lines suggested someone who at least knew what she didn't want, and made sure she didn't get. The only one hundred per cent resemblance between mother and daughter, so far as anyone could tell from a video, was in their mouths. Leila's mother's mouth was saying something now, laughing almost wholeheartedly from time to time, and constantly kissing proffered cheeks.

It wasn't as if I were picturing... well, who knows what? I liked Leila, and there was certainly nothing to dislike about her mother, or not for me. But it was only a film, and I was at home, and finding the woman was part of my job – until she looked into the camera. I've no idea why, but her eyes looked out of the shot so long and so steadfastly that for a moment, no doubt a vodka-fuelled moment, I was convinced she was looking at me. Me and no one else. And I was looking back.

'You like, OK?'

'Hm?'

'My mother – you like?'

'Yes, er, but she...', I said, not exactly stammering, although my tongue and my lips had been known to function better, '...but to all appearances she doesn't seem to be enjoying herself very much...'

'To appearances...?'

'I mean, at first it looked as if something was getting on her nerves.'

'Yes, I know…' Leila dismissed this. 'She want small, quiet party. But my father give big surprise. Lots of people there, my mother not like that. See that old cow?' She pointed to a young woman of about twenty, tossing her head in pique at something. 'She hate my mother. But my father invite everyone. Is always like that.'

And now the man she was talking about came into the picture. Objectively, you had to admit, he looked dazzling. Large, soft, brown eyes, a firm chin, straight nose, and a pop singer's haircut, shoulder-length, airily casual, it would probably fall perfectly into place even in a hurricane. Holding hands with a roughly five-year-old Leila, he made his way from guest to guest, greeting them, kissing them, evidently an amusing character. At least, people were laughing at him, and when they weren't he kept on laughing himself. He accompanied his remarks or jokes with sweeping gestures and a changing play of expression, expansive as everything else about him. If he hugged someone he seemed to be taking a run-up to do it, in kissing he smacked his lips first as if a kiss were more ardent the more obviously it was delivered, and when he picked up Leila for her to be kissed too he raised and waved her in the air like a trophy. The clumsiness that went along with this and was not, I thought, entirely spontaneous, presumably appeared 'cute' to a large part of the female sex.

'Is me,' came an impatient voice from the floor.

'I recognised you at once! I kept wondering if I'd ever seen such a pretty little girl before.' I didn't want to inflict any more belly-dancer disappointments.

'Hm.' A self-evident observation. 'With my father. My father very funny. You see?'

'Yes, anyone can see that.'

'But…' She stopped, and then her voiced tipped over, suddenly had a touch of desperation in it. 'But like I said, has big mouth too. So in prison. Because soldiers not see jokes, they…'

'Only hear the big mouth, right?'

'But if my mother do good work for Ahrens, my father get out.'

'Did your mother say that?'

Leila nodded. 'And so another thing: if my mother gone…'

'Your father stays in prison.'

'Uh-huh.'

She looked at me, downcast. Automatically I promised the kind of thing anyone would promise. 'I'll find your mother, you can be sure of that.'

Her eyes went to the floor. 'You know, sometimes she… well, not angry, but not amused either, like at wedding.'

'You mean she could get across Ahrens?'

'Get across?'

'Annoy him. Tell him he's an old cunt.'

'Yes. Like that.'

There was a pause, and I had the impression that Leila was waiting for more assurances that her detective would cope with everything. But for some reason or other I didn't want to give them. Perhaps out of respect, perhaps out of superstition. Finally we looked back at the screen.

The guests were now drinking aperitifs. The cameraman went from group to group, filming everyone as if for the records, and many of them felt obliged to put on some kind of silly show in front of the lens. I wondered whether

Leila was more worried about her mother or her father. Since he had come on screen there was pain in her eyes. Suppose her mother had simply run away? No more child, no more husband riding bikes on one wheel, a new life, new happiness?

I lit a cigarette. After a while Leila came over to the sofa, sat down beside me and took one too. The first sheep was being taken off the spit in the video, and people were beginning to gather around the tables, full of anticipation – but there was no fun in it for us. Lost in thought, Leila watched her smoke rising, and all I wanted to see was her mother, who had apparently left the wedding party for the time being. But instead of switching off the box and thus perhaps providing an opportunity for another conversation leading to more rash promises, I sat where I was, drinking vodka, letting the pictures run past me, thinking of this and that and waiting for Leila to fall asleep.

After finishing her cigarette she drew her feet up inside the baggy trousers, nestled into the sofa and put her head against my leg. For a moment she looked as if she were weeping secretly into her hands, and I stroked her hair. A little later she was asleep. I carried her into the bedroom, covered her up and put the light out. Alone in the living-room, I wound the video back and looked at her mother again. She really did have very light, very inscrutable eyes and skin you wanted to touch. Then I lay down on the sofa and tried to go to sleep myself. I wasn't too worried now about what Ahrens might be doing to her. She didn't look as if trying to force her to do anything would be much fun. And certainly Ahrens had enough on his hands just now without bothering with a reluctant female. Or if she wasn't reluctant, then I really didn't need to worry about her.

I tossed and turned for a while, smoked a few more cig-arettes in the dark, and finally just stared at the ceiling. From time to time the greengrocer walked around his flat, and Leila twice talked in her sleep. I lay awake feeling strangely peaceful. When I looked at my watch for the last time, it was just before three.

Chapter 14

We were having breakfast, and I was carefully explaining to Leila why I wanted to go looking for her mother on my own. It would be dangerous, if she came I might have to think about her more than the search itself, and I didn't like company while I was working anyway, certainly not my client's company. But what finally made Leila give way and stop arguing with me was my threat that if she didn't I'd chuck the whole thing up. In the end education is no big deal.

'So we're agreed. Good.'

I smiled warmly at her. She was still tousled from sleep, she was wearing my dressing-gown, which was much too large for her, and gloomily nibbling half a piece of bread and butter.

'And as I can't slink into Ahrens's place until it's dark, I thought we'd do something I'm sure you'll enjoy this afternoon.'

'Oh yes?'

'You like dogs, don't you?'

'Why?'

'Well, when the dogs were chasing around in the video yesterday, you liked that, didn't you?'

'Are my father's dogs.'

'Yes, well, we won't be looking for them, but we'll be looking for a lovely German shepherd dog called Susi.'

I smiled warmly again, while she looked at me as if I were Frau Schmidtbauer.

'Are you drank?'

'You mean drunk, sweetheart, and no, I'm not. If you come with me I'll tell you about it on the way.' I looked at the time. Twelve-thirty. 'In half an hour. Think it over.'

Then I got her to tell me her mother's surname, picked up my cup and moved into the living-room to phone. The phone was answered after the first ring.

'Afternoon, Herr Höttges!'

Perhaps it was something in the air, or perhaps they'd started mixing happy-drugs into instant coffee, the way I'd read they did with cat food. Anyway, the deep, heartfelt sigh at the other end of the line that followed my greeting filled me with genuine liking.

'I know, I know: you don't like me to ring your office.'

'I'm expecting an important call.'

'I'll be quick: I need to know by this evening whether a woman called Stasha Markovic has been arrested for any reason over the last few days. She's a Bosnian refugee, mid-thirties, green eyes, very bright.'

'Where can I reach you?'

'At my home number around six.'

Then I called Slibulsky. He was doing his accounts, he said. I could hear Formula One engines in the background.

'You sound glum. What's the matter? The dinner's tomorrow evening.'

'I think people can look at me without losing their appetite.'

'Sounds great. How's it going with the Army?'

'If everything works out I'll have them nailed on

Saturday. Until then I'd be very glad if you could put up a charming little girl in your guest bedroom.'

'How come you know any charming little girls?'

'She's my client.'

'Have you turned into some kind of youth social worker? This rock 'n' roll character turned up here yesterday, saying you sent him.'

'Zvonko.'

'Yes, he can start next week. What about the little girl?'

I told him briefly how Leila had become my client, and said I didn't want to leave her alone in my flat.

'OK. Do we have to cook her spaghetti or play the memory game with her and so on?'

'Well, she's not all that little and charming. Just sit her down in front of the TV set and give her some of your Western videos.'

'Girls don't watch Westerns.'

'With her, I wouldn't be so sure. Anyway, she'll be agitated and pretty distracted. I'm hoping to get her mother back for her tonight.'

'Are you sure you'll find her with this – what's his name?'

'Ahrens. I believe I will. The problem is, I must find her without being found myself. But I think I can do it.'

'That's funny. You don't sound like a man who thinks he can do anything. What *is* the matter?'

I muttered something like, 'Slept too well,' then we fixed to meet at seven and hung up. For a moment I wanted to tell Leila the news at once, but then I thought it would be more in line with educational principles not to tell her until there wasn't much time left for objections and nagging.

Twenty minutes later Leila and I were getting into the car, and for the first time since Frau Beierle had hired me I really set out in search of Susi, equipped with a stack of photos.

Looking in the rear-view mirror, I was just in time to see the greengrocer rush out of his shop, waving excitedly in our direction. Luckily we hadn't met in the stairwell. He would have taken his supposedly desperate situation as a reason to break our tacit agreement and look me in the eye. But now that he was even calling me by my proper name, I wanted to avoid getting close to him more than ever. It might have led to a flowering of sympathy setting us back years. For now I was going to try keeping our relationship going purely by phone.

The afternoon, spent in assorted animal rescue centres – in Fechenheim, Hanau, Egelsbach, Dreieichenhain – turned out much as I'd expected. Endless rows of pens, any amount of barking dogs, and all the German shepherds looked just like Susi. To me, anyway. After complaining of anything and everything during the drive – my beat-up old car, my shitty dog, even my wet weather – Leila brightened surprisingly quickly at the sight of the first bundles of fur looking soulfully at her. Soon she took over the photos and the investigation. She had nothing but a shake of the head for my technique of calling 'Susi!' to whatever dog we were looking at, and hoping that Susi would then identify herself by turning somersaults or some other such means.

'Must look their eyes. Susi have so stiff eyes.'

'Big eyes, you mean.'

The keepers or attendants or whatever were either grouchy alcoholics muttering incomprehensible remarks to themselves who presumably liked to kick the dogs in the face by way of saying good morning, or ladies in their mid-forties who truly loved animals. They didn't love their fellow men as much.

'You're looking for a dog for dogfights, right?'

'No, a German shepherd.'

'Because I can tell you, we don't give dogs away to all comers.'

'Quite right too.'

'You think so? But your daughter speaks hardly any German.'

'Well, I'm sure there's a lot to discuss there, but the fact is that we're looking for a German shepherd, and we don't have all the time in the world.'

Four unsuccessful hours later we drove home. I still had four animal rescue centres on my list. I'd try them another time. Or maybe not. The closer evening came, the less prominently Susi featured in my mind, and presumably in Leila's too.

I parked the car round the corner, and we reached the flat unobserved by the greengrocer.

While I packed a bag with a chisel, a flashlight, a hooded jacket and my pistol, Leila sat on the edge of the sofa, jiggling her toes nervously up and down and eating sweets that smelled like room spray.

'You think my mother come back today?'

'Well, at least I believe I'll find her.' And I did. At times you get a sense of certainty that something is bound to succeed. Goal-scorers have it when they get the ball while facing the serried ranks of defenders, and they know: I'm going to shoot right through them and score the deciding goal. And they do. Or bouncers: OK, they tell themselves, that bastard is much larger, broader, stronger than me, but right now I'm flinging him out on his ear. And they do fling him out on his ear. Or just people looking for something: I'll find it today, they say. And they find it.

'Without me not very good detective.'

'I'm better with human beings.'

'Hope so. What about Susi?'

'There are other refuges.'

'When my mother back, you take me with you?'

'Yes, sure. I'd be lost without you.'

The phone rang at six on the dot, and Höttges told me that no Stasha Markovic had been either arrested or done anything to get into police records since Sunday.

'Listen, Leila.' I sat down on the sofa beside her. 'It would be better if you slept with some friends of mine tonight…' I could have spared myself the educational approach. To my surprise, she agreed at once.

'Not be alone better, you know?'

'I understand.'

I dropped her off at Slibulsky's just before seven.

Chapter 15

Ahrens's white teeth and the slogan *Ahrens Soups: Pleasure On Your Plate* shone through the twilight. I was standing in a phone box opposite the dark brick building, pushing expired phone cards into the slot. Now and then there were situations which made me forget what a luxury not having a mobile was. It happened two or three times a month, when I had to rely on public phone boxes, or when one of those waiters who act as if they thought their place would run better without any guests declined to change a note for me, or when I needed a phone box and there just wasn't one anywhere in sight. But the rest of the time not having a mobile was a little like always being on holiday. I had Slibulsky constantly going on at me: if a message could be left people felt insulted if they didn't get called back at once; if no message could be left then they felt *really* insulted. And as one of those things was only occasionally switched off, because of the possible important incoming calls which was why you'd bought it in the first place, a ring tone was assaulting your eardrums every twenty minutes or so as if a fire had broken out. Maybe because of some misguided quota ruling, they use deaf people to develop new ringtones. Or maybe the whole mobile phone business was a kind of human experiment: can we make almost everyone who has over a few hundred marks a month available, independent of origin, religion, sex and education, into a poor idiot terrorising him or herself? As I saw it, they could.

The next card slotted in, and I dialled the greengrocer's number.

'Kayankaya here. Everything all right?'

Heavy breathing, trembling voice. 'Herr Kayankaya, what luck, I'm completely...'

'I'm sorry,' I interrupted him, 'but I'm in a really very important meeting at the moment, and it will go on for quite a while longer. So you'll have to turn to the police today if anything happens. And if they don't arrive in time, then I'd advise you, from my own experience, that facing up to the situation man to man, with a chair or a hammer handy, is more likely to be successful than covering your ears and waiting for the explosion.'

'Oh... oh dear...'

'Look, I must go back. I'll be in touch when I get home. See you soon.'

'Wait a minute, please, I... I was thinking about it today, if it goes on like this, well, I mean, perhaps it would be better for me to give up this flat and...'

'Move house?'

'...There, you see, I do admire your way of going about these things, oh yes, very much, but... well, bombs and chairs and man to man – I haven't eaten a thing since yesterday evening, and my poor heart, oh, I don't know, but if it goes on beating like this much longer I'll explode of my own accord.'

'Yes, I understand. But of course it would be a big step to take. My instant reaction would be to say maybe a sensible one too. But let's think some more about it. Perhaps – who knows? – well, perhaps so. Possibly that's the best solution – but I'm so sorry, now I must...'

'Yes, of course. But you will ring me, won't you, when you...?'

'When I get back, yes, of course.'

I hung up, feeling glad that Leila was with Slibulsky. The greengrocer might perhaps work all right for raising the alarm, but as an obstacle to any characters who wanted to get into the building he certainly wouldn't. Instead, I had a brief vision of a brand-new, friendly, humorous, civilised neighbour who would be wonderful in every respect.

I picked up my bag of tools, left the phone box, and walked past the entrance of Ahrens's soup company and down the street. About a hundred metres further on I climbed over a tyre dealer's fence, quietly crossed the yard, and approached the back of the brick building. Up on the first floor, faint light was falling through an open doorway into one of the offices. I climbed up a stack of tyres chained together, swung myself up on the wall, wriggled through the barbed wire stretched along the top of it, and let myself down on the other side, landing on a pile of gravel. A paved path led round the brick building to the metal factory shed where, I assumed, the soups or sweets or whatever were made. But perhaps nothing was being made there any more. Perhaps the shed now served only as a meeting place for the Army, and the tables were already laid for Saturday.

There was an entrance, locked, a lot of closed doors, and presumably an alarm system. I went once round the shed and found a loose flap over a gutter running down to the ground beside it and disappearing under a piece of metal. I raised the flap and listened. Nothing happened. There was a gap about thirty centimetres wide between the flap and the gutter. I got through it easily enough up to my waist, but then two things almost made me faint: first my breath was taken away, and second such a strong smell of urine met me as if they were boiling the stuff up to obtain its essence. Gasping, I squeezed my way on, centimetre by centimetre. Lack of air was bad enough, air smelling like that was even worse. Who pissed this kind of thing? Packet-soup manufacturers? The fat Hessian? The pretty secretary? Once I was inside the toilets I hauled the bag after me, straightened up and switched my flashlight on. Perhaps I'm more idealistic or I believe in authority more than I'd like to think – but the state of the toilets of this works, which did after all produce foodstuffs of a kind, staggered me. It wasn't just that the pans were a little dirty, they'd obviously been competing to see who could leave the most filth behind in here. Used loo paper was piled in the corners, the once white tiles round the urinals were covered with a dull, stained layer of stuff that looked crystallized, and the floor was covered by a slimy layer of something either thick or deep, but at least it gave slightly as you stepped on it. I got out of there fast.

Outside the toilets there was a coffee-break corner with a drinks machine, a small glazed-in office next to it, and right behind that the first of countless areas marked off only by partitions nearly two metres high. While I walked past enormous cauldrons, equally enormous and presumably computer-guided shovels for stirring them, conveyor belts, pipes leading from one area to another, stacks of plastic bags, pallets loaded up with cartons, a fork-lift truck and all kinds of other items, I came to the conclusion that the strong smell in the toilets must come from the equally strong and almost identical smell of the powdered soup hanging about in all the rooms. Well, obviously, what else did the employees eat at lunch time? So what else did they piss? But then I noticed the absence of any kind of soup powder and anything that might be its ingredients, and I sniffed myself with distaste. If I managed to find Leila's mother this evening and take her out of here, she was going to get a fantastic first impression of me.

In the back area of the factory shed a second horrible smell mingled with the stink. Something rancid and very faintly reminiscent of chocolate. And there was also another difference: work had been going on until quite recently in the rooms I reached now. Small, unwrapped pieces of something dark lay on a conveyor belt, then the belt disappeared into a cavern containing all kinds of mechanical devices and presses, to reappear two metres further on with wrapped items on it. Red lettering on black paper: Mars bars. I took one, tore the wrapping away, bit off a corner and spat it out again at once. If this was what Ahrens sold as a chocolate bar, maybe the fillet-steak dinner was going to be held in the factory toilets. I'd never had anything like it in my mouth before. If you took the worst, almost cocoa-free chocolate made mainly of very dead animal fat and colouring agents, and kept it for a few weeks in a closed, switched-off fridge, then possibly the end product might be something tasting like this stuff. As an antidote I immediately lit a cigarette. I could happily have eaten the tobacco.

The storeroom was near the entrance. Crates were stacked to the ceiling, sealed and labelled. Mars Bars, Snickers, Milka, Werther's Original, as well as new names like Berlin Sugar, Oktoberfest Choc Pretzels, Mercedes

Power Bars, Sweet Steffi, and last but not least Orchard
Fruits from Germany, Blackcurrant Flavour.

I spent the next two hours in the small glazed office
beside the toilets. I read files and correspondence, examined bills, clicked my way through a computer. Locked
filing cabinets and passwords were obviously thought
unnecessary in Sheikh Soup's domain. In the end I had
worked out the following: Ahrens brought in reject
products from all over the world – chocolate that had had
a shot of engine oil added by mistake while it was being
stirred in the vat, cocoa powder from a plantation next
door to a chemical works that had blown sky-high,
mouldy nuts, egg on the turn, flavouring agents contami-
nated for some reason or other, and just about any fat
liable to leave you sick or dead – mixed it all together,
formed it into bars, stuck a famous or invented name on
them, and sold them in countries where Mars or Oktoberfest apparently sounded good enough to make market-
ing the product worthwhile. Mars, Snickers, and Werther's
Original went to Romania, Bulgaria, Serbia, Albania and
the western part of Russia. Berlin Sugar, Mercedes Power
Bars and Sweet Steffi went to Croatia and the Baltic states,
as well as Siberia and the Volga, areas where large com-
munities of Russian Germans lived. I imagined a simple
young fellow whose great-great-great-grandfather had
come to Russia from Swabia, so now he was indulging in
a Mercedes Power Bar imported from the West, and not
cheap either, in celebration of the day. Perhaps the taste
surprised him. Perhaps he dreamed of a land where con-
vertibles sprouted from the ground.

It was to the credit of Slibulsky's palate that, as the
computer recorded, the blackcurrant-flavour fruit sweets

were the only product not to originate in Ahrens's kitchen with its rubbish ingredients. A perfectly normal sweets manufacturer supplied them free every month, packaged to Ahrens's specifications. As far as I could work it out from allusions and barely veiled threats in letters and notes, Ahrens knew about some incident in the manufacturer's life which, if made public, would not quite ruin him but would have a far from innocuous effect. You couldn't say that Ahrens missed much.

I put the files and papers back, switched the computer off, and set out in search of a door to break down. There wasn't one. As I might have known in advance, they were all secured by alarms. I smoked two cigarettes to anaesthetise my sense of smell, which was working well again after the treatment the Hessian had given my face – was working too well, in fact, just now – then I gritted my teeth and went back to the toilets.

I stood up and gasped for air for a while.

There was still a light on up on the first floor of the brick building. I went over, tried in vain to open the front door, went round the building, pushed all the windows, and finally set off in search of a ladder. After I had used my chisel to break into a shed belonging to the tyre dealer next door, I found one among all kinds of other junk. A worm-eaten ladder with rungs missing. I put it up against the wall, where it wobbled and creaked, but it held for now. Through the barbed wire again, then down on the other side and over to the window where a light was showing. To look in I had to climb to the top rung of the ladder. Slowly and cautiously I hauled myself up by the window sill. What I saw next moment almost made me step off into the void. The room was nearly dark, with light coming in only from the corridor, a TV in the corner was showing the regular programme about film stars and celebrities presented by a famous former woman newsreader, and the fat Hessian was sitting on a chair in front of it tossing himself off. Every element of this scene was far from engaging in itself, and in combination they were a complete nightmare. However, I thought that for the first time I understood the secret of the woman presenter's success. Obviously her bony face with its small eyes, plastered with pink cosmetics, a sly smile suggesting she'd do anything for money like a shot always on her lips, seemed just attainable enough for someone like the Hessian to work up his fantasies. And sure enough next moment, when a young woman – Sandrine Bon-something, the text under her said briefly – appeared on the screen he paused in his activities. She was just too attractive for him to fit her and his paunch into any kind of functioning scenario together.

Considering the state in which he would be found, this was a tempting opportunity to take instant vengeance for my smashed face. Perhaps they'd establish the exact time of death and compare it with the TV schedules. What headlines there'd be!

Of course nothing would come of it. Ahrens would have that fat bag of lard buried somewhere, and in the worst case he might cancel the meeting of the Army on Saturday or hold it somewhere else. I climbed down the ladder and looked through window after window on the rest of the first floor. After more offices I found a conference hall. As far as I could see by the beam of my flashlight, crates of champagne and cognac were stacked against the walls. Next door there was a kitchen, containing a huge electric grill standing at an angle which suggested that it had only just been delivered.

Apart from the Hessian there didn't seem to be anyone in the building.

I took the ladder back to the tyre dealer's place, climbed the fence into the street, sat down on a ledge by the wall and lit a cigarette. It was just after ten-thirty. Either I drove to Ahrens's home now, or I hoped that something else would happen here this evening. A photograph had been printed to accompany the report of the Croatian economic delegation's visit, specially mentioning the Ahrens company. It showed Dr Ahrens and his wife amidst a crowd of smiling men in suits. His wife was a strong woman in her late thirties, chin jutting assertively and with a huge pile of bottle-blonde hair. She looked amiable, but not amiable enough to let Ahrens play around with other women at home.

Just as I was becoming only too well aware that everything I had intended to do and imagined happening this evening was based on a possibly completely mistaken assumption that Leila's mother was somewhere very close to Ahrens, headlights at the end of the street fell on to my shoes. I jumped up and pressed close into the shadow of the wall. Next moment a BMW purred by as quietly as if the whole thing had been a dream. When it had turned into the entrance to the Ahrens premises, I followed it on tiptoe and peered round the corner. The doors opened, and out came two men who, from a distance, looked just the same as the bodies that Slibulsky and I had buried last week. Blond hair, short back and sides, cream suits, totally silent. They went up to the door, pressed the bell and waited. After a while the Hessian appeared and let them in. It was about ten minutes before they came out again. At least, I supposed it was them, for by now they had dark hair and wore jeans and leather jackets. They took two bicycles from a bicycle stand, and next moment they were cycling past me towards the city centre. The Hessian drove the BMW round behind the brick building, came back, cast a glance around him, adjusted his balls and went back inside. Half a cigarette later the next BMW purred in. Bell-ringing again, the disguised men let in again, they rode off on bikes again. Then came the third BMW, and the fourth, and the fifth. Business was booming.

When the sixth pair of headlights appeared at the end of the street, I just nodded, feeling bored with the show by now. But after the car had stopped in the yard and the doors had opened, I heard voices for the first time that evening.

'Right, lads, see you Saturday. Work in the morning first, pleasure in the evening!'

By now I was back at the corner of the wall, and I saw Ahrens laughing. Two huge hulks in suits stood beside him.

'Don't worry, boss, the faggots will get what faggots always hope for – they'll die in their sleep.'

At that moment the passenger door opened, and at first I was simply amazed – the way you're amazed when something turns out almost exactly as you imagined it. Black hair loosely braided at the back of the neck, slim body, economical movements. I saw her only from behind, in a light-coloured coat, but it had to be her, no doubt about it. Hesitantly, like a woman facing something disagreeable but inevitable, she approached the front door.

'Wait a minute, pet!' Ahrens waved to the two hulks, turned and followed her. As the doors of the BMW closed, Ahrens came up to the woman from behind and put his Michelin man arms around her waist. Then the BMW drove out of the entrance, I had to retreat into the shadows, and when I next looked round the corner the door was just closing behind them.

I stood there for a while motionless, as if my head had been swept empty. Finally I lit a cigarette and paced up and down for a bit. I couldn't make it out. Leila's mother might not have looked happy, but she certainly hadn't looked as if he were mistreating her either. And what did I know about her – about her relationship with Ahrens, any deal she might have made to get her husband out of jail, or her chance of getting hold of a great deal of money? Certainly not enough for me to shoot my way in through the door here and now, and get her out of there. The one thing I was sure of was that, although she was obviously relatively free to move about, she hadn't sent Leila any news of herself since Sunday. And if she could find the time to screw around with Ahrens, you'd have thought a quick call to the refugee hostel wasn't too much to ask. With Ahrens, too! Even if it was a case of getting hold of large sums of money, or for all I knew freeing the most wonderful man in the world from jail – surely no human being with the faintest aesthetic sense could do that...

I stood there in the entrance, looking up with revulsion at Ahrens's desert domain, now bathed in warm yellow light. Was he telling her something about the constellations on the ceiling? Or the wonderful world of the children of Nature? No, she'd know all that off by heart. It would be romantic hits on the CD player, and rumpy-pumpy among the coconut and banana cushions!

I turned away, striding fast, picked up my bag and marched down the street to my car. She could wait till Saturday. Which might even suit her. And after all, I had something more important to do. I was in the business of chasing a Mafia gang out of the city, I couldn't waste time bothering with a woman who had, perhaps, looked hesitant, but had gone straight from the car to the front door of the building. And that was the whole point: do you go to the front door of a building or don't you? There are always reasons. Reasons are the most tedious things in the world.

I roared the engine, put the car into gear, and stepped on the gas.

Chapter 16

'Saturday evening, I'm just about certain.'

'Just about...' repeated the Albanian. But it didn't, like his usual repetition of a word, sound like a sign that he was paying relative attention, or like a way of unsettling whoever he was talking to; it sounded distrustful. I was standing near the toilets in the Owl, holding the telephone receiver and a glass of cider, and I wanted to get this conversation over with as quickly as possible. Phoning the Albanian, but not really caring in the least what he thought and thus possibly striking the wrong note, wasn't the kind of thing you really wanted to try in this town.

'Well, you can't be absolutely sure until you're there watching the lads eat their dinner.'

'Ah, I see. So you can't. Tell me, is this case proving a little too much for you?'

'Too much for me? How do you mean?'

'Well, you sound so... oh, I don't know... agitated, nervous. Not a good state to be in for pulling off something like this.'

'That's nothing to do with it. Private business.'

'Fine. I'm relying on you...'

That, in his mouth, wasn't reassuring. I cleared my throat. 'So if nothing else happens, I'll meet you in the New York on Saturday morning.'

'Are you sure you don't want to tell me where this Army of Reason will be meeting? You have my word that everything will go as you want. But suppose something happens to you…'

'Nothing's going to happen to me.'

'I lost two more of my men last night, and a woman who sells sausages over in Sachsenhausen died.'

The bit about the sausage seller was a lie. They had said on the radio that a snack bar had been blown up, but the proprietress got out alive. And if his boys couldn't get their guns out of their trouser pockets fast enough, that wasn't my problem.

'Sorry to hear that.'

He audibly breathed in and out. 'I just want to make sure that if we have to wait until the day after tomorrow to get after this gang, we'll really be able to strike hard then.'

'Look, I'll have to go. My small change is running out.'

'Small change…?' he asked, as if I had told him I was planning to fight with a bow and arrows on Saturday. 'Don't you have a…'

I pressed the rest of the phone down. Another discussion of mobiles and I might actually have forgotten my respect for him, just for a moment. Wiser to break off in mid-conversation.

I bought another glass of cider and called Slibulsky.

'How's it going? Where are you?'

'In a phone box.' The Owl was one of the bars we patronised. It more or less stood for relaxation after work, silly jokes, cheerful boozing. To say I was here would have been a lie.

'In a phone box? Since when do you hear loos being flushed from a phone box?'

'Since when did I have to tell you exactly where I'm calling from?'

'Oh, what a great mood you're in. Was there anything else, or shall we ring off?'

'How's Leila?'

'Lying in front of the TV. Like you said, she's all strung up but OK otherwise. Have you found her mother?'

'More or less. I'll tell you tomorrow. And how are the two of you getting on with Leila?'

'I'm on my own. Gina's at the museum. But we're not having any problems. She says what she doesn't want, and I can guess the rest. You're right, she's delightful in her way. She even watched half an hour of table tennis with me just now. If she keeps this up she'll be someone's dream woman in a few years' time.'

'Bring her to the phone, would you?'

A moment later a breathless 'She there?' came down the line, and I couldn't help smiling. It was good to hear her voice.

'No, sorry, but I know where she is. Now, listen carefully…'

I told her that at the moment her mother was moving heaven and earth to get her father out of jail. That meant she was negotiating with Ahrens and some powerful Croatians, she was going to meet people in other cities, of course she was under severe pressure the whole time and hardly had a minute to herself. All the same, as I had found out by devious means, she kept leaving phone messages in the refugee hostel, but Frau Schmidtbauer obviously wasn't passing them on – silly old cunt that she was.

Leila listened to all this without putting in a word, and when I'd finished there was a pause. Then she asked gravely, 'Why Schmidtbauer not tell me my mother call?'

'Well, I strongly suspect she's jealous. Don't you

remember the way she went on about your mother in her office? Schmidtbauer is in love with Ahrens and thinks your mother wants to pinch him from her. But that's just nonsense. All your mother's interested in is getting your father out of jail.'

'You think?'

'Now listen, what's all this? I don't just think so, I know. At the moment, so I've been told, she's in Munich meeting an industrialist from Zagreb. But she'll be back by Saturday at the latest, and then I'll manage to get word to her that you haven't been getting her messages because of that stupid cow.'

'Saturday.' She made it sound like 'next year'.

'Two days. They'll pass quickly.'

'Oh, well,' she sighed, and fell silent.

'OK, look, I still have something to do this evening. I don't think I'll be able to drop in. How about I fetch you tomorrow morning, and we'll go to those other animal rescue centres and look for Susi?'

'Hm.'

'Was that a yes?'

'Don't know.'

'Then I do. So… see you tomorrow. Sleep well.'

'…You too.'

I hung up, stared at the phone for a moment, picked up my glass and went upstairs to the bar. What I still had to do this evening was find a free seat in a quiet corner. The bar was beginning to empty at this time. People playing cards still sat at the long, rough wooden tables around me, a pair of lovers and a small birthday party lingered on. No one I knew.

I leaned back against the wall, drank cider and smoked.

With every glass the truth I suspected became more like the story I'd spun Leila. Soon I felt there could be no other explanation of her mother's behaviour. I couldn't believe the woman I'd seen in the video yesterday would simply abandon her daughter just to screw around with Ahrens and get her hands on a few marks...

I took a large gulp and waved to the waiter for another glass.

... If they were screwing around at all. They had gone into Ahrens's office building – and if she had to negotiate with him, why not? As for the way Ahrens was pawing her from behind, well, that was hardly surprising with a man like him. Any more than it was surprising for Schmidt-bauer to fail to pass on messages. On the phone I'd simply been making it up; by now I was sure I'd hit the bull's-eye... I nodded to myself. There was a good reason for everything.

'Last orders, please!'

I ordered a last glass, and as I smiled at the waiter I realised how a few ciders had brightened my spirits and my general mood. I emptied the glass, and decided they'd be even brighter if I had another drink. I went round the corner to a run-down bar that stayed open all night. When I somehow, some time, got home, my spirits and my general mood must have been as bright as a dazzling summer sky. Unfortunately I couldn't remember anything about it next morning.

Chapter 17

Around twelve I woke up beside the sofa, surrounded by video cassettes, packets of cigarettes, and an empty vodka bottle. The blue of the video channel shone out of the TV screen. I lay there for a moment, working out where I hurt and where, as I gingerly felt myself, I seemed to be all right. Then I heaved myself up and launched into the usual routine: Alka Seltzer, cold shower, smart clothes for my battered body, a litre of water, open the windows and off to the nearest café to get some food inside me.

An hour later the ground beneath my feet was still making peculiar swaying movements, but I felt fresh enough to get into the car and keep my appointment with Leila. Obviously all the drivers on the streets today were learners. As I managed, with some difficulty, to avoid their strange manoeuvres I couldn't shake off the thought that I'd forgotten something during my phone conversation with the Albanian yesterday. Forgotten to tell him something... ask him something... no, I couldn't pin it down. And then I found that I'd reached Slibulsky's place.

The afternoon passed much like the last Susi-search, except for Leila's compliments on my suit and her way of moving my chin aside every time I spoke to her directly.

'Smell like rubbish from party.'

While Leila looked at dogs I spent most of the time sitting on the nearest crate and drinking bottle after bottle of water, unable to believe how long, loud and painfully those animals could bark. In the Kelkheim dogs' home a passing keeper groused at us suspiciously as if we were gypsies. Perhaps because of my suit, perhaps because of Leila's brightly coloured dress or her silver bracelets and earrings, don't ask me which. When we didn't reply he stopped, planted himself in front of us, chin jutting, and asked if we were planning to eat the dogs. Good heavens!

'No, drink dogs,' said Leila, winking at me.

The keeper narrowed his eyes, turned his head first to her and then to me, and jerked his thumb. 'What'd she say?'

I sighed. 'You heard. We boil the animals, then we distil the liquor and get tanked up. Do you have any problem with that?'

Obviously he hadn't expected an answer, or at least not one in complete sentences. He stepped back, looked from one to the other of us, shook his head, and turned away with a sour expression, as if we were suddenly none of his business.

Then, in Oberursel, a shrill cry of delight drowned out all the barking. I almost fell off the crate where I was sitting. Next moment Leila came racing up, gabbling something excitedly, grabbed my arm and hauled me over to one of the pens. To me, the dog looked like any other German shepherd, but Leila was convinced that the animal leaping up and down in there was my last two weeks' salary. The dog did in fact react to the name of Susi with enthusiastic howls and tail-wagging. I congratulated Leila, who was bursting with pride and excitement, and gave her a hug. Then we went to the office, settled the formalities, I bought a dog-leash, phoned Frau Beierle and told her we were on our way. Half an hour later we drove off: Leila as happy and exuberant as if she'd won the lottery, I full of respect and almost hangover-free by now, and Susi with her head out of the window greeting the entire Rhein-Main district with loud barking.

'I'm going to introduce you as my niece from Bosnia.'
   'What for?'
   'Because otherwise explaining you will be too complicated for her. She likes things clear. And try to look sad. When I mention Bosnia you could cry a little, or cover your eyes with your hands.'
   'Like rip her off?'
   'Not really. She'd feel more ripped off if we *don't* rip her off...' I saw Leila's baffled expression, and dismissed the whole thing. 'Forget it. Just look like a sad Bosnian girl, and you'll catch on to the rest. And if you could put your jewellery away while we're there...'

Soon after that I parked the car, we got out, and Leila took Susi, who was now yowling euphorically and tugging at her leash, off the back seat. Frau Beierle lived in a villa with a small park of a garden and a drive up to it. I rang the bell at the wrought iron gate, the buzzer sounded, and while Susi took off and raced ahead Leila and I marched up the pale gravel path. We were halfway between gate and villa when Frau Beierle came out of her front door and flung her arms round Susi.

As a former politician once famously said, you can run a concentration camp on virtues such as doing your duty, loyalty and obedience – and on Frau Beierle's hairstyle too, I was thinking. It was dark blonde, smooth, cut in a line precisely between her ears and her shoulders, and so

strictly parted to the left of her forehead that a straight
line of white skin ran across her scalp. To the right of the
line a metal clasp held some of the hair back. The rest of
it fell neatly, hair beside hair, as if it had been trained. Presumably hair that didn't grow in exactly the right way had
no future on her head. Her face was square and rather flat
with a turned-up nose, quick little eyes and a small mouth
that she was always twisting into a slightly ironic smile, as
if she were observing everything said and done in the
world from an extraordinarily high vantage-point and,
from up there, saw human weaknesses and crazy connections which ordinary mortals didn't even guess at. She was
wearing a grey trouser suit, a white silk scarf round her
neck and flat, sexless shoes polished to a high gloss. After
she had shaken hands with us, expressed her thanks at
length, and told us again how happy she and of course
Susi were, she asked us into the house and offered biscuits
and drinks. A little later we were sitting in her conserva-
tory drinking cherry juice and eating wholemeal vanilla
pastries. The little park beyond the windows had a foun-
tain and what I assumed was an Egyptian statue in it. Susi
was frolicking around there, celebrating her reunion with
the trees and bushes by lifting her leg to baptise them with
short, quick jets of urine. To the right you could see the
freshly mended hole in the fence through which she had
got out two weeks ago. Perhaps someone had taken her
away, perhaps she had simply been too stupid to find her
way home.

'So you're Herr Kayankaya's niece.' Frau Beierle gave
Leila a friendly nod. 'Do you live in Frankfurt too, if I may
ask?'

Leila let the corners of her mouth turn down in what

I thought was rather too theatrical a way, and looked at me as if she had been beaten.

'Er… she's only been here two months. My brother married a Bosnian woman, so you see…'

'Bos-nian!' repeated Frau Beierle slowly, and sketched the movement of clasping her hands over her head in distress. 'Oh, the poor child!'

'Yes… well, it hits some people one way, some another. I'm trying to get her into a private boarding school while she has to stay here. State schools don't take pupils short-term just like that, and after all, the child can't sit at home all day alone and… well, she prays a lot, but she must go back to learning something too.'

'Quite right. At her age learning's what matters most. Particularly learning how to learn.' She emphasised this last sentence word by word, while her friendly glance conveyed her doubts of whether I knew what she meant.

'You put that so well. Just what I think myself. And the way things look, I'm afraid, she won't be able to go back to Bosnia in a hurry…'

Leila did something in between sniffing and swallowing and passed her hand over her face, leaving a heart-rending pastry crumb there.

'I'm sorry, darling.' I bent over to her. 'But those are the facts. That's why you're going to that nice boarding school. Remember how much we liked it when we went to see it?'

'What kind of boarding school is it?' asked Frau Beierle.

'Oh, well…' I leaned back and sipped my juice. 'Well, it's a cross between a Koran school and a grammar school specialising in sport. Very recently founded. In the middle of the forest, very secluded, only women teachers on the staff – wonderful. Not yet recognised by the state in Germany yet, unfortunately, but as you said, learning in itself is the greatest good of all.'

I had no idea how she managed it, but Leila now had real tears running down her cheeks.

I gave Frau Beierle a look that appealed for understanding. 'We'd better go now, I think. If we could just settle up first…'

While she went into the next room to fetch her cheque book, and Leila drank her juice in short order, perfectly unmoved, I said quietly enough for it to sound like a whisper, but just loud enough to be heard in the next room, 'I know you're unhappy because I can't pay the boarding school fees at the moment, dear, and you'd like to be back at school so much. But as your father may have told you, what we say where I come from is: bring a thirsty man a glass of water and he'll reward you with rain. And my job is to bring people back what they're missing, the way the thirsty man misses a glass of water. Do you understand? It's not always a sweet, clever dog like Susi. Sometimes it's only a bicycle I find, but because it's worth so much to the owner he pays me as if I'd found him his Mercedes. Of course that kind of thing doesn't often happen in Germany, because the culture here is different. But now and then it does turn out like that, perhaps I'll strike lucky in the next few weeks or months, and then…'

Suddenly Leila's face assumed that downtrodden expression again, and I turned to the door. 'Oh, Frau Beierle, there you are. I was just telling Leila where that beautiful statue in your garden came from…'

The slightly ironic smile became a knowing one, she shook her head, put a hand on my shoulder, and said as if to a small child who's trying to act like a grown-up, 'Oh, Herr Kayankaya, you don't have to pretend to me. I know you can't think of anything just now but your niece and your family. Even if you weren't what I expected in some respects, I mean in the qualities arising from your origin – perhaps rightly, I don't want to be dogmatic about that – I'm well enough acquainted with your ways of thinking and feeling to be able to work out that you weren't giving your niece a lecture about an old statue.'

'Well... er... I...'

'Now, you listen to me...' With two firm strides she went over to the table, made out a cheque, waved it energetically in the air to dry the ink, and pressed it into my hand. 'And no argument. Of course this is mainly for your excellent work – you can't imagine how happy I am to have my Susi back – but it's also a little contribution to help you out in your present situation. Your niece,' she added, nodding and smiling warmly at Leila, who now looked as if she were on a course of depressive drugs, 'is such a delightful girl, and I'd be really glad if you can get her into that boarding school.'

For a moment I hesitated, then I moved as fast as I could. Effusive thanks, put the cheque away without looking at it, get to my feet, unobtrusive sign to Leila to hurry, step by step to the front door accompanied by a never-ending farewell monologue, final handshake: 'If there's ever anything else...' '...Oh, of course, I'll certainly turn to you', then down the gravel path, into the car, stop round the next corner to look at the cheque... five thousand marks!

'Is OK?'

'...Yes, it's OK.'

'What we do now?'

'Now...' I put the cheque away and beamed at her. 'Now you wipe that chicken-feed off your face and we go and drink champagne!'

We sat in the bar of the Hilton Hotel for almost two hours, polished off two bottles of champagne, ate caviar on toast and laughed over Frau Beierle. Leila imitated all three of us in turn, and explained how she'd managed those tears.

'Easy, I think hard of sad thing, then they come. Do just like that!' And she snapped her fingers. 'Am going to be actress, you see.'

She enjoyed the champagne and so did I, and after we had given points from one to ten to all the alcoholic drinks the two of us knew, it was agreed that we had just been consuming the best of them all. Then we told each other about our first drinks. With me it was quick: alone in my room at the age of thirteen, putting back a bottle of apple brandy in one go. Instead of appearing at my heart-throb's party a little later, all relaxed and witty as I'd planned, I found myself in hospital next morning.

'Me, was my father's birthday. I twelve. I drink secretly in kitchen. Then I go at night to house next door where boy I love live, and I go to window like this...' She tapped the air with her hand. 'I take flowers too. Then I suddenly very ill, and the boy come, and I go like this...' She leaned forward, retching and letting her tongue hang out of her mouth. 'Was all over with boy. But good that way. He always so stuck-up, playing piano, top of class at school.

224

Later I am glad I…' and she did a little more heavy breathing '…all over him. Afterwards all were angry, my father, my mother. But I drink not often, I don't like because it make me tired, and when life normal, you know, I have soooo…' and she flung her arms wide apart '…so much to do, I not want to sleep.'

If it hadn't been for Gina and Slibulsky's dinner at eight, we'd probably have ordered a third bottle.

On the way to the car Leila linked arms with me.

'When my mother come, we drink champagne again?'

'You bet we will. The three of us will drink the bar dry.'

And then, for a moment, I was breathless. Tomorrow the crunch would come – whatever the outcome. I'd been trying not to think of that all day. Suddenly it almost knocked me flat.

As we drove through the empty evening streets to Sachsenhausen, the radio was playing Van Morrison's *Whenever God Shines His Light*, and there was a fine sunset glowing behind the tower buildings for the first time in a week. As if everything was all right now.

Chapter 18

Not much was all right for Slibulsky this evening. Ten minutes with the assembled company in the living room around a buffet of aperitifs and nibbles were enough to show me why he was so keen to have me there. His concerns about my private life might be one reason, but first and foremost it was probably so that he wouldn't be delivered up alone to this bunch of Mickey Mouse scholars who thought the world revolved around them. Not a chance was missed to trumpet names or professional terms through the room, not a refill of white wine came without a little Latin joke, presumably on the subject of liquor, and there were always surprised, slightly embarrassed smiles when, since I was there anyway, I contributed something I myself knew to the conversation. Now and then Gina's glances suggested that much of her guests' behaviour seemed to her pretentious to say the least, but the choice between her partner the ice cream vendor and ex-drugs-dealer and her museum acquaintances had clearly been made for this evening. Sometimes Slibulsky looked at her as if in pain. The obvious centre of attention was Gina's new boss, the museum curator. A tanned, lean, good-looking man of around fifty who wore a sports jacket with a hood, flared workman's trousers and trainers like cruise missiles similar to those favoured by Gregor, as if showing that he for one didn't look his age. He liked to drop little references to that into the conversation now and then.

'…I think I told you how they wouldn't let me into the conference building in Tunis the other day – priceless! Even though I had my pass for the occasion, they really refused to believe for a whole half an hour that I was the museum curator from Frankfurt!'

So far so priceless, but of course Gina, who was putting all her efforts into gaining the title of Silliest Female of the Evening, had to make it even more so.

'But why not?' she asked in surprise.

Or perhaps she wasn't being quite so silly after all, perhaps she was actually being rather clever, she knew her boss and how to act with him. For he was only too ready to answer her question. 'Well, I mean, look at me…' Laughing, he indicated his person. 'To one of those Arabs, I'm a total freak.'

In fact the members of the museum staff present were pretty freaky anyway. They were free and easy in their language – 'Oh, Iris, you wino!' – they weren't taking any thought for the morrow – 'Well, then I'll be there half an hour late, makes no difference to me!' – they respected no one – 'The old bugger who wrote that article may be a big name in Italy, don't ask me, but I'd rather not say what I think of the article itself' – not even their boss. 'Listen, Heiner… you, listen up! I thought for a moment when I saw your back view, hey, there's Lukas, you know, the work experience lad who's always trying to get us to techno parties. I mean, really, you want to wear something more respectable!'

The boss reacted vigorously to this. 'On the day I wear what you'd call something respectable you can turn me out of the curator's office! But you'll have to wait a long time…' He shook his head, grinning. 'However, to be serious – and it's really nothing to do with a man's trousers – just take a look at the way other curators run their museums. All by the rules laid down in the last century, know what I mean? Yes, yes, I know: as my colleagues see it, I just don't fit their ideas, but to be honest I can't imagine things any other way. Sorry, but that's where I stand.'

In which case I'd have to go and stand somewhere else. I refilled my glass, put a cracker with cream cheese in my mouth, and set off in search of Slibulsky. He was sitting in the kitchen with Leila, the pair of them peeling garlic. Leila smiled at me and I smiled back. Champagne allies.

'How's it going?' asked Slibulsky without looking up.

'Oh, wonderful.'

'Hm.'

'Those elegant ladies you were talking about…'

'All right, all right, drop it.'

I sat down at the kitchen table with them, lit myself a cigarette and watched them peeling away.

Suddenly Slibulsky put his head back and asked, 'What's up? Why that silly grin? Was there someone out there after all?'

'Out there? Nope.'

'Aha.' He turned back to his garlic-peeling. 'Where'd you meet her?'

'Wait and see.'

'I know,' said Leila, beaming knowingly as we both looked at her in surprise. 'Heard how you watch video again.'

'Video?' Slibulsky frowned. 'Is this some kind of a joke? Julia Roberts, maybe?'

'I said wait and see.'

'What *is* this video, Leila?'

But when she realised that we, and particularly I, weren't dismissing her notion as lightly as perhaps she expected, her glance suddenly became uneasy, and she quickly played things down. 'Is only idea. Don't really know.'

Probably it really had been only an idea. The notion that there might have been something in it didn't exactly simplify our situation. Not a good subject.

'Come on.' Slibulsky wasn't letting it drop.

'Suppose I'm just having a kind of second honeymoon with Deborah? You ought to be glad that after all the attractions you held out in advance I wasn't pinning all my emotional hopes on this party.'

'I hadn't seen them then.'

'Elegant ladies, you said.'

'Well, what you'd take for elegant ladies among museum curators. A little education wouldn't do you any harm. Anyway, we were talking about something quite different. What was the title of the film? You can tell me that at least.'

'Can't remember. Some kind of erotic thriller. Deborah had a small part.'

'You're having me on, right?'

'Oh, shut up.' I stood up. 'What is there to eat? Garlic bread?'

Slibulsky sighed. 'Go and make that sort of joke out there. A lot of them are only just out of college. Someone may laugh.'

'Why would they? They would be glad to get French cuisine.'

On the way to the living room Gina ran into me. Like

last time, she was dressed up to the nines and her eyes were shining, as if she still had a lot to do today.

'Sorry I haven't had time to say hello properly yet.' She kissed my cheek, stepped back and examined my face. 'Everything all right again?'

'Keep taking plenty of fluids, the doctor said, and I've stuck to his advice. You're looking wonderful. Like always… recently. What is it – in love?'

I meant it facetiously, but when Gina suddenly froze and blushed red the question instantly assumed uncomfortable weight.

'Er… I didn't mean anything. What would I mean?'

'What indeed?' she replied in a slightly husky voice. 'I expect I'm a little nervous about the meal. I haven't known these people very long.'

'Hm. And how's it all going at the museum?'

'Oh, great. Really fun. That's why recently I may have been so… oh, well.'

'You get on all right with the boss?'

'To be honest, I don't have all that much to do with him. I look after my own department, and now and then we discuss things. Sometimes we have a coffee together, or we…'

'That's all right,' I interrupted her. 'I didn't want to know all the details of how little you have to do with each other.'

She stared at me, and a trace of anger came into her eyes.

'Not exactly a nice guy, is he? Well, what the hell, between you and me he's a world-class arsehole. Best to avoid him as far as possible, I'm sure.'

She stood motionless for a moment until her mouth

twisted into a grim smile. 'Thanks for the advice, but luckily I'm grown up. I can decide for myself who I'll avoid and who I won't.' With which she left me standing there.

It's a funny thing how some women always make a really big deal of their independence just when they're about to mess things up. Or what I'd call mess things up.

There was little I could do but go back into the living room and mingle. In the process I took plenty of fluids and let a small, crisp woman in glasses deliver me a lecture on sexual stimulants in classical antiquity. Interesting the way she did it in a tone of voice as if she were reading aloud the instructions for using an electric iron. Then there was supper, and I found myself sitting at one end of the table between Four-Eyes and a man who kept saying 'Tasty, tasty'. Now and then I cast a surreptitious glance at Gina. She was sitting at the other end of the table beside her boss talking exuberantly. But occasionally she fell silent for a moment, and I thought I sensed her looking at me. Slibulsky was between a young man with rings on his fingers and a shaved, spotty neck, and a woman who kept putting her head on one side as she listened, smiling as if she were talking to a set of soft, pink stuffed toys. They were conversing with each other across Slibulsky, discussing who would be appointed to a post about to fall vacant. Slibulsky stoically put forkful after forkful in his mouth and didn't look as if he planned to follow any conversation for as much as two sentences together. He must have been envying Leila, who had retreated to watch TV in the bedroom.

Iris, the bespectacled woman, seemed intent on having a serious conversation with me during the meal. She didn't seem to mind what the subject was. In her instructions-for-use tone, which did not change in spite of her increasing tipsiness, she moved from the digital future of archaeology to the destructive effects of popular tourism, and from the subject of what I did in my holidays to the relationship between the sexes in general.

'Do you agree that the crucial mistakes, the mistakes that will lead to a rift some time later, are made at the very beginning, perhaps even at the first meeting?'

'Hm, er… I don't know. Perhaps sometimes.'

'Aha.'

'Why aha?'

'Interesting: perhaps sometimes. Conversely, that would mean: perhaps sometimes not.'

In one respect she was phenomenal. So tight by now that she was practically squinting and her remarks were really sheer nonsense, she kept on uttering them in the same slightly slurred, entirely unemotional way, without any intonation at all, as if talking was her job, and a badly paid one at that.

When we left the table and sat down on sofas and chairs I took my chance to slip away from Four-Eyes, and went into the bedroom to say goodbye to Leila.

'As soon as there's any news tomorrow I'll call you.'

'OK. Went well?'

'Of course.' I stroked her head.

'That in the kitchen, just joke, you know?'

'I know. Try to sleep a bit.'

She nodded, and we smiled at each other.

'See you tomorrow.'

As before, I found Slibulsky in the kitchen. He was sitting at the table drinking schnapps.

232

'I have to go. There's a lot to do tomorrow.'

'You're telling me,' he muttered to himself, sounding sozzled.

'Is it just those people annoying you, or is there something else?'

'Aren't they enough to annoy anyone?'

'Yes, sure. Well... look after Leila.'

'Don't worry.'

As I left I waved to Gina, received a cool nod in return, and then I was on the stairs at last. Although it wasn't very friendly of me, as soon as the front door of the building closed behind me I'd forgotten Slibulsky and Gina.

Chapter 19

At ten in the morning on the dot I got into the car and drove off to the station district. The sun was shining, and it had turned warm again overnight. In the streets people were strolling about, talking, doing their Saturday shopping or having the first drink of the weekend outside cafés. I had wound the window down. Laughter, children's shouts, and fresh air smelling of flowers wafted in. Frankfurt this morning felt like a mixture between a meadow by an open-air swimming pool and a busy village square.

But when I turned into Kaiserstrasse the atmosphere changed. At first it was simply quieter, although it was usually noisier in the red-light and gambling district than anywhere else in town. Especially on Saturdays, even in the morning. After all, the weekend customers from *Little Whatsit* and *Lower Thingummy* wanted value for their petrol money. They rose with the lark and were up and down the corridors of the brothels from nine in the morning onwards.

The closer I came to the Albanian's headquarters, the New York, the emptier the pavements became, until there was almost no one around at all any more. Here and there a druggie who'd been kicked aside, or a few travellers with their bags on the way to or from the station. They too sensed the curious atmosphere and were looking around nervously. Only when you looked closely could you see all the heads crowding together behind the dark windows of bars and half-open striptease club doors, looking down the street. Suddenly a siren broke the silence, and next moment an ambulance raced past me. The siren faded into the distance, and it seemed even quieter than before. Then I saw at least twenty blue lights flashing outside the corner building of the side street where the New York stood. I drove slowly up, stopped at the police barrier, and lit a cigarette with trembling hands. Instead of the New York – a three-storey disco with a restaurant and billiards room, adorned outside with a profusion of neon tubing – I saw blue sky. The building opposite which had been the German boss's residence lay in ruins too, and there wasn't much left of two of its bars apart from the last wisps of smoke. But there were any number of charred bodies. They were being carried out of the ruins by firefighters and doctors with protective face masks, and laid in a row on the pavement. I couldn't see the end of the row.

'You out of your mind? Get away from there!'

One of the army of policemen standing about, all of them looking helpless and unable to take it in, had spotted me. Tapping his forehead, he came over.

'What d'you think this is?'

'All right.' I waved him away and drove to the next corner. There I stopped and tried to get my breath under control. Now I knew what it was I'd forgotten to tell the Albanian. Outside the Ahrens office building in the evening: 'Right, lads, see you Saturday. Work in the morning first, pleasure in the evening!' – 'Don't worry, boss, the faggots will get what faggots always hope for – they'll die in their sleep.'

What with thinking about Stasha Markovic, it had simply slipped my mind.

No one must ever know, I prayed, as someone opened the left back door of the car and I felt the muzzle of a pistol on the nape of my neck.

'Get moving.'

I saw the Albanian's bloodstained face in the rear-view mirror. He smelled of smoke.

I said nothing, and even if I'd wanted to say anything I probably couldn't have uttered a sound. All my concentration was bent on driving fairly fast and not causing an accident.

'Turn right up ahead there.'

I obeyed orders, and vaguely realised that we were driving out of town.

'At least you were punctual.'

I cautiously nodded.

'Keep going straight ahead. My God, what a frightful car!'

Quarter of an hour later we were standing beside the car surrounded by fields of potatoes and cabbages, the Albanian still had his pistol pointed at me and was demanding to know everything I knew about the Army of Reason. I told him almost all of it.

'Croats?' he exclaimed, and for a moment I was sure he was going to pull the trigger. 'Why didn't you tell me? I'd have found out who exactly was behind it in half an hour! And I have people down there, just a day and the Army would have been...!' He flung his hand heavenward.

By now I could think reasonably clearly again. Clearly enough to realise why the racketeers extorting protection money had to look like a delegation of men from Mars. In addition, today's attacks showed that the Army was not intended to be a temporary outfit, and after their day was over Ahrens and his partners did not plan to slip off with their pockets full. They were in the process of taking over the quarter much more brutally than their predecessors but after thinking it out better. Get people nervous first, wear them down, then strike hard and grab undisputed possession of the goldmine. And if they were really crafty, in the end they'd take off their make-up and wigs and make out they'd managed to rid the place not only of the old bosses, but also of the Army of Reason that had spread such fear and terror.

'Where's the meeting?'

And I understood one more thing: if I told him that, the last thing I saw in this world would be a potato field. All he wanted to do today was kill, and in a way I could understand him.

I shook my head. 'I'm sorry about what happened this morning, but it's not my fault. Either we go through with the thing together this evening, or Frankfurt will be no place for you.'

'You want to threaten me now?'

The muzzle of the pistol was within a few centimetres of my nose.

'No, I don't want to threaten you, but I don't want to hang around out here either. And you probably couldn't drive my car. It has its own little ways.'

He looked me in the eye, his lips opened, his incisors together, and held the pistol without the faintest tremor.

'How many men do you have left?'

His eyes widened, and briefly his glance was like a lunatic's. Once again I thought, this is it. But then he took a deep breath, closed his mouth, stepped back and slowly lowered the pistol.

'Any more shit and you won't be the only one to get it, it'll be your family too, all your friends, and whoever else is worth anything to you.'

I nodded. 'I understand.'

'I certainly hope so.' He looked at the ground and sighed. 'About ten men. But I have friends in Mannheim and Hanover. They can be here by this evening.'

'Then let's drive back into town. I'll tell you where the Army's banquet is taking place, and we'll meet near it around six.'

'Why would I meet you?'

'Because I'm asking you for two things: first, to let me have a brief word with Ahrens, and second, that no harm will come to a woman who has nothing to do with any of this. She's close to Ahrens at the moment because he's been blackmailing her.'

'Is she the reason for your interest in the Army?'

'That's how it's turned out.'

'Aha. So she would be the first to suffer for it if you're planning anything clever.'

'That's right.'

'Very well, come on...' He gestured towards the car with his pistol, we got in and left the field behind. As we drove into Frankfurt and the familiar high-rise buildings slipped past us, I felt I was coming home from a long journey.

Late in the afternoon the first BMWs arrived. I was sitting with a pair of binoculars on the junk-dealer's roof, where I had a good view of the yard of Ahrens's office building and the conference hall on the first floor. The tables in the hall were arranged in a rectangle. White tablecloths, flowers, three different glasses for each table setting. A flag with horizontal stripes of red, white and blue hung on the wall. Looking down the open passage to the kitchen, I could see Zvonko's uncle in a white apron busy with knives and pans. Two men wearing black and white waiter's suits were sitting on a freezer near the passageway, drinking beer and watching Zvonko's uncle at work. Now and then Ahrens came into the hall and seemed to be asking if everything was going all right. No sign of Leila's mother yet.

Along with the BMWs, Ahrens's hulking henchmen and the fat Hessian came into the yard. All three in blue trousers, red jackets, and some kind of silly garrison cap. They opened the car doors and escorted the guests to the conference hall. The waiters began going round with trays.

Twelve cars rolled up in all. As far as I could tell, there were no refugees among the guests. At least, none of them looked as if they would be happy in a visitors' room with rubbishy old chairs screwed to the floor. One man seemed to be particularly important. A small, sturdy figure, and those standing around him always laughed heartily when he said something, but they almost always took half a step backwards too.

Just after six-thirty the Hessian drove the last car round behind the brick building. He came back, sat down on a bench near the entrance to the yard with the hulks, and all three lit cigarettes. As they were obviously the only guards, Ahrens must be feeling pretty sure of himself. And he had good reason, really: during the afternoon the TV and radio had kept reporting on the incident in the station district where buildings and clubs belonging to two of the most prominent businessmen in the area had been blown sky-high, and it could be assumed with great probability that both the businessmen themselves were among the many victims burnt beyond recognition. The third 'important businessman' of the locality, the Turk, had been found shot in his villa in Oberursel during the afternoon. And if the BMW with its real number plate hadn't fallen into my hands and Slibulsky's, I was sure no one would have been looking for the man behind these incidents in Dr Ahrens's packet-soup factory today. Presumably the Hessian was responsible for changing the number plates. Perhaps he'd neglected to do it that evening. Perhaps he'd been in a hurry to get to the TV set.

And then I saw Leila's mother. She was one of the few women in the conference hall, standing among a group of guests with her back to the window. Sometimes I thought I caught a brief glimpse of her profile, but most of the time she was facing whoever was talking to her and stood almost motionless. She had pinned up her hair, she was wearing a pale blouse and the pearl necklace I knew from the wedding video. While I turned the binoculars on the nape of her neck and hoped she'd turn round some time, the air began buzzing very quietly. As if a huge swarm of deep-voiced insects was approaching. I turned my binoculars to search the industrial yards, metal factory halls, containers, office buildings and the clear blue sky, but I couldn't find anything to explain the noise. Only at second glance did I see the line of cars moving past the gap between a detergents company and a haulier's firm as if in slow motion, bumper to bumper.

I cast another quick glance at the cigarette-smoking guards, who obviously hadn't heard the buzzing sound, and then I climbed down from the roof and over the fence and went to the place where we'd arranged to meet.

Along the street outside a container depot about fifteen dark, high-class cars were parked, occupied by about fifty men. At the head, a small group stood round the Albanian, the rest were sitting there on the de luxe leather upholstery waiting, or stretching their legs with their feet in bright white trainers or gleaming black, hand-made Hungarian shoes. The car engines were turned off, and when no one said anything it was so quiet that you could hear the click of their Dunhill lighters.

'We need a short fat man and two big toughs to replace the guards.'

The Albanian nodded to an older man beside him. The man turned, walked down the line of cars, and a little later brought us three men of the required stature.

'Did you tell your men not to touch the black-haired woman?'

The Albanian nodded.

'And that I must speak to Ahrens?'

'How will we know him?'

'You'll know him when I buttonhole him. I only need a moment after that.'

'Good.' He gestured to the cars, and next moment half a hundred heavily armed men were there in the street. There were a few nervy, chain-wearing characters among them, but most looked as cool and reliable as a military special unit.

The Albanian said something in Albanian, five men stepped aside to stay with the cars, then the unit started moving. While the majority stopped at a part of the wall that couldn't be seen from the brick building and put up a ladder, I, the small fat man and the two big toughs went quietly to the entrance. The three of them were really impressive. It took them less than two minutes to break the necks of the Hessian and his two companions, drag them into the street outside the half-closed front door, take the suits and caps off the bodies and put them on themselves, and then stroll back into the yard chatting as if nothing had happened.

I was probably simply inured to it after the events of the last week. At the latest since I'd seen all those burnt bodies outside the New York, killing Ahrens's men had seemed to me inevitable, almost natural. But without thinking about it I distinguished between those who were biting the dust or about to bite the dust here and now, and the protection money racketeers from the Saudade. Whether it was because the racketeers had died at a time when I wasn't yet used to the idea of all these warlike confrontations, or because I felt solely responsible for their deaths – well, anyway, in my mind they had faces, whereas even while they were alive the Hessian and the two hulks hadn't been much more than a mass of grey armed with pistols.

As I reached the ladder the last men were just climbing over the wall. I hurried so as to get to the Albanian at their head. We went into the building and up the stairs without a sound. A vanguard of two men stabbed another guard who had been sitting by the door to the first floor playing with a Gameboy. Then we filed quietly into the corridor, and heard confusion of voices and the clink of glasses.

The Albanian gave a sign to stand still, took me by the shoulder and indicated the open door ten metres away.

'The field's yours. Get the woman and Ahrens and take them into the next room. You have a minute.'

I must have looked surprised, and if there'd been time I'd probably have thanked him.

'Right, off you go!'

I set off, putting my pistol in my trouser pocket on the way, and entered the conference hall. For about twenty seconds no one really noticed me, and I had time to get over the shock of seeing that the black-haired woman with the pearl necklace had a fat nose and dark eyes.

Someone asked me something in Croatian, and at the same moment I spotted Ahrens. First he just looked surprised. Then he frowned, probably wondering how I'd got past the guards. Then his face muscles set, and he came towards me with slow, menacing strides, his head lowered.

'Do you want to die?' he asked quietly. Obviously he wasn't keen on having any fuss during the party.

'No, but you probably do. Or you wouldn't have left such idiots on guard.'

His eyes automatically went to the door.

'Don't look that way. And keep your mouth shut. There are forty heavily armed men out there. Men whose mates were blown up this morning and...'

'What?'

'I said keep your mouth shut. The Albanian survived.'

'Survived?'

'Didn't you hear what I said? Anyway, there's about to be a bloodbath in here, and either you come with me and answer a few questions, and then maybe I can put in a good word for you, or you take a last look at this world. I'll count to three and then I'm going. On the count of five you'll be dead.'

All the hardness had gone from his face. Nothing was left but a pale splodge with a slack hole in the middle of it. I grabbed his arm and pulled him out into the corridor. As I drew my pistol and propelled him forward, I heard a hissing from the other end of it and thought I felt the building begin to vibrate.

We were at the door of the first office when I heard the Albanian's voice and the sound of glasses breaking as they fell. Someone answered in a placatory, almost friendly tone. Obviously they knew each other.

I pushed Ahrens into the room, closed the door behind us, and while all hell broke loose in the conference hall next door I shouted in his ear that I wanted him to give me the names of the two dead racketeers and tell me where to find the mother of the girl I'd taken out of the refugee hostel three days ago.

'What?'

'Surely Gregor or the two clowns with the broken legs will have told you about it?'

'Yes, sure, but...'

And then a whole lot happened almost at once. First, Ahrens suddenly began to laugh. Hysterically, in view of the situation, but also with entirely inappropriate and malicious glee. Piqued for a moment, I heard, too late, that at least part of the fight had moved into the corridor. The door burst open, and Zvonko's uncle, streaming with blood, made for me with a long kitchen knife in his hand. Of course his main idea was to get away from someone, but that didn't make much difference where I was concerned. Without hesitating, I fired a few more bullets into his belly, and the man literally burst apart. Behind him, eyes wide open and frenzied, face covered with dark

splashes, came one of the chain-wearers. By now Ahrens
had reached the window and was pulling at the catch. In
this situation, it was unlikely that I could have got many
of those here today, wanting revenge, to be quick to grasp
the fact that the windows wouldn't open fully, but with a
jittery chain-wearer I wasn't even going to try. I lowered
my pistol and watched almost indifferently as he emptied
his entire magazine into Ahrens. While he was firing away,
and Ahrens, lying on the ground, was looking more and
more like a suit stuffed with sausage-meat, I couldn't
shake off the picture of his gleeful smile. I turned my eyes
away from the horrors and looked out of the window. The
setting sun was reflected in the junk-dealer's shop sign.
Something about that bothered me.

Soon afterwards the operation was over, and a torrent
of footsteps clattered down the corridor to the stairwell.
The chain-wearer had taken his leave a few minutes ago,
giving the thumbs-up sign, and when the Albanian came
into the office I was sitting at the desk alone, smoking. He
was holding the black-haired woman's thin arm. Her
blouse was torn, tears and saliva gleamed on her pale face
with its broken veins, her mouth was trembling, and her
eyes were moving like pinballs shooting around at speed.

The Albanian cast a glance at what was left of Ahrens
and then nodded to his side. 'Didn't you forget something?'

Perhaps he'd have let her go, but I wasn't sure of it. And
since she could hardly have played a greater part in the
whole business than that of Ahrens's latest safari partner, I
said as convincingly as I could just now, 'I didn't have
time.'

'Didn't have time. So you preferred to take him?' He

pointed to the floor, looking at me with a touch of contempt.

'Oh, leave me alone. It's the wrong woman, OK? But she's only some tart, she won't have anything to do with all this.'

'Right.' He let go of the woman, took a handkerchief out of his jacket pocket and wiped his hands. 'All things considered,' he said, putting the handkerchief away again and nodding to me, 'thank you.' Then he turned and went out.

I looked at the open door and listened to his footsteps. At some point a shadow flitted by, but only when I rose and moved slowly to the corridor did it strike me in passing that it must have been the woman.

'…What did you mean when you said your mother had been gone since last Sunday? Sunday as in Friday, Saturday, Sunday, or the last time it was a sunny day?'

'Last time it was sunny day.'

'OK…' I kept perfectly calm. It was only my eyesight that was changing. I was beginning to see only the things I was thinking of at any given moment, and I was thinking of nothing but things. The phone receiver, the cradle. Everything around them blurred, went grey or simply disappeared. 'I'll call you back.'

'What about my mother?'

'I didn't find her. It's all rather complicated. I must go. See you later.'

'See you later.'

Telephone receiver, cradle, car. I crossed the street. Key, ignition, gear change. It was just before eight. I filtered into the Saturday night traffic, people out to enjoy themselves. Lights, car in front of me, green light, accelerator, indicator, bend. When I left Frankfurt behind, all I saw was the grey ribbon of tarmac moving faster and faster towards the Taunus. Then the forest began. Headlights, woodland paths... *the* woodland path. I turned off the road and parked the car. Tree, root, earth compacted after the rain of the last few days – hands, claws, shovelling. It was dark in the forest. Cigarette lighter, stains on plastic bin liner, a few more clods of earth, a head... I didn't hesitate for a second, to do that I'd have had to think about more than things, there was only one thing in my mind, and next moment I had the wig in my hand. Long black hair fell over the face disfigured by a week of lying in the earth of the forest floor. Unstrapping the bulletproof vest was purely mechanical after that. A bra.

I can't remember how I got home and exactly what I did then. The vague outline of the greengrocer came to meet me in the hall of our building, and I think I told him he could sleep easy, there was no threat from the Mafia any more. Only later in the evening, with a bottle in my hand, did I realise that I must speak to Leila as soon as possible. I couldn't let her sit around hoping any longer. I looked at the time. Ten-thirty. I rang Slibulsky and asked him to stick around. I was going to drop in and see Leila. Half an hour later we were sitting at the kitchen table, and I told her that after her meeting with the Zagreb industrialist, her mother was in a car accident on the way back to Frankfurt and had been fatally injured. That seemed to me the least painful explanation for Leila. After I had held her in my arms for a while she said she wanted to be alone, and disappeared into the living-room. Slibulsky promised to look after Leila, and tried to persuade me to stay the night, but I wanted to go home.

He went to the door with me. 'It *was* her?'

'I think so.'

'And it was an accident?'

'At least it wasn't done on purpose.'

Chapter 20

Two months later Romario opened his new bar, Rommy's Irish Pub. We had met by chance on the underground just as I came back from four weeks in Corsica.

'Why an Irish pub?' I asked, baffled.

'Because there isn't one around here yet, and people like pubs. Guinness, whiskey, Irish music – goes down great.' Romario was wearing a new, slightly shiny suit with big leather buttons, coloured trainers with about four layers of sole, he had blow-dried the hair above his forehead into a surfer's-paradise wave that enclosed a large hole full of air in its tall curve, and was beaming as if embarking on the project of his life.

'I got the money from the insurance, see?'

'What will there be to eat?'

'In the pub? Did you ever eat anything in a pub?'

'No, but I've only ever been in one two or three times, and then only because I had to. The beer's like gnat's piss, but you still drink it to help you put up with the music.'

'Oh, you…!' He laughed, and brushed his finger-tips on my shoulder.

'And now I'm naturalised I had no trouble at all with a licence and rental agreements. Honest, Kemal, you've no idea how grateful I am to you. It all went so well with Höttges: fast and friendly, no trouble at all. We even went out for a drink together a few times, and he'd have come to the opening, but now he's had himself transferred to Braunschweig.'

'Oh yes?'

Romario waved it away. 'Family business of some kind. A pity, eh? The two of you could have met again. I still haven't quite worked out how it is you know each other, but I can give him news of you if you like. We sometimes talk on the phone.'

'You talk to one another on the phone?'

'It's just that, among Frankfurters,' he said, winking at me, 'and I'm a Frankfurter now, I've got it all in black and white. Well, anyway, he misses the city a lot.'

'Tell me, Romario, is it that I've been away so long, or is there something different about you?'

'What...? Oh, I must get out here. Right, I'm counting on you and Slibulsky. You'll get written invitations. See you.' He got out of the underground train and set off, waving.

The party was a typical Romario occasion. The invitation card was adorned with a shamrock leaf which had eyes and a smiling mouth, and said: *Rommy's Irish Pub, Guaranteed Good Company and a Happy Atmosphere*. The card added, with an exclamation mark, that you had to show it to get in. Either he had really imagined something like bouncers on the door, massive men who had to stay on watch outside, and a pub full to bursting with the rich, beautiful and famous, or else possession of a German passport had given him a taste for border checks of every kind. In fact he could think himself lucky if a few curious passers by came in from the street during the afternoon to join our small party and not let the atmosphere bother them. I've no idea if the place was really anything like an

Irish pub. But it did resemble the kind of bar that you seldom remember next day, because you went into it only at the end of an evening's boozing when everywhere else was closed. Halfway sober, hardly anyone would choose to sit in a tunnel twenty metres long, with only one window, beige woodchip wallpaper and dark brown, wiry wall-to-wall carpeting. Little blue globes like nightlights with yellow shades stood on the tables, providing minimum lighting and making it feel as if the committee of the local euthanasia group normally met here. In addition, at least to start with, the music was that typical Irish hoppety-hop fiddling and yodelling that always made me wonder whether the Irish listen to it themselves or just produce it for export as part of their successful folklore myth, advertising the fact that there may be nothing to eat in the pub but it's cheerful.

Slibulsky and I were sitting on one of the corner seats upholstered with imitation green corduroy, drinking whiskey, and Slibulsky was working out how much we might get for the BMW still standing in his garage, always remembering the smashed the stereo system. Next week the ad appeared in the paper with an asking price of eighty thousand.

Zvonko and Leila were sitting on another upholstered corner seat, their heads close together, and seemed to have entirely forgotten the presence of the chattering Brazilian transvestites, former Saudade customers putting back Guinness for all they were worth, and a handful of people who looked as if they wished they'd been invited somewhere else. Leila was working three times a week as an ice cream vendor now, and that was how she had met Zvonko. In the mornings she took a language course, and after the summer holidays she was going to start school. Slibulsky and Gina had seen about enrolling her and getting her a residence permit, had given her a room of her own in their flat, and more or less adopted her. We didn't see each other often, and when we did it was in company. Once we had gone for a walk alone together, had found almost nothing to talk about, and we had probably both been relieved when we said goodbye. Those few days together – the hopes, sometimes the fun – belonged to another time and were only in our way now. Occasionally, when I came to eat a meal or fetch Slibulsky, our glances met for longer than necessary, and it all came back to me.

Slibulsky had told me that Leila had hired a colleague of mine to find her father. She had enough money. One of the two suitcases we'd taken away from the refugee hostel was full to the brim, as I also learned from Slibulsky, with gold plates, jewellery and banknotes. Stasha Markovic must have been fairly raking in the money on her own account. The video cassettes were still at my flat. When I came back from holiday I finally managed to clear them away into the back corner of my wardrobe. Lying there in the dark at night, I sometimes felt as if they were enriched uranium or some such thing, and would send invisible radiation through the wood of the wardrobe and the whole flat. Leila didn't ask about them. Perhaps by now she had guessed at some of it, and was deliberately leaving the cassettes with me. Or the thought of what they showed hurt so much that she was simply blocking out their existence for the time being.

I hoped it would never occur to Leila to hire any reasonably competent detective to find out in exactly what accident, how and where her mother had died.

While Slibulsky got us another drink, Zvonko was talking to Leila and making her laugh. Even through the dim light, I could see her eyes shining, and her overcrowded-bistro-table face changed for a moment and wore an enchanting expression of pure, relaxed happiness. I quickly looked away.

'And how's things going with Gina?' I asked when Slibulsky came back with two full glasses.

'Oh, we don't see much of each other at the moment, working too hard, both of us, but it's OK,' he murmured, dismissing the subject, and moved swiftly on to talk about the World Cup. France were perfectly acceptable as world champions, we agreed, although we'd both been betting on the Dutch. A Zinedine Zidane poster had been hanging in Slibulsky's office for the last week, and we neglected no opportunity this afternoon to rib Romario about the Brazilians: instead of playing football, we suggested, that admittedly good-looking team would do better to earn a living advertising men's fragrances or diet fruit-juice drinks – just so long as they didn't keep monopolising every other sports programme with claims of how they always won in the final. Unfortunately none of that really bothered Romario much; he wasn't particularly interested in football. Possibly he was backing the German team these days. Or the Irish.

After a while Slibulsky took over as DJ. In honour of the occasion he stayed with Irish music, but it suddenly sounded different, and soon the first couples were dancing to *Carrickfergus* by Van Morrison and the Chieftains. I drank whiskey at the bar and was talking to a drag queen about the proposed move of Frankfurt Central Station to an underground concourse when a set of fingernails painted turquoise appeared beside my elbow.

'Well, did you get your million packet soups?'

I turned and saw Miss Chewing-Gum's smiling face, slightly flushed with alcohol.

'Well, what a surprise! Where've you been? When I next went to see Ahrens there was no one on the switchboard.'

'I gave notice. I wasn't staying in a place where the clients come out looking like you did. And I'd have reached that point soon anyway. What happened to you wasn't the only thing I wasn't supposed to see. The whole business was probably a gangster outfit. They hired me just to sit around so that it would look halfway straight on the surface.'

'Halfway is the right word for it. Are you reading your women's mags at home now?'

'I'm reading them at my new desk in my new job with a haulage firm. And as you like words, you ought to understand these: a place is nothing but a gangster outfit if anyone and everyone, without exception, right down to the woman on the switchboard, is a gangster who works for the firm or wants anything from the firm. What were you planning to feed your earthquake victims, cream of cocaine soup?'

I shook my head. 'Forget it. Anyway, I never did any business with Ahrens. What would you like to drink?'

She hesitated, and looked inquiringly at me for a moment. Then she said, 'That Irish stout of theirs, I haven't eaten yet.'

'Hey, Romario, a Guinness.'

I excused myself to the drag queen and guided Miss Chewing-Gum to one of the upholstered seats.

'So as I see it, you find fulfilment in your work during the week and go to exciting opening parties at the weekend. Do you live here?'

'Round the corner. You forget the delightful men I meet at the opening parties.'

'Ah, yes. Do they invite you out later to smart restaurants when you haven't eaten yet?'

'They go on their knees to me for that.'

'I'd get scratch-marks, on this carpet.'

'That's all part of it.'

It turned into an evening which gave neither of us any cause for complaint. On Sunday we watched nature films and comedy shows on TV, and on Monday I set out in search of a new office.